Once Upon a Christmas Castle

by

Virginia Barlow

Christmas in the Castle Series

Once Upon a Christmas Castle

Cover Art by *Debbie Taylor*

The Wild Rose Press, Inc.
PO Box 708
Adams Basin, NY 14410-0708
Visit us at www.thewildrosepress.com

Publishing History
First Edition, 2023
Trade Paperback ISBN 978-1-5092-5037-0
Digital ISBN 978-1-5092-5038-7

Christmas in the Castle Series
Published in the United States of America

Cousin Lucius left Thomas and Ulysses with the nanny and escorted Rosalind to her chamber.

"Until dinner." Taking her hand in his. He maintained eye contact as he bent his head. His hot lips slid over the cool flesh of her hand, weakening her knees. Her breath caught in her throat as his mouth moved against her skin, making her tremble in her satin slippers. His earlier conversation about kissing made her wonder what his firm mouth would feel like if he slid his lips over hers like he did the back of her hand, and the fever of desire caught her blood on fire. Fluttering filled her belly as she wilted against the door jamb, willing this moment to last for an eternity.

At last, he lifted his head. "Good day, Rosalind."

Praise for Virginia Barlow

"I loved this book (Coconut Macaroon Scandal)! Lots of twists and turns, with all the characters getting exactly what they deserved at the final denouement. The chemistry between the main characters was very believable and I loved Emma's grandmother's ghost stepping in to help her. This is a great story and I couldn't put it down."

~ Net Galley Review

"Fans of both historical romance and paranormal romance will love The Witch of Rathborne Castle. Reminiscent of Jude Deveraux's historicals, The Witch of Rathborne Castle will sweep the reader away. Highly recommend!"

~ N.N. Light's book Heaven

"If you love mermaids, you're going to want to read S'mores Siren Song. A sweeping, summer paranormal romance, S'mores Siren Song will whisk you away. Highly recommend!"

~ N.N. Light's Book Heaven

Dedication

For Katelyn. You have such a beautiful heart.

Chapter One

Yorkshire, England
Late November 1813

Lady Rosalind Chatham's first view of Weston Castle took her breath away.

Gazing out the little window of her stepfather's luxurious carriage as they turned a corner on the winding road, the trees of the dense forest fell away to reveal a magical, ethereal structure rising high above them. Standing tall against the dark foliage of the forest, the heavy stone castle sparkled in the afternoon light. Rosalind blinked up at the elegant towers and spires caressing an azure blue sky holding communion with fluffy white clouds and sighed with appreciation.

The relatives spoke of the beauty of Weston Castle, but their lavish praise in no way prepared her for this glorious reality.

Allowing her gaze to roam the enchanting scene before her, she wondered how the gate to her private hell could resemble the entrance to heaven. Such a thing should not be allowed, for it played with her mind and heart in a most unpleasant fashion. Shaking her head at the irony of the situation, she turned her attention back to the lavish grounds surrounding them.

The cobblestone road they traveled on meandered through acres of manicured gardens strewn with glistening diamond-studded droplets of frost to an impressive outer wall made of stone and curved metal. Guards dressed in blue, gold, and black stood at attention beside the arched entrance welcoming her stepfather and mother in the forward carriage before waving the rest of the entourage through. Their warm breath hung suspended in the frosty air as they acknowledged their visitors.

Rosalind's heart skipped a beat as their carriage wheeled past the guards. She had never been so happy and so distraught for a journey to end.

Her ancient, newly acquired fiancé, the Earl of Gloucester, would arrive within a fortnight for the wedding, planned for Christmas Day. Feeling as though she received a lump of coal in her stocking, a shiver of revulsion skated down her spine when his wrinkled face and snowy white hair popped into her head. Bushy white eyebrows dipped low over dull brown eyes accompanied by thin lips and nose. An inch shorter in stature then she, with a rounded belly and hunched shoulders, he hobbled when he walked because of swelling in his left foot. When she left this glorious abode, she would do so as his wife. Anxiety twisted a knot in her stomach as she shoved the thought aside.

Two London seasons, a handful of half-hearted suitors, and a less-than-favorable reputation later, she received one proposal, his, a fifty-four-year-old widower anxious to make her his brood mare.

She often wondered where the term "love of my life" originated from. Did one have more than one? She concluded one must after taking her mother into consideration. Mama claimed Rosalind's father held the title until his untimely death, and following her marriage to Lord Timothy Weston, now claimed her stepfather to be her one true love. Thus, reason dictated each person must have at last two, perhaps more. And if there were so many about, why had she not run into at least one of hers?

"Is this Cousin Lucius' castle?"

Her five-year-old half-brother's question jerked her back to the present as he squinted his nose at the drawbridge. "If I knew we were this close, I would have waited to stop."

The heavy wooden beams groaned under the weight of the carriage.

One of the many reasons her stepfather and mother traveled in their own carriage with Rosalind and Thomas in another had to do with her brother's frequent stops to relieve his bladder and constant chatter. When her brother grew bored, he invented reasons to stretch his legs. She would join him if not for the fact she must behave as a lady.

Shaking her head, she replied, "Next time, be patient."

He gave her an eye roll and studied the scenery with interest. "Do you think Cousin Lucius has a pond?"

Gazing at his angelic face, she smiled. The child's big blue eyes stole her heart the second he appeared in this world as a tiny babe, and she held him in her arms for the first time. She alone possessed the fortitude to deal with his precocious behavior.

"Papa says he does." Although Lord Timothy did not father her, she called him Papa since she had no recollection of her real father.

"If I had patience, I would not have found Admiral Georgeous Frederick Alexander Junior the Third." A wiggly, croaking object appeared from the inner pocket of his jacket, clutched tight in a chubby hand.

Rosalind's eyebrow rose. "Who? What is this? You caught a frog?"

He nodded with a wide grin and set the amphibian down on his best linen trousers.

She frowned in alarm. "He will ruin your breeches and make Mama upset. Put him back in your pocket until I decide what must be done."

Their carriage rumbled across cobblestones once more and drew to a stop. She shot a quick glance out the window, noting the parents disembarking. Somehow, she must deal with the frog before his presence became known or risk her mother's fury.

Frowning out the window, she eyed red carpeted stairs leading upward to a tall, dark-haired figure wearing a royal blue jacket with gold braids on the shoulders and black breeches standing cold and aloof at the top. A regal white and gray dog sat at attention beside the duke, eyeing the newcomers.

The gentleman must be Cousin Lucius, the Duke of Weston. His face remained expressionless, and his manner impeccable as the parents approached. Then with a slight nod of his head, his grace welcomed them to Weston. The dog lay still like a statue, and the only movement arose from the breeze ruffling his thick fur.

The parents spoke with the duke for a moment, and then her mother dipped an elegant bow low enough to impress royalty while her stepfather shook hands with the impressive figure before them.

Masculine, powerful, wealthy, and distant Lucius Alexander Phillip Weston became the fifth Duke of Weston five years prior upon the death of his grandfather. As head of the Weston family, the duke invited one relative per holiday season to stay at his castle.

This season, their turn arrived with an extravagant and very expensive, gilded invitation signed by the duke's own hand. Fortuitous considering her recent engagement? Perhaps. Rosalind suspected the duke invited them out of sheer despair at the thought of opening another of her mother's hundred-and-one letters begging for the honor.

Mama obsessed over impressing Rosalind's fiancé and exaggerated their financial situation to the point a wedding in the castle was necessary to keep the earl from guessing the true nature of their circumstance. Her mother believed if the earl had knowledge of their lack of funds, he would withdraw his proposal, and she would be pitied by the local nobility for failing to obtain an advantageous marriage for her only daughter.

Frantic to maintain the façade and her social position in their little village, she sent a new letter every day, entreating her husband's distant cousin to allow them the privilege of the upcoming nuptials.

The present returned with a bump when the parents turned and motioned toward their carriage. What if the dog smelled the frog? Panic flared as she gazed from her brother to his wiggling, jumping companion still sitting in his lap and returned to the forbidding scene on the stairs. The amphibian must go.

"Mama and Papa want to make a good impression on his grace. You must leave the admiral in the carriage so we do not disappoint them."

"But he is part of the family now. Why can he not meet Cousin Lucius?" The boy held his pet up to her nose as he asked his question.

"Your friend might shock the parents since he is so new to our household. Put him on the carriage seat, and we will return for him later." She jumped when the carriage door opened, and a footman set the step stool on the ground, holding his hand out to offer her assistance.

"But I want him to come!" The boy's voice grew in volume, and his lower lip stuck out, threatening a full-blown mutiny.

If Thomas did not calm down, Mama would scorch her ears later. "Fine." Thinking quick, she stuffed the frog into the left pocket of her gown where she could monitor the situation and hopefully hide the scent from the great beast beside the duke. "He shall ride with me. Now behave."

The child's rebellion disappeared like a foul scent in the breeze, followed by another wide grin as they stepped from the carriage. "You should call the duke *cousin*, too. I am sure he will not mind."

Mama frowned. "Who, Thomas? Who will not mind?" Casting a quick worried glance in Rosalind's direction, she took two steps toward them.

"Everything is fine, Mama. Thomas expressed his opinion. Nothing more." She kept her hand against her pocket to hide the wiggling bulge and prayed no one would notice.

Her mother visibly relaxed and held her hand out to the boy. "Come." Catching her brother by the hand, she turned to their host. "Your grace, I would like to introduce you to our son, Thomas Hutchinson Weston."

Rosalind stopped a foot behind and waited her turn, her gaze on the dog

To his credit, the child executed a perfect bow in

6

response to the duke's deep voice bidding him welcome to the castle.

"And this?" The deep voice drew her gaze to his, and her knees clacked together as their host's gaze lingered on her hair and face before perusing the rest of her.

Stepping forward, she swallowed and waited for the parents to make the introduction.

The duke stood six feet tall if an inch, possessed dark wind-swept hair, piercing blue eyes, a broad forehead, straight nose, and a dimple in his chin. His jacket emphasized the breadth of his shoulders and the narrowness of his waist. His muscled thighs strained against the fabric of his breeches, and his boots gleamed in the sunlight. No man of this caliber had stood this close to her before, and Rosalind snapped her gaping mouth closed, dropping her gaze before her expression gave her fascination away.

"Lady Rosalind Chatham, daughter of my wife's late husband, the Earl of Chatham." Papa stood beside her, gripping her elbow.

She dipped a deep curtsy, and the frog jumped in alarm, straining against the fabric of her pocket.

The dog let out a low growl, and cold sweat broke out on her forehead.

The duke's cool, impassive gaze dropped to the pocket of her gown while he snapped his fingers at the animal beside him. "Silence, Ulysses."

The white beast did not make another sound but kept his gaze fixed on her pocket.

Clasping her hand against the opening to keep the amphibian from escaping, she rose to her feet and pinched the edges of the fabric together with her left hand, hoping she adopted a believable level of disinterest in the dancing fabric at her hip. Casting a worried glance at the dog, she smiled, ignoring the panic in her chest. Mama would never forgive her if something went amiss, and this situation contained enough potential to effect ancestors yet unborn. She inched backward, praying the breeze blew her scent away from the massive dog, not toward him.

"Do not be shy, Rosalind." Mama nudged her forward, and with her attention on the dog, she tripped on a stair.

"Ah, the bride." The duke's gaze traveled over her a second time, and a smile touched his mouth. "Welcome to my home, Lady Rosalind." He bowed from the waist and took her right hand in his, kissing her gloved knuckles.

The dog leaned forward, staring at her pocket.

"I call her Ruby. She is *my* sister." Thomas stepped to her side to establish ownership, tugging on her left hand, the one holding her pocket closed, and glared up at the duke.

To her extreme consternation. she lost her grip on the edges of the fabric, and Admiral Georgeous Frederick Alexander Junior the Third made his debut into the family by jumping out onto the duke's bent windswept hair!

Everyone reacted at once.

The dog barked and leaped at the duke, jumping around his master for a better vantage point.

Anxious to contain the situation, Rosalind made a dive for the frog while Mama screamed for help. Thomas yelled and dove in to retrieve his pet at the same time she did. They hit heads, falling to the ground in a heap. She groaned in frustration.

Papa burst out laughing, offering no assistance whatsoever, to Mama's verbal dismay.

While the duke snapped his finger at the dog, captured the amphibian with one hand, and surveyed the group before him as if this were a common occurrence. "Heel, Ulysses."

The dog whined and dropped to his belly, keeping his gaze on the frog.

The liveried butler, two steps behind, hurried to the duke's side to relieve him of the green wiggling creature while Papa continued to chuckle, wiping tears of mirth from his eyes.

"You owe me twenty gold coins, Amelia. We have not been here a full ten minutes, and already we have an incident."

Her mother sputtered apologies as she fluttered around the duke, trying to help but unwilling to touch the loathsome creature he held. She gave the dog a wide berth.

"Cease this fuss." The duke's quiet voice stopped everyone mid-stride. He held his free hand down to assist Rosalind to her feet before studying her and Thomas.

Silence filled the cobblestone area around them as the duke gazed from one to the other. "To whom does this creature belong?" Blue eyes narrowed on her face as he waited for her answer.

Her heart beat loud in her ears, and a band tightened around her chest as she considered possible repercussions. His grace might send them home in shame. And if he did, Mama would send her to a convent to hide her embarrassment from the world. No one wanted the social disgrace of having a spinster for a daughter, least of all her mother. Marrying the earl was her one chance for acceptance and approval.

Anxiety turned to nausea and rose in her throat as her future loomed before her sending fear skittering down her spine. The punishment would be far worse for Thomas. A convent, she could escape from, but a boarding school for him would crush his spirit, and without her, he would be unmanageable.

Swallowing, she lifted her chin to meet the duke's piercing gaze and take responsibility. "He belongs—" She squeezed her brother's hand, stopping short when Thomas stepped forward.

"He is mine. Ruby kept him safe in her pocket so he would not embarrass Mama." The child stood with his head thrown back, his gaze unwavering as he faced their host.

"I see." The duke held the frog out and glanced down at the boy. "And did you plan to carry him into my home?"

Thomas nodded. "We must because we named him, and he is part of the family now. He cannot stay in the carriage. He will get lonely."

Mama groaned as if she could hold back no longer. "For God's sake, Thomas, frogs do not belong in castles nor in carriages. Really, Rosalind, I should think you would discourage him rather than abet him in his nonsense. His grace will no doubt want us to return home now, and I warned you of the repercussions if he did. How can this happen when I worked so hard to get us here?" Flushing with embarrassment, Mama dipped down in a swooning curtsy, addressing their host. "Your grace, I do apologize for all this." Waving her hand toward her two children and the frog still wiggling in the duke's fingers. "What can we do to make this up to you?"

"May I have him back?" The boy held his arms up to retrieve his pet, not at all repentant.

The dog whined as if unable to bear the tension of the frog being so close and having to obey his master and stay.

Rosalind held her breath and waited as the duke studied the boy's face, her mother's fawning curtsy, and Papa's jovial laughter. Thinking he meant to be stern with them all, he surprised her by dropping to his haunches, becoming eye level with the child.

"You may have him on one condition. While you are here at the castle, you must ask before you invite any more creatures into my home whether they are part of the family or not. I like to know who occupies my castle. Do I have your word?"

Thomas did not hesitate. "Yes, your grace. Thank you, Cousin Lucius."

Their host handed the frog back to the boy and rose to his feet. Holding out his hand to help Mama to hers, he offered her his arm. "If I may voice my opinion, do not be too harsh with them, my lady. The boy meant no harm. Frogs do possess a certain charm for lads of his age. As for Lady Rosalind, she meant to defend the boy. A kind heart is an admiral trait in a young lady."

Mama gaped and then snapped her mouth closed as she allowed him to lead her up the stairs to the heavy entrance door while monitoring the large dog keeping pace on the duke's other side. "I pray you feel as lenient toward us by the time we leave, your grace."

Papa fell in behind them, clasping his hands behind his back as he strolled along, still chuckling. "I agree, Lucius. Both with you and my wife. I remember a time or two we were sent to our chambers for such antics."

"Quite right."

The three approached the open door to the castle and disappeared inside.

Rosalind followed, bemused by the way their host dealt with her younger half-brother. "Come along, Thomas." She took his hand and hurried after the parents, trying not to envision the talk she knew her mother planned for later. The duke may be appeased, but Mama would not be until she had her say.

Chapter Two

"Cousin Lucius kissed your hand." The small boy squeezed her fingers. "I did not like him to touch you."

Risking a quick glance at their host, she prayed the child's voice did not carry to their subject's ears. The duke showed empathy instead of offense, and she joined her mother in hoping his opinion of Thomas remained so until their departure. "He gave your frog back and did not punish you. Most lords would have taken the admiral away and sent us home. He did not, and I should think you would like him."

When she thought of them leaving, she sighed, knowing she would not know if his grace changed his mind or not, for she would be on her honeymoon with a man old enough to be her grandfather. Her stomach churned at the thought, her previous nausea returning.

"I do like him, or at least I did until he stared at you. Most people do not know how pretty you are, but I do. I think Cousin Lucius does too. I could tell by the way he kissed your hand."

Heat rose to her cheeks. "What nonsense, Thomas." Her unremarkable red hair and pale skin held none of her would-be suitors speechless any more than her average body and average height. She possessed a passable singing voice, wrote average poetry, and struggled with stitching. Reasoning, math, and languages were her shining accomplishments. Something her tutors praised her for, and Mama cringed over.

Her mother's thoughts were quite evident when they ordered this year's gowns for her London season. "At the very least, we shall create a perfect wardrobe, so no one will notice how average you are. Sparkling brooches to draw the eye, a tuck here, or a pleat there, a sharp contrast with fabric and the right pattern will transform you into a butterfly, and the suitors will flock to you."

Mama's seamstress spent untold hours updating her wardrobe, pouring over patterns and ideas with Mama. But alas, the one suitor who flocked to her turned out to be a gray gull too old to fly and losing feathers by the handfuls.

"My lady." The duke's deep voice penetrated her thoughts, and she jumped when she discovered him beside her. He stood in the open door of the castle and ushered them into an exquisite entry hall.

Mama and Papa stood within, waiting.

"Make sure Thomas gets some rest, Rosalind. I will see you at dinner." After giving their instructions, the parents left the entry following a footman.

Rosalind turned back to their host, and his steady regard made her pause. Had she missed something? The heat of his body warmed her side, and her nose caught whiffs of orange, lemon, bay leaf, and sandalwood on his clothes. An unknown feeling settled in the pit of her stomach, and she shifted nervously. God, he smelled good. None of the young lords she met used toilet water of such a mouthwatering scent. Her fiancé, the earl, did not, either. Of this, she knew.

"Rosalind, this is my butler, John, and my housekeeper, Mary. Mary will show you to your chamber, where you can rest and freshen up from your long journey."

Portly with white hair, clean-shaven, brown eyes, and a crisp uniform, John bowed from the waist. "A pleasure, my lady."

Mary's round little body, covered in a severe black uniform, dipped a curtsy. Sparkling brown eyes surrounded by curly brown hair and pink cheeks smiled into hers. "I'm happy to make yer acquaintance."

"Can I pet the dog?" Thomas stepped forward until he stood in front of the beast sitting beside the duke's feet.

"Let us put the admiral out of harm's way, and then I will introduce the two of you." Taking the frog from the boy, he tucked him into his own pocket away from the dog before crouching down beside him. "Thomas, this is Ulysses. He is part Great Pyrenees, part wolf. Let him sniff your hand before you touch him."

The boy bowed and held out his arm for the dog to sniff before stroking the dog's head. "I like him."

"I trained him from a pup. Ulysses can be aggressive at times, so make sure you do not surprise him."

The distraction lasted for a few minutes before Thomas ran to the center of the room, looking up.

Rosalind's gaze followed him, widening in amazement. Cream plaster walls with gilt-edged mirrors and paintings surrounded them. Elegant tables held crystal vases of fresh-cut flowers, filling the air with their sweet perfume. A thick cream Persian rug lay at their feet, but the ceiling held her attention. Ice blue plaster framed in gold depicted angels engaged in various activities. One played a harp while another lounged on a cloud. One held a rose, sniffing the delicate perfume, and another shot golden arrows with a golden bow.

"How did they get up there?" Thomas' voice dripped with curiosity as he tilted his head all the way back to stare.

"I hired workmen to paint them for me." The duke nodded toward the ceiling from his position on her left.

"I know, but how did they get up there? It is too high, and there is nothing to climb."

The duke's lips twitched. "The workmen carried in wooden scaffolds to stand on while they worked. They were quite safe. Is there anything else you wish to know?"

She closed her eyes and held back a moan. Now the boy would never stop asking questions, and she did not want to test their host's goodwill further. Catching Thomas' hand in hers, she turned to follow Mary. "You can ask his grace more later. I think Mama wants you to rest."

Her brother kicked at the carpet. "I am too old to sleep during the day. I want to explore the castle. Those tall towers touched the clouds, and I wanted to see how to get up there. Come with me, Ruby. I bet you can see the whole world from up there."

Anxiety gripped her chest as visions of her little brother leaning out the turret window danced in her head. He had no sense of safety. "You must not, Thomas. Mama would not like it." This new worry distracted her from the duke's closeness.

"I have planned to take you around the castle tomorrow." Her host strolled to the child's side and handed him the admiral. "I shall make a special effort to show you the towers on the condition you never go up there alone. Agreed?"

The boy nodded, his grin growing wider.

"For now, I thought you could all rest and get settled in, as I have meetings I must attend to. Now be a good lad and go with your sister. I shall see you at dinner." With a nod in Rosalind's direction, he turned to walk away.

He had not gone two feet before her brother exclaimed, "Bugger!"

She gasped in horror. "Thomas!" The little rascal seemed determined to put the wrong foot forward with the duke. "You should not use swear words." Risking a quick glance at the duke's retreating form, she noted how he slowed as he neared the door to the corridor as if he waited to hear their conversation.

She flushed with embarrassment at the prospect.

"Why? Papa says them when he is happy."

"I have never heard him. If you cannot behave, I shall be forced to send you to rest your mouth." She meant every word and prayed the duke was far enough away he could not hear them.

Her brother's chin lifted in challenge. "Yes, Papa does. When his new racehorse nipped at him, he told Mama he was bloody happy the bugger did not take a finger off. You cannot be happier than bloody happy."

Loud male laughter preceded the duke down the corridor as he resumed his departure with the dog at his heels.

She sighed from the bottom of her soul. "Do not let Mama catch you saying those words, or she will put spice on your tongue."

"Okay." His voice sounded sincere but she had her doubts.

Gripping Thomas' hand, they followed Mary in the opposite direction. Rosalind thanked the gods the impassive duke possessed a sense of humor.

A young housemaid approached to relieve her of Thomas, to take him to the nursery where he would sleep. With reluctance and a great many warnings to keep a close eye on the lad, she let him go.

Men servants carried in her trunks an hour later, and three housemaids unpacked, airing out the gowns to her new trousseau.

When they lifted the gossamer lace wedding gown wrapped in paper from the trunk, Rosalind held her breath. As the maids removed the paper, they exclaimed over the delicate, intricate design of the lace. Made in Paris, the gown had a tight bodice with long tight sleeves. The skirt dropped in graceful lines to the floor, where a small, elegant train cascaded from the back waist. The back of the gown dipped low to her shoulder blades, trimmed in expensive hand-stitched lace edging. The gown should be worn by a bride in love, wedding the love of her life, not her, of average height with average red hair wedding an old man for the purpose of giving him an heir.

A wistful sigh escaped her as she sank onto the bed to oversee the unpacking.

The afternoon passed quickly, and soon her maid, Ellen, arrived to dress her for dinner.

"Which gown, my lady?" She held open the wardrobe filled with a rainbow of fashionable gowns purchased for this year's season.

Rebellion against her life and the choices made for her filled her heart. "The red velvet evening gown."

Ellen paused, shooting her a concerned glance. "Did yer mother not say to get rid of it? I did not know we packed the red one."

"I packed it, and I will wear it to dinner." Mama did not think the burgundy velvet gown with the scoop neck and high waist complimented her hair or coloring. Right now, Rosalind did not care. She liked the gown and the way she felt with it on. The velvet brushed her skin, the scoop neck made her average bust appear fuller, and the high waist made her average height appear taller. For some reason, she cared whether the duke thought her average or not. As a grown woman of nineteen, she should be allowed to make her own choices, and a girl must resort to whatever means necessary to accomplish the impossible.

With her hair curled high on her head and threaded with a string of pearls, she stepped into the gold salon the footman escorted her to and stopped.

Mama sat on a white settee dressed in lavender and amethysts beside Papa, resplendent in his wine-colored dinner jacket with black embroidery and black breeches.

The duke stood before the fireplace swirling a glass of whiskey in his hand and staring into the flames. Dressed in a black evening jacket etched with gold embroidery, he wore a snow-white pleated shirt, a navy vest, and black trousers. The masculine picture he presented made her stomach flutter with awareness.

She dropped her gaze to hide her expression and noted Ulysses lying before the hearth at the duke's feet, his eyes watchful.

Thomas sat opposite Mama in his best blue jacket and black pants, fiddling with his fingers. His expression stony with boredom and mutiny.

Mama caught sight of her first and gasped in disbelief. "You packed the burgundy velvet to wear at the castle? Why, Rosalind, when I forbade you to? You know how red clashes with your hair and complexion. Is your plan to embarrass me in front of the duke?"

Rosalind's chin lifted as she held eye contact, refusing to be ashamed of her choice for dinner. "No, Mama, I chose this gown because I like the color and style." *Please do not make a scene. Soon I shall be wed with no say in anything.*

"I think she looks pretty." Thomas got up and walked to her side, taking hold of her hand.

"I agree." The duke's deep voice broke into her thoughts, and she tore her gaze away from Mama, risking a glance at his face. He stood beside the mantel and took a sip of whisky as his gaze slid over her trembling body, resting on her heaving bosom and rising to her hair.

Their eyes locked, and the strange fluttering she experienced before filled her belly. She grew breathless at the prolonged contact and swallowed to ease the dryness of her throat.

"You are beautiful, daughter, like your mother. Come sit beside me." Papa rose and tucked her other arm in his, leading her to the settee beside him.

Mama glanced at Papa and then Rosalind, pinching her lips together. She would say nothing more in front of their host but would wait until she had a moment alone to express her opinion.

Rosalind accepted the small reprieve with a glance of gratitude toward the heavens. She and Mama had lots of little talks, and although plentiful, they never got any more pleasant.

At dinner, the duke sat at the head of the table with Ulysses at his feet, Mama on his left, and Papa on his right. Thomas sat beside Papa, and she sat beside Mama.

Every time Rosalind glanced up, she met the duke's

searching gaze and blushed, dropping her eyes to her lap or the top of the table.

The parents discussed the weather, travel time, and banalities until Mama brought up her pending doom. "A Christmas Wedding at Weston Castle. What could be more exciting or romantic?"

Rosalind made a quick mental list beginning with a groom more her age with hair and good teeth, who walked without a limp and loved her despite her clumsiness and ordinary ways. A man who challenged her and viewed her abilities as desirable assets, not flaws.

An intelligent mind should be a virtue, not something to be ashamed of.

"Have you had many suitors, Lady Rosalind?"

Her gaze jumped to the duke when his deep voice broke into her thoughts.

"One besides the earl." She did not know why it became important to say she attracted more than one elderly lord intent on procreation, but it did.

Mama swiveled toward her. "Tell us more, darling." A small smile twisted her lips upward.

Papa quit eating and set his fork down, his gaze on Mama. "I do not think this the time or the place for confessions, Amelia."

Mama shrugged. "I want to hear what she has to say."

All eyes focused on her. Even Thomas stopped chewing long enough to stare. A log settled in the fireplace, disturbing the sudden silence of the room.

Her mouth dried, and she swallowed nervously. "Richard Carruthers and the earl."

Papa's shoulders dropped as if he let out a pent-up breath of relief.

"Oh, pish." Her mother dismissed Rosalind's comment with a wave of her hand and continued eating.

Papa's gaze pinned her to her seat. "You mean Baron Richard Carruthers's from down the road? What connection did you have with him? I do not recall him expressing any interest in you, and did he not marry Miss Standish last summer?" Papa looked perplexed and gazed from Mama to her. "I have been underinformed on a great many subjects, it would seem. We believed both your seasons were unfruitful and accepted the first offer we received for your hand after what happened. Had I known another man held an interest, I would have considered the option. What happened, Rosalind?"

Wishing the floor would swallow her whole and damning her wayward mouth, she set her fork on the fine linen tablecloth and took a deep breath. She must share the same genetic mouth disorder her brother suffered from. "He made me promise to marry him when we were younger, but he grew up and asked Miss Standish instead." Of course, he wore knee breeches when he proposed, and they were in the middle of making mud pies when it happened. He did not like Cecelia Standish back then, teasing her with frogs and bugs until her skirts dropped to her shoes, she grew breasts, a waist, and hips, and her hair rose to the top of her head. Then, he transformed to a drooling half-wit writing sonnets to express his undying love for her. The baron did not qualify as a love of her life because they were five and six at the time, and her interest in him stemmed from his ability to catch dragonflies without destroying their wings. Not from a palpating heart.

"Oh. I see. Nothing quite as serious as the other." Papa resumed eating, and the matter dropped.

She did not realize her hand shook until she lifted her glass to take a drink and spilled a little.

Chapter Three

"Are you excited at the prospect of a Christmas Wedding at the castle, Rosalind? Most girls would be, I have been told by several dowagers in the area. I hoped to discuss the wedding decorations tomorrow or the day after so I can get my people working on them. Cook has put together a tentative menu for the reception, and I would like to discuss the number of guests, etc. at the same time. I have several dinners and a ball planned for neighboring gentry to meet the family over the course of the next few weeks. I thought we could keep you entertained until your fiancé arrives." The duke's blue eyes rested on Rosalind as he spoke, and heat rose to her cheeks.

"How very kind, your grace. I, of course, am delighted to go over any of these items with you whenever you wish. Rosalind has no sense of protocol or etiquette for these kinds of situations. So, I will be handling all the arrangements for her." Mama took a sip of her wine and smiled at their host.

Silence followed her announcement, and Rosalind shifted in her seat. Mama thought she would make a mess of everything and would not give her a chance. Granted, she did end up in situations out of her control, usually instigated by her brother, and since she had no say in the groom, she wished she could arrange the wedding to her taste.

"This wedding is hers. I think Lady Rosalind should decide."

The duke's quiet words wrapped around her heart, and she swallowed the sudden emotion in her throat.

"Really, you must accept my word in this matter. I am the best choice for handling this affair." Mama met the duke's gaze head-on, determined to get her way.

Papa said nothing, knowing better than to get in Mama's way when she made her mind up about something.

The duke arched a brow at Mama and turned to Rosalind. "My lady?"

She cleared her throat and met his gaze. "Thank you. I would very much like to plan the wedding."

"Then the matter is settled. Meet me in my study at ten tomorrow morning, and we shall go over the details."

Mama sucked in a breath, shooting her daughter a look of displeasure but said nothing more.

Rosalind ignored the thunderclouds hovering over her mother and smiled into the duke's eyes. "Of course. Thank you, your grace."

Dinner continued without further disruption until the admiral suddenly joined them, jumping from Thomas' pocket onto the fine linen tablecloth.

Mama screamed and shoved her chair back, upsetting a footman behind her with a tray of dessert. The tray flew through the air as the footman slipped, landing on his backside. Silver plates, forks, and cake flew in every direction. Whipped cream splatted onto the table in front of Rosalind, covered the back of her mother and the side of the duke's face, dripping onto the arm and shoulder of his gold-embroidered black dinner jacket.

The dog barked and rose to his feet to join the

confusion, running back and forth with his gaze on the frog.

John rushed forward with an army of servants, wiping, clearing, dodging the excited dog, and directing the flow of people coming and going, while he apologized for the mess.

The duke snapped his fingers, and Ulysses sank to the floor at his feet. Holding his hand up for silence, he surveyed the chaos.

Thomas caught the frog, tucked the creature back into his pocket and shot a sheepish glance toward the duke, who leaned forward in his seat with his hands steepled, a thoughtful expression on his face.

The silence lasted for long moments, deafening her, and her heart rose high in her throat. Their host dealt with the last episode in a calm, detached manner, and she hoped he did this one as well.

"I believe I mentioned how silent I found the castle just yesterday, Did I not, John?" Picking up his glass of wine, Cousin Lucius took a sip.

The butler grinned. "Aye, and how bored ye were, wishing for something to liven up yer life."

"I now realize my error in not being more specific in my wishes. Instruct the workman to make a small cage for the admiral and have someone lock him in while we dine from now on. Ulysses will be kenneled during meals so we do not have a repeat of tonight's entertainment."

"Are you going to make me stay in the nursery for dinner now, too?" Thomas eyed the duke in what she guessed could be interpreted as repentance, although she had never witnessed the child being so.

"Why would I do so when you usher so much life into this old castle? I dare say none of the servants have hustled so fast in the last five years as they have since your arrival. I welcome the diversion."

"You cannot mean it." Mama found her voice at last and sank into her seat, brushing cake and whipped cream from her once pristine lavender silk gown.

"But I do. I am happy you are here to share my Christmas, and I look forward to the coming weeks. I dare say they will not be boring."

Rising to his feet, he glanced at Thomas. "Come along, young man. I believe a distraction is in order. I have some soldiers, a drum, and a wooden sword you might enjoy."

Rosalind's eyebrow rose. Her ears cringed when he spoke of the drum but sword? Oh lord! The trouble her brother could create with such an item!

Thomas had the same thought, for as he passed her, he whispered, "Bugger."

****

The next morning at ten o'clock sharp, Rosalind smoothed the skirt of her navy silk day dress, and biting her lip, knocked on the duke's study door.

Mama's lecture the previous night rang in her ears, but she did not care. If her life were to be planned out for her, first by her mother, then by her husband, she would arrange her wedding to suit her own thoughts and bugger to them both.

The oak door swung open, and she faced the duke dressed in shirt sleeves and black breeches. His gold embroidered vest buttoned down the front where a gold watch chain dangled from the bulge in his vest to the front pocket of his breeches.

His gaze slid over her face and hair, dropping to her lips for the barest moment.

"Come in." He stepped back, leaving the door open, and strolled back to his heavy oak desk along the opposite wall.

The room boasted heavy leather settees before the marble fireplace and another in front of his desk with oak side tables on either side. Heavy navy drapes hung at the large window creating a dominant masculine atmosphere.

She took a moment to steady her racing heart before stepping into the room. Her mother forbade her to go to the duke's study without her, commenting on the impropriety of being alone with him.

"Should the earl learn of this, I fear what his reaction would be. We cannot return home with you unwed. Think what the villagers will say."

Rosalind knew full well and found the idea as distasteful as her mother. "The duke is no threat and wishes to help. What harm can come of sitting in his study planning my wedding? I will ask Ellen to join me."

"You will ask your mother to join you, or I go without you. The choice is yours." Mama used her serious tone so her daughter knew how much trouble she would be in if she did not submit.

And here she stood, making her choice.

"I took the liberty of inviting my housekeeper to sit in our conversation." He waved toward the door as Mary bustled in and took a seat. "Whenever you are ready, Rosalind. We can begin."

Her name rolled off his tongue like blackberry brandy, sweet to her ears and smooth to the palate creating flutters in her stomach. "Of course." Sitting beside the housekeeper, she folded her hands in her lap and lifted her gaze to his.

The duke leaned back, studying her. "Traditionally, we host two dinners during the holiday season. The first dinner is held the last week of November for the local gentry and any visitors. The second dinner is held the second week of December. This is for family and anyone they wish to invite. The third week of December, we host a Christmas Ball and invite everyone in the area. As a boy, my grandfather took me to the forest to pick out a tree for the ball the first week of December. The servants collect boughs of evergreen, holly and mistletoe, which we hang in the main living areas, down the corridors, and the ballroom.

"On Christmas Eve, we light the yule log with a remnant of last year's log for remembrance, and gifts are exchanged. Christmas day, we open our doors for servant and lord alike to feast in the main hall. The ballroom is used for dancing and entertainment until the sun sets, and then we close our doors until the next holiday season.

"With your wedding taking place on Christmas Day, we can either do away with the feasting and dancing except for wedding guests and open our doors the following week or offer the tradition at the ball the week before. What are your thoughts on the matter?"

No one asked her to speak her mind before, and she hesitated, unfamiliar with how to proceed.

"I say we do away with the tradition altogether this year. The villagers must understand an important member of your family is being wed and celebrate in their own homes." Her mother's voice rang out from the open door as she strode into the room and took a seat beside Rosalind. "I must not have heard you knock, darling. I am sorry I am late."

Ulysses lifted his head from his place on the floor

29

beside the duke and gave a soft growl.

The duke rose to his feet to welcome Mama, snapping his finger at the dog.

"I did not knock." Rosalind lifted her chin and met her mother's furious gaze. The heady sensation of speaking her mind for the first time exhilarated her, and with a shrug, she ignored her mother's warning look. "Although I appreciate your concern, the success or failure of my marriage rests on me and my wedding equally so."

Mama's mouth dropped open. "But how shall you know who to seat beside whom? Or what to serve for dinner for optimum effect? This event must convey the importance of your position as the duke's relative and the earl's bride. London Society must proclaim this the event of the year!"

"And all this time, I thought you planned to see me wed so I would not be an embarrassment to you and Papa." She could not resist the comment, for her mother brought the subject up often enough.

The duke steepled his hands as he regarded the women. "I have given countless parties which were all the rage in the London rags with Mary making all the arrangements. Do not worry, madame, about the intricacies of society. I think you will find the nobility quite eager to praise our efforts."

Anger flashed for the barest second in her mother's eyes. "I do not wish to stay if I am unwanted." She sniffed, waiting for someone to assure her they valued her opinion. When they did not, she shot a glance at her daughter and adopted a molasses-sweet smile to impress the duke. "I will oversee this event and inform you of any social missteps to avoid embarrassment. Yours or ours. I do wish to point out Rosalind's job is to see to the boy. I have no idea where Thomas is and think she should go search for him." Her mother's chin rose in challenge.

"I have employed a young woman from the village to keep an eye on the boy while you are here, to free up Rosalind's time. With your daughter's upcoming wedding, you might consider hiring a companion as well, for soon Rosalind will no longer be available to you." Leaning forward, he ignored her mother's gasp of outrage. "Now for dinner and the reception. Once we are finished here, I will take you through the rooms on this level before taking Thomas to see the towers."

Rosalind had no problem with the decorations he mentioned. She would miss Christmas at home and all the festivities in the village. Here, she would enjoy them on a grander scale before she succumbed to marriage and childbirth.

They discussed meats, wines, and desserts, deferring on several occasions to Mary's superior wisdom on the subjects. She suggested pheasant soup, puree of grouse, and stewed trout for the first course, followed by a haunch of venison, saddle of lamb, hot raised pie of mixed game, and spring chickens for the second course. Entrees of salmon, Christmas goose, braised beef, and fillet of pheasant and truffles would then be served, and the third course would consist of wild duck, snipes, golden plovers, and widgeons. Raspberry cream, cherry tarts, Charlotte Russe, and Madeira wine would complete the meal.

Rosalind sat back with a sigh, her mouth watering. Content to let Mary use her best judgment for the other dinners, her lips curved in a happy smile.

Her mother sat stiff beside her, her lips thinning every time her suggestions were ignored, and her daughter knew she would get an earful as soon as they were alone.

"I received a message from the Earl of Gloucester today. He plans to arrive earlier than anticipated and should be here by this time next week."

Her happy thoughts disappeared in an instant, and a bitter taste filled her mouth. "Oh. Thank you." She thought she had more time to enjoy her freedom, but the marriage gallows loomed in the distance, calling her name. Even with the enticement of Christmas in the castle, the thought turned her mouth down and filled her with anxiety.

"How wonderful!" Mama clapped her hands, her good humor returning. "Once the earl is here, we shall present the plans for the wedding and see if he approves. Then, we shall adjust them to our liking."

The knot forming in Rosalind's stomach grew as the foreboding shadow of her future weighed like a stone. She did not realize, until now, how much influence Mama had over her future, nor how much she valued her own opinion. Rising to her feet, she lifted her chin in defiance. "They are to my liking now. There is no reason to bother the earl with the details, and we shall proceed with things the way they are." Facing the duke, she smiled. "Will you show us the ballroom and dining room, please?" Anxious to divert the conversation away from her ancient fiancé, she smiled. "I wonder how tall a tree we can fit in the ballroom."

The duke rose to his feet and offered her his arm. "Come and see."

Rosalind did not glance back at Mama. She sensed

the disapproval in the click of her slippers against the stone floor behind them.

They walked several feet ahead of Mama and Mary, for her mother kept a good distance from Ulysses, who padded along beside the duke.

"You are not happy with your parents' choice of husband?" His keen blue eyes searched her face. He spoke low so she alone heard his question as they strolled down the corridor and around the next.

She thought hard and fast about her answer. He must not learn of her discontent, or Mama would never forgive her. "Has your grace met the earl?" A question seemed a better answer than the truth.

"Nay. I know him by reputation only. I confess I did not know the earl had a son old enough to marry. I remember my father mentioning the old man's third wife dying in childbirth. I had the impression the man had no children."

She swallowed the bile rising in her throat. "He does not. He marries me to provide him with one."

Several minutes passed in silence until she glanced up and met his unreadable expression.

"I find it hard to believe no one paid you court but he." His lids dropped over his eyes, concealing his expression as he made the statement. "You are quite beautiful, Lady Rosalind."

She risked a glance at his face to see if he jested with her. "I have endured two London seasons, two wardrobes with all the fittings, and too many failures with nothing to show for the effort but the earl."

"In failures, you mean…" He seemed determined to get all the humiliating details.

"I received the usual number of flowers and

invitations to dance but I am clumsy, unladylike, and headstrong, not to mention intelligent. I outthink most men of my acquaintance, and my would-be suitors found me offensive. In short, I am not the sort of malleable material most men seek in a wife."

"I see." Clearing his throat, he stopped before two ornate wooden doors and threw them open to reveal the perfect area for a Christmas ball.

Chapter Four

Four massive chandeliers hung from the gilded ceiling painted with scenes of angels with beautiful golden wings gazing down as if a heavenly host oversaw the proceedings. Gilt-edged mirrors and fabulous colorful tapestries adorned the cream silk lined walls, and though grand, the workmanship in the flooring drew her attention. Blocks of wood carved with intricate designs, each more fabulous than the last, nestled against each other in a sea of gleaming wooden splendor.

"Oh, my." Rosalind put a hand to her chest and blinked.

They stood on a platform with stairs leading down either side, and on the opposite end of the grand room, two curved stairways led up to double doors opening outward to the magnificent gardens beyond.

She did not have to close her eyes to envision a twenty-foot tree strewn with dried fruit, candy, nuts, and strings of cranberries. Holly and mistletoe would drape the handrails and adorn the walls. The orchestra would sit over there, and the refreshment tables would be over there. Swirling couples in bright colors would fill the floor with the strain of the music. The laughter, joy, and excitement of Christmas would permeate the air filling the guests with happiness and anticipation.

Her nose twitched as if she could smell the pine tree, roasted nuts, cider, and hot apple tarts. Excitement and wonder filled her soul as she envisioned the throng of holiday merry makers.

"I have engaged local musicians for the ball, and the vicar agreed to perform the wedding ceremony on Christmas Day."

Mention of her wedding dropped her back into reality with a thump as Mama stepped to her side. "We will set up the tree over there, out of the way." She pointed at the opposite corner of the ballroom. "Hmmm. I think the refreshments will go on the opposite wall in the corner."

"The tree will be twenty feet high and go between the curved stairs opposite us, where it will be the focus of attention." She would not dissuaded from the vision in her head.

Papa appeared with Thomas and stood beside the duke. "Excellent idea, Rosalind. I remember years ago, we put a tree there, and the whole castle took on an abundance of holiday spirit. As if putting the tree in the center of our festivities centered goodwill and joy in our hearts." He smiled in remembrance. "We hung mistletoe everywhere, and I kissed my first girl over there by the stairs."

"With mistletoe hanging all over the castle, some local lord might decide to make use of it and give Rosalind a kiss." The duke's deep voice broke into her thoughts.

Heat filled her cheeks as she risked a glance up at him. "Rest assured, once the mistletoe is hung, I shall walk a wide berth so no one makes a mistake."

"I think your decision wise under the circumstances, although I doubt the young man will consider such a moment a mistake. I did not." Papa laughed and slapped the duke on the shoulder. "Or you either, I will wager."

"My first kiss happened long before that Christmas, but no, I did not consider it a mistake."

His first kiss. What would such a thing be like? She mused on the subject for a minute and jumped when the duke cleared his throat. "The dining room is this way."

Though not as detailed as the ballroom, the dining room featured elegant pale mauve silk walls and a long gleaming rosewood table with silver vases and candelabras. Thirty guests could sit comfortably while an army of servants served them. A massive marble fireplace stood on one wall, and gilded chandeliers hung overhead.

"Very little will change in here but the decorations and the centerpieces. We have gold dinnerware and gold-rimmed glassware for the table."

Rosalind blew out a breath of delight as she imagined the scene. Liveried servants bearing platters of food, mouth-watering aromas, holly and mistletoe, a hearty fire on the hearth, and elegant guests, chattering while they ate. Her stomach rumbled as she envisioned the menu items.

"I want to see the towers," Thomas announced from his position behind them. "I rested yesterday so I could." He stood beside the Great Pyrenees, stroking his fur, and Rosalind fancied the dog leaning in to get more attention.

A chuckle escaped the duke. "Well then, we shall proceed to the towers. Come along, Ulysses."

Mama grimaced. "I have seen enough for one day. I think I will go to the salon and order tea."

Papa agreed with the plan and offered her his arm. "I will leave you both in Cousin Lucius' capable hands." With a nod at the duke, he said, "Thank you, cousin, for your hospitality."

"My pleasure." Warmth shone from the duke's gaze as he nodded at Papa and offered Rosalind his arm. "We go down this corridor."

"I agree with Papa and offer my gratitude for your kindness, your grace." The visons of holly and mistletoe in her head enticed her as nothing had in a good while.

The duke remained silent for a moment. "Since we shall be in proximity for the next month, I suggest we drop the formal salutations. I shall be Cousin Lucius, and you shall be Rosalind, agreed? I find there is too much confusion with formality when it need not be so. Imagine three duchesses taking tea together and their conversation."

A giggle rose to her throat. "I see your point and bow to your superior wisdom."

He led them to the east side of the castle, and together they climbed the steep, winding stairs to the top. Once they arrived at the door leading to the tower, Cousin Lucius lifted the latch and swung the door in. The hinges groaned as the heavy door opened, allowing them entrance.

Thomas ran to the tower window exclaiming over the view and laughing as the breeze ruffled his hair. "I knew you could see the whole world up here." Ulysses followed him and sat by his heels as if to protect him.

When Rosalind pointed out his behavior toward the boy, Cousin Lucius smiled. "He belonged to my late wife, Lucinda, and I trained him to look after her in my absence. I think he considers Thomas his new duty."

It would appear so for the animal positioned his body, so any threat had to pass him before gaining access to her brother.

They gazed out for more than an hour before Cousin Lucius turned to Thomas. "You must not ever come up here alone. I did once as a boy, and the wind blew so hard through the open windows the door swung shut, and I could not open it. Wet weather caused the wood to swell, and the latch jammed, making me a prisoner in my own home. I would have caught my death of cold if my brother had not searched for me. While waiting for rescue, I paced and leaned out the windows hoping someone would notice my distress. I will never forget the feeling of being locked inside and losing a miniature of my mother somewhere between the gold salon and the tower. I have not found it since."

"Why did you come up alone? Did your father tell you not to?" Thomas frowned at the duke as if he wondered whether he had a good father for not warning him.

"Aye, he did, but we received news my mother died, and I wanted to be alone."

She remembered Papa telling them the story. The duke's mother broke her neck in a riding accident and died, leaving her husband alone to raise their two sons. His father died eight years later, followed by his older brother, taken ill with consumption, leaving Cousin Lucius the surviving member of his family.

"I will not come up here without Ruby. I promise." The little boy nodded his agreement, and they returned the same way, closing the heavy door behind them.

Cousin Lucius left Thomas and Ulysses with the nanny and escorted Rosalind to her chamber.

"Until dinner." Taking her hand in his, he maintained eye contact as he bent his head. His hot lips slid over the cool flesh of her hand, weakening her knees.

Her breath caught in her throat as his mouth moved against her skin, making her tremble in her satin slippers. His earlier conversation about kissing made her wonder what his firm mouth would feel like if he slid his lips over hers like he did the back of her hand, and the fever of desire caught her blood on fire. Fluttering filled her belly as she wilted against the door jamb, willing this moment to last for an eternity.

At last, he lifted his head. "Good day, Rosalind."

****

John presented her with a glorious centerpiece for the dining table the next morning, weighed down with pine, holly, mistletoe, and red roses from the duke's hot house. "I am to get your approval or order whatever changes ye desire. There will be seven of them down the length of the table." He grinned at her amazement as she touched the petals of a rose.

"This is magnificent. I have never seen such a beautiful arrangement in my life. The silver base and red bow add a touch of elegance that takes my breath away. You have my approval."

"The gardener and Mary will be pleased. Thank you, my lady." He bowed and walked away, leaving her breathing in the exquisite scent of the centerpiece. Every item needed for a perfect holiday wedding lay at her fingertips and she could not help wishing the groom and her future were as well. She hated the uncertainty of what her life would be once the ceremony concluded. Would the earl be kind? Would he treat her well? Would she be allowed to visit Thomas or he her? How she would miss her busy, danger-seeking little brother and the messes he got into.

Swallowing her anxiety, she glanced up with a

tender smile when her little brother burst into the room with his sword in hand. "Come play with me, Ruby. I have not seen you for days."

"You sat beside me at dinner last night and breakfast this morning." She brushed a strand of red-brown hair from his brow and gazed into his blue eyes so like her own.

"Eating does not count because you have to do it." He stared up at her twisting his face into a frown. "Are you crying, Ruby? I see a wet mark on your cheek."

"Of course not. Why would I cry when I have you?" She gave him a quick hug, and to her amazement, he hugged her back. The child avoided hugging because he said they made him feel squeezed.

He shrugged. "Maybe you cried because you have not played today. I cry when I do not."

He made a good point. She glanced down at her mauve satin day gown and grimaced. She would be forced to behave like a lady soon enough. In the meantime, she had today and all the possibilities this moment contained. "I will come play swords with you but I must change my gown first. Mama would not like me ripping this one."

He nodded his head. "I will wait for you in the gold salon." Turning, he walked away as if he had an important mission to perform.

The boy could be both a terror and a gentleman from one moment to another, and one never knew which one would win.

Half an hour later, they retired to the ballroom for a rousing game of swordplay involving a pirate and the militia.

Rosalind hid behind a pedestal holding a Grecian

bust, waiting for the pirate to show his face so she could arrest him in the name of the king. She held a wooden sword identical to the pirate's in her hand.

The whisper of feet against the wooden floor made her smile. Her brother improved his ability to maneuver without making a sound.

"Hah!" Thomas rounded the corner, and they exchanged blows. He lunged, and she parried, blocking his attack.

Ulysses barked and jumped to join the fun, earning him a pat on the head from Thomas. Ending his assault as quickly as he began, her brother turned and ran up the stairs to the platform in front of the door leading to the corridor.

"You cannot catch me." His challenge rang in the silence as he charged out the double oak doors with her right at his heels.

She bound into the corridor and swung her sword with both hands at an object she glimpsed from the corner of her eye and stopped cold.

Her play sword rested level with the Earl of Gloucester's neck.

She gulped and lowered her arm, swallowing the tightness in her throat as she met his steely-eyed gaze and the stunned silence in the corridor.

The duke stood beside the earl, and her mother frowned with annoyance a foot behind them, holding tight to Thomas' shoulder.

Ulysses growled at the earl, showing teeth until the duke snapped his fingers. Dropping to the floor beside his master's feet, he stared at the newcomers with his ears flat, warning them to keep their distance.

"I did not know you had a dog in your castle,

Weston, or I would have stayed elsewhere. I am allergic to the horrible beasts, as is my man, Edgar."

A moment of silence greeted his announcement. "I shall have him kenneled while you are here." The duke summoned a footman commanding him to take the dog away.

Thomas stomped his foot in anger until Mama threatened to take him to the nursery.

A tall thin man with graying hair and a scowl stood one step behind the earl. Plain dark clothing proclaimed him a valet. His haughty stance and rigid demeanor proclaimed him trouble. Edgar, she surmised.

Once she had Thomas quiet, her mother turned to her. "Darling, we searched everywhere for you until one of the footmen heard noise coming from the ballroom. I must say we are quite surprised to see you…thus." Her eyes snapped with disapproval as she made the dry statement.

"I apologize." Rosalind turned her attention back to the earl and dipped down in a deep curtsy sucking in air to calm the furious beat of her heart. "My lord, I believed you would not arrive until next week."

"As I see." His tone dripped with displeasure. "Hand me the toy. I believed you to be above childish games, but now I understand my error. I await your apology for not meeting me upon my arrival and instead find you behaving in an unseemly manner."

She turned the handle of the wooden object toward him and dropped her hand when he took it.

He handed the sword to his valet. "Edgar, dispose of this worthless object."

The thin man took the toy between two fingers as if the object were infested with the black death. "Aye, my lord." His narrow gaze bored into hers as he held the toy away from his person.

Rosalind tightened her lips. "I apologize, my lord. I entertained the boy, nothing more, and meant no disrespect. Had I been informed of your arrival, I would have been in attendance." Her mother would have ensured it. Judging from the way the earl's eye twitched, she doubted her apology appeased him.

"A kiss of welcome is in order to prove your delight with my presence and your repentance for embarrassing me." His dull eyes challenged her, and she swallowed hard pinching her lips shut.

Playing toy swords with a child embarrassed him? The future did not bode well for her, for she envisioned hours of play with a child of her own.

"Of course." Bending from the waist, she placed a quick kiss on his leathery cheek and resisted the urge to wipe the contact from her lips with the back of her hand. "Welcome, my lord. Please accept my apology." She choked on the words and smiled to hide her reaction.

"Hhmp." The earl placed both hands on the top of his cane and surveyed her from head to toe. "I will forgive you this once, but in future save your energy for the marriage bed. I like a woman with a little spirit. Makes the bedding more enjoyable. Eh, Weston?" He nudged the duke with his elbow and received a quirked eyebrow in response.

The nauseating, sweet scent of the earl's toilet water, coupled with images of being in bed beside the wrinkled old man, made her eyes water and nausea rise in her throat. Choking, she bent her head, hoping to get her wayward stomach under control before she emptied her breakfast all over her aging fiancé.

"Shall we adjourn to the gold salon for tea?" The duke's deep voice calmed the nervous flutter in her belly.

"If you excuse me, I will go change and meet you there." Not waiting for approval, Rosalind escaped to her chamber, where her breakfast catapulted into her chamber pot from her gagging mouth. Retching until her sides ached, she leaned back against the side of her bed and closed her eyes. Dear God, how could she go through with this arrangement if the scent of her fiancé made her sick to her stomach?

Tea would settle the unruly ripples in her belly and give her fortitude in her dealings with the earl, who would no doubt send a footman if she took one minute longer to change than he deemed appropriate. Rising, she rang for her maid, changing into a lavender silk tea gown and white gloves.

Chapter Five

She found the three of them plus Papa, in the gold salon sipping from delicate porcelain cups and making small talk.

Edgar, the earl's man, stood behind her aging fiancé with watchful black eyes. The earl sat on a settee alone while her parents occupied the second, and the duke sat in a velvet armchair.

Rosalind hurried in and sat in the other armchair before anyone could suggest different, smoothing the skirt of her gown with nervous hands. She dared not make eye contact with any of them as she poured a cup of tea and added a sugar cube.

"Sweet tea is for children, not grown women." The earl remarked. "I prefer you to sit by my side. I have missed you."

She had no idea why he would. They met once, at a ball at the palace, before he sent flowers and asked to speak to Papa, who accepted his proposal of marriage with surprising speed. Afterward, they danced at one other ball and ate dinner side by side at another. He could not miss her because he did not know her.

She added another cube for effect and stirred her tea with slow, methodical circles. "There is a chill in the air, and I am closer to the hearth where I am." She had no intention of sitting beside him or anything else until she must.

"I must insist. Come sit beside me, and I shall warm you." His whiny, high-pitched voice took on a note of command, and she blanched when she met Mama's furious gaze.

"Take my place, my dear. I am too near the fire and must retreat, or I fear I will melt. I will trade you places, and everyone will be happy. The earl enjoys his space to rest his leg and invites you near him to show you favor. We shall allow him his freedom while he can." Papa rose to his feet and strolled to her chair, giving her a small smile when she mouthed *thank you* as they passed.

Sinking down beside Mama, she placed her teacup on the table at their knees and held her hands to the blaze. God bless Papa and his good heart. She could have hugged him when he made his suggestion, turning an awkward situation into a better one.

The earl frowned but said nothing more.

When Rosalind glanced up, she met the assessing gaze of the duke and flushed. Did he think her childish as the earl did?

"When you are settled in, my lord, I would like to go over the wedding arrangements with you." Mama did not miss an opportunity to get her own way as she gave the duke a challenging glare.

But the earl waved his hand in dismissal. "Let the girl decide. She has too much idle time if she can run around like an urchin playing swords. She must learn to manage my household in a manner to please me, and the experience will be healthy for her."

"Thank you, my lord. I have made all the necessary plans and will proceed as I see fit." She could not resist a glance at Mama's face to gauge her reaction.

Mama's pinched lips revealed her agitation. "My

lord, are you sure allowing Rosalind to make the decision is wise?"

The earl spared her a glance. "I can see where the girl gets her cheek. I say, let her deal with the planning, and may the devil take her if she fails."

"Of course, my lord." Even Mama hesitated to anger the old man for fear he would withdraw his proposal. She took a hasty sip of her tea and switched the topic of conversation to the chill in the weather.

Anxious to escape to her chamber, Rosalind waited twenty more minutes and then made her excuse, setting her teacup down and hurrying to the door.

"You will sit beside me at dinner, Rosalind." The earl's command made her miss a step before she dashed down the corridor and up the flight of stairs to the guest wing.

Bolting her chamber door closed, she sank onto her bed and stared at her shaking hands. If she married the earl, her life would be hell.

Any intelligent person could see his domination of her would grow once they said their vows, and she doubted her rebellious nature could stand much more. Being submissive to him for ten seconds ruffled every fiber of her nature. She had been so for nineteen years with Mama and did not plan to be anymore. Having spoken her mind proved quite addictive, and she planned to feed the fire.

Freedom shimmered like gold in the distance tantalizing her with unknown pleasure and delight. There were so many things she yearned to experience and places she longed to visit. How could this be the end when she had not yet begun?

No way would she stay solitary, bearing the old man

children, while her life fluttered away before her eyes without doing the things her heart yearned to do. She gave up the idea of love and a young husband after her first few encounters with them. None of the younger men she met could keep up with her mentally, and their conversation bored her to the point she nodded off a couple of times while they spouted their sonnets and poems. Offended, they drove away, vowing to never return, and she earned a reputation among the younger set in London of being a half-hour lady. Something she took exception to. Using her intelligence did not make her a fraud, and if no man could see the advantage of such a situation, who needed them?

Remaining a spinster contained elements of unpleasantness. Mama threatened to make her join the convent and devote her life to God. And to her surprise, Papa gave no argument. The more mellow of the two, he championed her cause often, except on this one point. A frown furrowed her brow. How could she disappoint him after all he did for her, taking her in as his own and loving her the same as if she were? How could she let him down when he depended on her to make an advantageous match so he could hold his head up with pride? With no other offers in the wings, she had little choice but to accept her fate

A small knock on her door startled her. She opened the door a sliver and peeked out at Thomas, twisting his cap in his hands.

Opening the door, she stepped back to allow the boy to enter.

"I wanted to see you because I thought you might cry when the old man made you give him your sword."

"No. I am made of sterner material than to let the

earl cause my tears." She smiled so the boy could see she meant what she said.

"But your lips pinched together like they do when you scold me, and Mama said you made the earl mad. I waited to see if you got mad back, but you did not." He took a seat in her armchair and swung his legs back and forth as he studied her face.

"I wanted to, but getting upset would not make the situation better." The child would never understand the pressure she endured to walk the marriage plank.

"Mama said the earl might give you a talk."

She gave the boy a quick glance, concerned about his involvement in Mama's conversation. "I should like to see him try. To whom did Mama say all of this?"

"Papa. I do not like the earl. I think Cousin Lucius is nicer." The child nodded his head as he imparted his opinion, and Rosalind hid her smile.

Thomas acted a lot like Papa when he made his mind up to speak about something.

"I do, too." She agreed with his assessment of both men. "Did Mama take your sword?" She had no idea what Thomas would do without her or her him.

He nodded. "I am not to disturb you anymore, and when I told Mama I do not, she got mad."

"I am sure she did. Her idea of disturb and yours are two different things." She resisted the urge to frown and studied her brother's mutinous expression. "You must not disagree with Mama anymore because I will not be there to help you." Her heart ached for the boy for she had always been his champion, and now Papa would have to intervene.

"I must go. Good-bye." The child slid from the chair and strolled to the door. "Mama said I have to eat in the nursery while the earl is here, and I want him to go away."

She swallowed the lump in her throat. She wanted the earl to leave, too, but such would not be the case. When he left, she would go with him to a whole different life. And the way things were looking now, her life would not be pleasant.

Dinnertime arrived too soon, and Rosalind sat beside the earl, enduring his foul breath and sweet toilet water while swirling her food around on her plate, too nauseated to eat. Edgar, once again, stood a foot behind the earl with watchful, narrowed eyes as if he expected her to accost his master when least expected.

The meal lasted forever and an eternity while she managed to swallow a couple bites of food. When the ordeal ended, the earl leaned close, and she snapped her mouth shut, trying not to breathe in, or she would gag.

"I order you to be in the morning room at ten tomorrow following breakfast. I heard whispers of you while in London. Some of the men in my club commented on your ability to do sums in your head. You must know, my dear, this is not acceptable in a gentle wife, and so I arrived early to learn your true nature. I am saddened to discover you running about with your hair a mess playing with a child. There is no other avenue to take but to tutor you in proper etiquette every day until the wedding, beginning tomorrow. Good night, Rosalind. Do not be late."

The earl rose to his feet and left the room, followed by his man, leaving a smiling Mama, a frowning Papa, and a quiet, thoughtful duke.

Rosalind took the moment to breathe in some much-needed oxygen and picked up her fork. Her appetite appeared with the fresh air. She shoved the thought of tutoring sessions with the earl from her mind and took a bite of pheasant and new potatoes.

Mama frowned. "Have you forgotten your manners as well, Rosalind? We have finished, and the servants wait to clear the dishes."

"She has not eaten a thing all evening, and the servants are happy to prepare more should she desire." Cousin Lucius broke into the conversation with a wave of his hand at the hovering, nodding menservants.

She shot the duke a quick glance of gratitude, surprised he took note of her lack of dinner.

His grace merely took a sip of his wine and motioned for more. "You are excused, Madame. I will wait with Lady Rosalind."

She caught his formal address with a grimace. No longer were they Cousin Lucius and Rosalind, but your grace and lady. Sighing, she took another bite of food.

Her mother protested, but Papa took her by the arm, suggesting they go to the gold salon to enjoy the sunset, and she at last acquiesced.

When they disappeared down the corridor, Rosalind smiled. "Thank you for coming to my aid once more. I could use a champion."

"And I should like to be yours if I could think of a sound solution for your plight." The words rang in her ears for days afterward, ushering warmth and hope into her dreary world.

****

She stepped into the elegant cream and mauve morning room at precisely ten in the morning as commanded, praying the gods kept her rogue tongue from giving voice to the rebellious words surging in her head.

Snow fell during the night, coating the ground in a frozen blanket, and Thomas appeared at her chamber door ten minutes prior, begging her to come outside and throw snowballs. At home, she would be there now, making them and throwing them as fast as she could. But here, with the earl present, she must act as a proper lady should.

The parents lectured her after the duke retired the previous evening on the disaster of a broken engagement and pleaded with her to behave as they wished until Christmas Day. She could withstand Mama's entreaties with ease, but when Papa asked with such gentleness, she succumbed.

Now, sitting in the morning room, Rosalind regretted her submission to their pleas twenty minutes into the earl's speech. "How long is this lesson to last?"

"You may leave when I have finished reading and not before. Now, pay attention." With a glass of port at his elbow, he adjusted his spectacles, opened the latest book on proper female etiquette, and read the first page. His nasal, high-pitched voice grated on her nerves like a pesky fly, making her want to swat him away.

She ground her teeth as he instructed her on the proper way to shake hands and greet her female peers but never extend her hand or invite a conversation with a man unknown to her.

Glancing at her over the rims of his glasses, he gave her a stern look. "This includes the duke. He is no relative of yours and is therefore unknown to you." Clearing his throat, he continued with the horrors of appearing out-of-breath, too hot, or too cold. "You must refrain from showing anything other than a pleasurable smile, graceful posture, and a light step." His voice droned on about the proper way to sink into a chair and how to sit.

Biting her tongue to keep the unruly thing in check, she glanced at the window and hid her smile when she spotted Thomas' bulky jacket dash through the snow toward a small hill. His laugh and then cry of surprise when he fell face first in a drift of snow made her chuckle.

"I do not see the humor in learning how to walk as a proper lady aught. Your unruly behavior last eve convinced me you needed training if I were to be spared embarrassment as your lord. Your flushed face, mussed hair, and booming voice took me aback. Not to mention your wide strides and spread legs as you brandished the toy." He shuddered. "There are two acceptable times a woman may spread her legs, for mating and for birthing. Since you were engaged in neither of those activities, you appeared quite wanton. And so, I shall tutor you on how to present a graceful, gentle bearing. Now, I wonder if I started on the wrong chapter. The evils of interrupting an important man such as your husband or father are not discussed until chapter three, and a far more serious offense." He frowned. "We will read chapter three and then restart with chapter one. My instinct tells me we will go through this book many times in our marriage."

Rosalind grimaced and dropped her gaze to her lap. Any hope she harbored of a quick visit to the morning room vanished like mist in the morning sun. She would give quite a lot to be out in the snow with Thomas right now and risked a quick peek out the window. The boy made it to the top of the hill and rolled down, squealing with delight and cold.

She dropped her head when the earl set the book on the table by his elbow and took a sip of port, shooting her a sharp glance.

The more she knew of him, the more she wanted to run away. Her future loomed like a dark cloud over her horizon, and she knew she would never be the countess he envisioned but did not care. Who could live with all those rules? Not her.

Clearing his throat to get her attention, he shot her a sharp look and continued reading.

Rosalind meant to listen and keep her promise to Papa, but after two minutes of more mind-numbing rules, she gazed at freedom just beyond the window glass and sighed.

"And shall not interrupt the dominant male in her life with inconsequential female emotions and ailments…"

Rosalind bit her lip to keep her rage in check. Women had as much right to express their opinions and views as men did. And she planned to interrupt the dominant male in her life every day with more than just her inconsequential female emotions and ailments. A lot of her opinions would erupt with them. And would be now if she had not promised Papa.

His high-pitched voice droned on and on with more rules and shall nots. Rosalind wondered if the male author responsible for the book lived or if his wife choked him in his sleep. She would have if she were married to the fool.

Chapter Six

Turning her head, Rosalind gazed out the window at Thomas out of sheer desperation. The acres of snow-covered grass bordered by hedges and tall, graceful trees made the perfect winter picture. If she closed her eye, she could feel the nip of the wind and the ice of the snow.

She smiled when Thomas laughed again and froze. Did the earl see?

The silence caught her attention, and she risked a glance at her future jailor.

His gray head drooped above his left shoulder, and drool dripped from his flabby lips. His closed eyes and snoring produced a smile on her lips. Even the earl got bored with etiquette, and she swallowed her chuckle. If she woke him, her chance of freedom would vanish. Gazing over her shoulder at the closed door where Edgar waited outside in the corridor to maintain their privacy while the earl instructed her. She held her breath. No sound could be heard.

Glancing toward the window and freedom, she rose to her feet and tiptoed across the distance separating them. The window to the morning room had to be six or seven feet from the ground, but if she were careful, she could shimmy out the window and run change before the earl discovered her absence.

Sliding the catch open, Rosalind pushed the pane out in front of her and sucked in a freezing breath of glorious freedom.

The earl still slept, and his snoring grew in volume.

Careful not to make a sound, she sat on the window ledge and slipped her feet out the window. Turning to face the interior of the room, she inched her hips over the window ledge. She slipped on the ice, frozen to the brick outside the window, and slid down faster than she intended, cringing when the silk of her day gown ripped. Panic gripped her like a cinched corset. She did not fear falling. No. The fine sheen of terror covering her brow appeared out of fear she might wake the earl.

Catching the edge of the brick where she lay against it halfway between her bosom and her waist, she sucked in a deep breath, conscious she must present a sight with her skirts bunched up and wedged between her and the window ledge. Her white pantalets and silk-stockinged legs dangled as she maneuvered her hands so she could drop to the ground. Thank the gods no one wandered the flower gardens beneath her to see her unladylike display.

Her prayer of gratitude stopped dead, and she received the shock of her life when a large pair of hands caught her about the waist!

She froze in terror, not daring to breathe.

"Lady Rosalind, how unexpected of you to drop by like this." The duke's deep voice laughed at her as he held her still.

She swallowed her cry of surprise ad choked. God, what Cousin Lucius must be thinking about her right now. She thought he chuckled but could not be sure, for she could not hear much over the pounding of her heart. "Please do not make a sound. I must escape the tiresome lesson before I do something regrettable like speak my mind."

A few deafening seconds ticked by while she risked a glance at the prone figure in the armchair, who snorted and then resumed his snoring.

Rosalind blew out a breath of relief.

"Then, by all means, let us get you down and avert disaster." The duke lifted her away from the window and set her down on the snow-covered walk in front of him, holding her steady.

Ulysses sat at his feet, observing the scene with interest.

Trembling with fear, elation, surprise, and the excitement of being free, the emotions pounded in her head keeping time with her thumping heart.

"So, your lessons progressed well?" The duke chuckled, turning her to face him, amusement twinkling in his eyes.

"Not so much." She glanced down at her ripped gown and grimaced. "No one could sit still for so long and listen to such drivel without going mad. The gown is worth my freedom."

Glancing up, she met his steady regard. "You must think me awful to destroy such an expensive gown in such an unladylike fashion." She shook her head. "Believe me when I tell you my escape is life-preserving."

"Yours or his?" The duke chuckled again. "I am no tattle tale and swear to never reveal how you escaped." He clapped a hand over his heart and bowed. "Although I believe the open window will give you away." He glanced around as if checking for unseen observers. "If you are to be successful in your quest, might I suggest the back stairs?"

"Pardon?" She could not believe he meant to help

her but smiled up at him with gratitude, just the same.

"My great-grandfather had a series of corridors built into the walls allowing the servants to pass from one area to another without detection. My valet can traverse the kitchens to my chamber undetected. A valuable bit of information for a growing lad who enjoyed his nighttime forays into the larder. I suspect the back way might come to your aid in this situation. Come with me, Rosalind, and I shall show you the way." He patted the dog. "Ulysses, see to the boy." The dog jumped to his feet and raced toward Thomas without hesitation.

Her heart tripped at the way his eyes crinkled when he smiled down at her. "Thank you." She had not meant to sound so breathless and grimaced over her lack of self-control.

"My lady." He offered his arm, and together they strolled around to the kitchens.

Twenty minutes later, she scooped a handful of snow and sent it sailing through the air toward Thomas, laughing at his surprised cry.

"Are you here to play?" He tossed a snowball back, grinning when it hit her in the head.

"Aye, you little scamp. Prepare for battle." She laughed aloud as she bent to make more ammunition. "We shall see who the better snow warrior is." Shrugging off the gloomy morning in the crisp cool air, she took aim and sent another snowball at his head, delighted with his howl of displeasure when she found her mark. Grinning, Rosalind retreated as he pelted her with half-formed balls, rounding the nearest tree and scooping snow into a tall heap for her first line of defense. Crouching behind the wall, she made more ammunition. The exercise, Thomas' delighted squeals, and the playfulness of the dog livened her spirits and helped her forget her dismal morning and the problems of her future for a few moments of fun.

****

Lucius studied the pair from a distance as they engaged in their snow battle and smiled. Such a spirited boy would be hard for his mother to handle without Rosalind. The boy doted on his sister, and the duke suspected he paid more heed to her word than anyone else's. And the girl, though not a classical beauty, possessed an impish grin and an energy for life he found quite intriguing. The old fool asleep in his morning room would destroy her with his tenacious demand she conform to the rules of society. If his unrighteous dominion did not suffocate her, his temper would break her. Rumors at his clubs said the earl had a heavy hand with a whip and several pairs of fine horses lost their lives to his foul disposition. Lucius hoped the earl drew the line where women were concerned. If he kept his punishment to reading to her from the various books on manners, Rosalind would be fine. Bored out of her mind and rebellious, no doubt, but fine.

He noted the earl's man guarding the door earlier on his way to the stables to check on one of his mares. Shaking his head over the situation, he rounded the corner of the castle in time to see her lower half appear out the window directly in front of him. Long shapely legs encased in silk stockings held up with delicate, pink satin garters and slippers swung above his head as she worked her way over the edge. Silk drawers peeked out from under bunches of rose-colored satin skirts until, with a shove, she slipped further into view. Her feet dangled close to his face, and glancing up, he had a full view of her curved behind. Her whispered prayer for help made him smile. If she scooted out a little more and let go, she would drop to the ground unharmed. Unable to resist the temptation, he clasped her around the waist and chuckled when she let out a gasp of surprise. Holding her with great care, he lifted her to the ground, surprised by the narrowness of her waist and blue of her eyes when they met his.

The lords in London had no idea what they let slip through their fingers. But he did. His late wife Lucinda would no doubt enjoy this morning's lecture in the morning room, adding her opinion on which rules should be stricter and the reason why. The book the earl read from hailed from her collection in the library, still resting on the special shelf she commissioned near the hearth for volumes of greater worth, as she called them. He had no idea how much he adhered to Lucinda's rules of proper behavior until the boy yelled, "Bugger," the day of their arrival. Rosalind's shocked reaction and the child's defense of his actions still made him chuckle when he thought on the subject. Lucinda would have put pepper on the boy's tongue and sent him to the nursery without dinner. Thomas had no idea what a kind sister he possessed. No lady of quality would pocket a frog for anyone for any reason. And yet Rosalind did, even stepping forward to take the punishment brewing in their mother's eyes.

She deserved better than the earl but breaking a marriage contract had far-reaching consequences. The fines and scandal would be great for whatever lord took on the task. Although, if the man in question were enamored enough, he would be willing to pay the price. True love solved all problems, or so he had been told.

Lucius frowned as he considered which direction to place his influence. He would help her any way he could to avert the disaster asleep in the overstuffed chair inside. Perhaps a local lord would become enticed by Rosalind while attending the traditional dinner next week. The idea had merit, and more mistletoe arrangements may be in order. As head of the family, the responsibility lay with him to see things done in the proper fashion.

Speaking of proper, the earl would no doubt notice the open window once he woke, and one could never be sure what the proper punishment would be for escaping in such a manner. With one more glance at the battling siblings, Lucius strolled in the kitchen door and took the back halls to the morning room. Opening the panel in the wall, he closed the window without a sound and returned the way he came. Let the earl figure out how she escaped. For once wed, the girl would bolt from more than mere windows or accept her fate. He bet on the first scenario and refused to dwell on the second.

****

"My lady, you are wanted within."

The footman's deep voice drifted to her position behind her snow wall, surprising her to her feet. "Who asks for me?" Rosalind cast a quick glance around the perimeter for the earl and sighed when she discovered the area empty.

"His grace. He mentioned *naptime* ended and wondered if you would like to return to your chamber to change for tea."

Glancing at the sun overhead, she sighed. Time flew when she played with Thomas. "Thank you. I shall return in a moment."

The footman took a step forward, his voice

dropping. "His grace mentioned the matter quite urgent. He instructed me to see you to the door of your chamber unobserved."

The earl must be awake and searching for her! "Of course." She caught the skirt of her old gown and approached Thomas, ducking as he tossed snowballs at her head. "I must go now, dearest, and change for tea."

The snowballs ceased, and a freckled face appeared above the snow pile he hid behind. The red tint in his brown hair gleamed in the light of the sun as he squinted at her. "I do not want you to go."

"I know. I do not want to go either, but I must. I will see you at dinner." Her face softened as she ruffled his hair. "I had a good time today. I am going to miss our little battles." Turning away before Thomas could see the sadness in her eyes, she hurried after the footman.

"Me, too."

The two little words spoken with such emotion seared her heart and soul. She could bear the unpleasantness of the situation but worried for the boy. Mama would demand obedience, and he would defy her as sure as the rain arrived in May. The future did not bode well for either of them.

No sooner did the door close and she turn to allow Ellen to untie her wet gown than quick footsteps filled the corridor outside.

"Where is Lady Rosalind? The earl demands her presence forthwith." The thud of boots on the wooden floor of the corridor grew louder as Edgar approached and stopped.

The deep, muffled voice of the footman who escorted her to her chamber answered, followed by profuse swearing. "Get out of the way. His lordship commands I escort the girl to him at once."

Ellen muttered something about Edgar knowing his place and helped her out of her sodden underskirts. She made quick work of the corset and other undergarments while the footman argued with the earl's man.

"I will give her ladyship the message." The footman's dry tone made no secret of his opinion of Edgar and his message.

"No underling will keep me from my duty. Stand aside." A loud rapping on her door followed. "Lady Rosalind. I have a message for you from his lordship. Bid your maid to open the door."

Rosalind kept her gaze on the latch, fearing the fool might try to breach. "Tell your master I shall come when I am ready and not before. I will not be summoned as if I were a trollop waiting for his favor."

A moment of silence followed her announcement.

"His lordship will not be pleased." The dry unamused tone of the valet drifted toward her.

"I do not care. When you pound on my chamber door as if you have a right, you encourage me to dawdle. I shall order a bath and not appear before dinner if you continue to harass me."

The tone of her voice must have angered the earl's man for the door latch shook, and Rosalind froze, her mouth dropping open in shock. "How dare you!" She clasped her discarded undergarments to her naked body in alarm.

"Stand aside, or I call for assistance." The footman's voice filled the corridor as he ordered the valet to leave the area. "His grace will hear of this."

Their arguing ensued.

"The door is bolted, my lady. I know what I am

about." Ellen's firm tone eased the stone in Rosalind's belly as the maid helped her into clean, dry undergarments and laced up her corset.

She kept her gaze on the door as they hurried through the process of dressing her.

Men's boots thumped up the stairs toward them, and Edgar's footsteps hurried away in the opposite direction.

She released her pent-up breath when the evil little man left. A frown marred her brow. If he were this bold in the duke's castle, what would he be like once she wed his master?

"I am not worried, Ellen." She strove to lie with an even tone while her ears twitched at every sound outside the heavy door.

"Yer clenched hands, and trembling say ye are." The maid's matter-of-fact tone as she dropped underskirts over her head caused Rosalind's gaze to swing around.

"The earl does not frighten me. My marriage to him shall be dull and uneventful at best. He is more interested in protocol and manners than me, and I have plans should he become an outright bore." Her chin rose as she spoke. Saying the words aloud did not make them true, and she winced when her voice wavered.

"Let us hope you are correct. I am not one to spread stories, but I have heard a few things about the earl I do not like. On any other occasion, I would not listen, but when they pertain to my lady, I take note. I must say, I am surprised your father agreed to the match." Ellen's lips thinned with disapproval as she helped Rosalind into her bodice and tugged the laces tight.

Papa's agreement surprised her, too, although she never voiced her opinion on the subject.

Chapter Seven

"What things have you heard?" Rosalind's voice broke as she struggled with her bravado.

Ellen's eyebrows rose. "He has a temper and strikes out in rage. I spoke with her ladyship about my concern, and she assured me you would not be in danger. I hope her ladyship knows him better than most. If he strikes you, I swear on my mother's grave I shall come fetch ye. Ye have my word." Ellen turned her toward the dressing table. "Now sit. So, I can help ye with yer hair."

The duke's deep voice broke the silence outside in the corridor as he spoke with the footman, and Rosalind sighed. If only Cousin Lucius had appeared a few moments earlier and caught Edgar in the act. She doubted he or the earl had the fortitude to withstand the duke's disapproval. Although he could prove a powerful ally, he could not fight her battles for her. She must do this on her own.

"Once we are wed, the earl can do as he pleases, and no one shall interfere. You know this, Ellen, and I thank you for the offer to assist me should the need arise." Lifting her chin and straightening her spine, she sighed. "Whatever happens, I shall deal with the situation, pleasant or no. One cannot evade their fate but must embrace the outcome to the best of their ability."

Ellen snorted. "Unless fate is an evil old man twice yer age with a temper. Ye run if ye must, and I will help ye. Ye are my darling girl, and yer Mum may be content to let ye deal with the devil, but I am not." She said nothing further as she pinned curls and added a string of pearls.

Rosalind dropped her gaze, saying nothing. She must believe her fate held a happier ending than the one presenting, or she would go insane.

Staring at her reflection in the mirror, she sighed. The lavender tea gown complimented her fair complexion and drew the blue from her eyes. With her red hair pinned high on her head, she presented a vivid, elegant picture, but without the gleam of hope or happiness, she may as well be dressed in rags.

"I wish ye luck, my lady." Ellen's fierce expression softened as she touched Rosalind's shoulder. "I meant what I said. If ye have need of me, I will come for ye." The older lady sighed and shook her head as if unwilling to accept the changes they all knew were coming.

"Thank you, Ellen." Kissing the wrinkled cheek beside her, she opened the door and stepped into the corridor.

The temperature in the teal salon hovered just above freezing. The earl glared when she entered, and Mama frowned, shaking her head with disapproval. Edgar stood behind the earl, his nose high in the air and anger shooting from his black eyes. Every taut muscle in his body depicted rage boiling beneath a thin veneer of civility.

Rosalind gave them all her sweetest smile and dipped a curtsy. "Good afternoon."

The duke turned from his stance beside the hearth and ran his gaze over her from top to bottom. A smile tugged at the corner of his mouth. "Good afternoon,

Rosalind. Now we are all here, I would like you to act the part of hostess and pour today."

Mama gave a gasp of outrage, her gaze darting between the two as anger thinned her lips. "Since I am the elder female relative, the duty is mine." She leaned forward on her white satin seat and planted both hands on her hips.

The earl tapped his cane against the wooden floor. "Rosalind is not a relative at all, Weston. Her place is beside me. Let her mother pour." The earl's sneer of displeasure twisted his face into a grotesque mask as he patted the seat beside him and waved her forward.

She hesitated, not wanting to get trapped beside the earl and hoping for a miracle.

Her gaze swung to Papa sitting alone facing Mama. He crossed his legs and leaned back, giving Rosalind a smile as he patted the seat to his right.

She would sit beside him and solve the entire matter. Hurrying across the room before anyone guessed her intention, she stumbled when the duke addressed her.

"Well, Rosalind?" Cousin Lucius arched a brow in her direction, waiting for her answer and ignoring the others.

She sank down beside Papa, grateful the settee held two, and nodded. "I am delighted to pour, Cousin Lucius."

The earl grunted his disapproval, and her mother glared.

Papa squeezed her fingers. "You will make a beautiful countess, daughter."

The warmth of his approval wrapped around her heart, and she glanced up in time to see her mother frown.

"What matters is she marries and gains a title. I thank the gods I had but one daughter. I do not think I could go through all of this again." Her mother wilted into her seat as if overcome with fatigue.

"Perhaps another daughter would not be as difficult as Rosalind. She requires the stern hand of an experienced man to deal with her frivolous nature. You have the gods to thank for sending me to deal with the task. One can imagine the disaster a young buck would make in the same position. Many young girls count marriage a blessing. I cannot think why this one does not." The earl's dry tone answered as he narrowed his gaze on Rosalind's face.

Could he not? Her chin lifted a notch. He thought she had a frivolous nature and marriage to her would be a task? What did either of them know? She had wonderful qualities and character another daughter might not.

"I am considered quite a catch by the most influential hostesses in London." The earl wagged a finger in her direction before folding his hand back over the head of his cane. "You should count my interest in you a great blessing."

Not bloody likely. If he were so popular with the hostesses of London, let them marry him.

An awkward silence filled the room until the footman opened the door and the tea trolley arrived. The man lifted the tray of biscuits and cakes to the table at their knees and set the teapot in front of her before standing back at attention.

"Thank you." Giving the servant a smile, she took hold of the silver teapot handle, hoping no one noticed her trembling. Their opinions did not matter in the slightest.

Only the clink of silver on porcelain could be heard as she poured tea and handed out cake.

The moment she finished, the earl cleared his throat. "I require a few moments alone with Lady Rosalind in the morning room. I waited as you asked, your grace. But tea is poured, and I have much to say." Setting his teacup on the table, the earl rose to his feet. "Come, girl, this cannot wait." His face flushed with anger and his knuckles grew white where he gripped the head of his cane. The stiffness of his posture and furious flashing eyes told her what he had to say would not be pleasant.

"Of course." Swallowing the lump in her throat, she set her cup down, ignoring the rumbling in her stomach. With a lift of her chin, she stood. Her hour of reckoning had arrived sooner than she anticipated.

Mama smiled, her good humor returning as soon as Rosalind rose to her feet. "I will pour in your stead. I imagine the two of you have much to speak about after this morning."

She shot her mother a glance. Mama never rose until noon or one and had not been awake during all the excitement. At home, she supposed the servants kept her informed, but who would do so here?

"I shall accompany you." Cousin Lucius set his cup on the trolley and straightened, his gaze on the earl.

Rosalind shot him a grateful glance, surprised he intervened.

"What I have to say is for her alone. Rosalind is my problem, and I require privacy." The earl snapped the words out between clenched teeth and stalked toward the door, turning to glare back at her. "Stay two paces behind me, Rosalind. You must learn your place so you are well versed before we marry."

She took a step and stopped when the duke placed a hand on her arm.

"As head of the family, the duty to see things done in proper form falls upon me. Rosalind is unwed, and I deny your demand to be alone with her. She shall be properly chaperoned until her wedding day and shall not be allowed alone with you or any other man. Until you are wed, your man can relay any message you have for Lady Rosalind to her maid. After what occurred today, you and your man are both banned from the corridor outside her chamber. Protocol shall be observed for her benefit, not just her education." His gaze never wavered from the earl's furious face.

"God damn you, Weston. I have the right to take the girl to my bed if I desire. The marriage contract has been signed. She is as good as mine." He scowled and took a step toward the duke.

Cousin Lucius straightened, his voice dropping silky soft. Danger clung to him like a cobra weaving before the strike. "You shall not touch her without the blessing of the priest. If such is your attitude, you will leave my home. I will not tolerate abuse of my relatives." The air hung thick around them filling the room with an awkward silence.

Rosalind held her breath and waited, trembling from head to toe. The duke's hand on her arm comforted her and calmed her racing heart. She glanced at her parents to see their reaction to the earl's outburst and swallowed.

Mama frowned into her teacup. "The earl is correct. He *did* sign a contract, and Rosalind is his responsibility now. I do not understand what all the fuss is about. He wishes to discuss her behavior, and I cannot fault him or his reasoning. As for the other, they are all but wed."

Rosalind's mouth dropped open as she stared at her mother. Disbelief raced through her as she gaped. Did Mama value her position in their village so high she cared not for her daughter's virtue? How could she be so callous about her reputation and welfare?

"Cousin Lucius is right."

Her gaze swiveled to Papa, and relief filled her soul. He offered love, compassion, and support every day she lived in his home, and he did so now.

Setting his cup down, her stepfather stared at the earl. "After what has occurred, my daughter shall be chaperoned until the wedding so there can be no complaint about her purity after the ceremony."

Tense moments passed as the three men eyed each other, and then the earl capitulated. He smiled and took another step toward Rosalind. "Come to the morning room, my dear. I have a few questions to ask you. Edgar shall accompany us so we are not alone."

His smile frightened her more than his threats, and she doubted Edgar would do anything other than hold her down should the earl decide to ravish her. "All right." Her knees clacked together, despite her best effort to appear nonchalant. Thankful that Cousin Lucius stepped closer, she placed her hand on his arm and followed the earl from the room.

The change in her fiancé between the teal salon and the morning room took her by surprise. He seemed almost tranquil when he took his seat facing them and gripped the head of his cane as he studied her face. "Why did you leave this morning? I woke to find the room empty and had no idea where you were."

Edgar took up his position behind the earl and gazed

down his nose at her. She risked a quick glance at the duke where he stood in front of the hearth and straightened in her seat. Something about the earl's man frightened her, and she thanked the gods Cousin Lucius accompanied them. Facing the earl, she answered his question. "You gave permission for me to leave when you finished reading. When you stopped reading, I left." Snoring meant he advanced to more pressing matters. She folded her hands together and met his gaze with fortitude. No withered old earl would get the best of her in any situation.

"How did you get out? Edgar denied allowing you to exit and suffered my wrath for his error." The earl's gaze narrowed as he stared at her.

Her stomach tightened. No wonder Edgar clenched his hands when he gazed at her as if envisioning them around her neck. She experienced the same feeling she did when Cook caught her sneaking a sweetmeat without permission Christmas Eve. "I had no idea you planned to keep me prisoner in the morning room with the doors locked and guarded, or I would not have joined you."

The earl shifted in his seat as he glanced at the duke. "You were not a prisoner and could leave whenever you desired." His nasal tone rubbed her nerves the wrong way, and she knew he lied. He posted Edgar outside the door to keep her inside.

"Then when I left should not matter, should it?" She gave him her most innocent look and smiled. No man would keep her prisoner against her will. "Have you more questions?"

The earl glared for a moment or two and then shook his head. "No. You may go."

Edgar's gaze grew icy as his black eyes stared into

hers from his place behind the earl, but she ignored him. They could both bugger off. With a nod, she rose to her feet and sailed from the room, wondering how the earl missed the open window and then laughed aloud as a new thought occurred to her.

"Something amuses you?" The duke spoke right behind her, and she turned.

"Thank you for closing the window and sending a footman to summon me to tea. I owe you a favor in return." The smile twisting the corner of his mouth told her she guessed correctly.

"My pleasure, Rosalind. I gave aide of my own choice. You owe me nothing." He glanced behind them. "If you hurry, Master Thomas finishes his tea in the nursery around this time, and no one will see you if you go up the back way."

She stopped in her tracks and turned to face him. God bless his soul for knowing what she needed most. Throwing her arms around his neck, she kissed his cheek with a sound smack and raced away, overjoyed for another opportunity to be with Thomas.

Had she bothered to glance back, she would have seen the duke touch the spot she kissed with a curious expression on his face as he stared after her.

The rest of the day passed without incident.

But the following day, Edgar stopped her as she left the morning room. "If you are going to the nursery to see young Thomas, he is not there."

She stopped in her tracks, her eyes narrowing. The man made no secret of his dislike for her when others were not around. "Where I go is none of your concern. What have you done with my brother?" She planted her fists on her hips rather than his nose and waited.

"Nothing. The boy climbed the stairs to the tower about an hour ago. I caught a glimpse of him as I made my way here for your morning lessons."

Terror tightened around her chest like a bowstring. "Why did you not tell me sooner?" She wanted to throttle the man.

"And interrupt his lordship's lesson? I think not." The thin nose rose high as he dealt the final blow. "I do not worry him with trivial things."

"Trivial?" Her anger burned like a bonfire catching a field of straw alight. "If anything happened to my brother while I sat in there listening to drivel, I will tear you to pieces!"

After delivering her threat at the top of her voice, she sped down the long corridors, turning left, then right, dodging servants and footmen until she arrived at the circular stairs leading to the tower. Climbing the steep winding stone stairs as fast as she could, she stopped at the top and pushed the heavy door. Nothing happened. Rosalind lifted the latch and discovered, with a heavy twist of her heart, the mechanism jammed. "No!" With her heart in her mouth, she wrenched the offending latch and shoved with all her might.

Fear lent her strength, and after a moment, the door gave way. Climbing through, she raced into the round room and gazed around. She alone stood in the empty space.

With a cry, she sped to the open windows gazing over the side to the ground far below, terrified of what she might see. Miles and miles of countryside spread out before her. Flat fields dotted with trees, the village down below the castle, and the massive forest stretched as far as the eye could see.

Her brother was not here, and no sign of him could be found!

Chapter Eight

The crisp gusty wind pummeled her face and tugged on her sleeves. She hesitated. Why would Edgar tell her Thomas climbed up here when he did not? A creak of a hinge made her heart jump to her throat, and fear tingle her senses. Turning, she lunged for the door as it swung shut with a loud bang. Catching the handle, she tugged as the sound of the latch being bolted from without filled her with dismay.

Someone locked her in the tower!

No! How could this be? Who would do such a thing, and why? Footsteps thumped away as she shook the latch and yelled for help. Terror gripped her chest, making it difficult to breathe, and her heart beat fast in her head. Time after time, she called for help with the same result. Anxiety gripped her hard as she assessed her situation.

High in the tower, no one would hear her call for help. No one but Edgar knew her location, and the knowledge terrified her. Did he orchestrate this whole thing, and if he did, why? What if she died? Shaking the horrible thought from her mind, she paced. Surely Papa or Ellen would notice her absence before too long and search for her. They had to.

An hour passed before she noticed the cold and shivered as the wind picked up speed.

Glancing up at the sun, she frowned when she discovered the storm clouds and gathering darkness.

Fearing lightning would strike the tower at such a height, she dropped to her knees, keeping her gaze on the window.

Two more hours passed as the storm broke into crashing thunder, flashes of lightning, and sheets of freezing rain pelting the open tower room.

Rosalind huddled on the floor with her arms wrapped around her legs in the driest, warmest spot, praying someone would notice her absence.

Her gaze wandered to the door, and she closed her eyes, wishing with all her heart the duke would appear to rescue her. He alone ventured up the tight winding stairs to the tower. She knew from Ellen's prattle the servants avoided the place.

Another hour passed. Dripping wet and afraid she might catch her death of cold, she curled over on the floor. As her gaze skimmed the boards in front of her, a glimmer of gold caught her eye. With an exclamation, she dug a finger between two boards and drew out a locket. Flipping the clasp, she gazed down at the angelic face of Cousin Lucius' mother. All this time, the precious piece lay hidden between two coarse boards on such an angle one could see the chain from the floor but not from above.

Holding the locket up in the flashing light of the storm, she shivered and tucked the object into her pocket for safekeeping. Assuming they found her before Christmas or her death, she would have the piece cleaned and gift-wrapped for the duke.

Rosalind must have dozed off as she envisioned the delightful moment when Cousin Lucius unwrapped the locket. For the next instant, she dreamed a large warm male held her close and whispered soothing words into her ear.

A dog's cold nose sniffed her hand before the animal whined.

The warmth of her rescuer's hard body against hers brought a smile to her lips. In her dreams, her hero had black hair, piercing blue eyes, and spoke very like the duke. She must be hallucinating out of hysteria, she decided. His warmth felt so real she shivered and wondered what would happen if her one true love appeared to rescue her. Would he hold her close and whisper sweet words in her ear, telling her of his quest to find her? Of his desire to be with her and his fear of losing her? Frightened and yearning for comfort, she said the first thing which popped into her mind.

"Will you kiss me?" All true loves did so, and she longed to know the pleasure of one real kiss before her sentence of marriage was carried out. The girls she knew in London spoke of thrilling moments in the moonlight with ardent young lords desperate to steal a kiss or two, but no one attempted such a thing with her. Knowing she dreamed made the words come easier to her lips, and she trembled in anticipation as she met the intense regard of the man holding her.

"I do not think such an act would be appropriate." His deep voice rumbled beneath her cheek as he held her tight, descending a set of tight spiral stairs.

What better place for a forbidden pleasure than a dream? "None of this is real, and I must find out what a real kiss is before I am doomed to a life of misery. As the hero of my dream, you must comply with my wishes because this *is* my dream. I shall never have this chance again. Please, kiss me, so I have something to remember in the time ahead."

He hesitated for the barest second before his hot mouth covered her own, sliding against her lips the way the duke kissed her hand. She could not breathe and wrapped her arms tight around her rescuer's neck, giving her body over to the wonder filling her heart and soul.

When he lifted his head, she protested. "Do not stop. For soon, I shall be the chattel of a man old enough to be my grandfather from whom there is no escape. I will never know passion or love except in the arms of a make-believe lover. Please kiss me again."

"I cannot, Rosalind. You are out of your head with delirium and know not what you ask." His deep voice vibrated beneath her cheek, and the heat of his embrace soothed her despite her desire to argue over the propriety of kissing.

In her dream, the man placed her on the warm, soft bed in her chamber and commanded someone to build up the fire.

"She is freezing through and through. Send for the doctor." Her hero bent to stroke her cheek, whispering. "You are strong. You can fight this."

She did not want to fight anyone and told him so. If she remained in this warm, wonderful world of pretend, she need never marry the odious earl and provide him with an heir. In her fantasy, she would love and be loved as she wished to be for so many years. She must have given voice to her thoughts, for her rescuer gazed at her for a few seconds and left, closing the chamber door behind him.

She had a vague memory of heated blankets, bitter herbs, and people speaking in whispers beside her bed before the darkness claimed her once more.

When she next opened her eyes, Thomas lay two

inches from her face, staring at her with his head in his hands.

She blinked. "Thomas! You are safe!" Catching him to her, she gave him a fierce hug.

He tolerated her for a moment before wiggling free. "I am not supposed to bother you, but you do not mind if I come in here, do you?"

She frowned in confusion. "Why would I mind?"

"Because you have been sick for four days. Cousin Lucius found you in the tower the night of the rain and carried you down all those stairs. He told me the door got stuck, so you could not open it."

She remembered parts of the dream and flushed when the child mentioned her rescuer. Surely, she did not beg the duke for kisses in her delirium. Other memories ushered a rush of heat to her cheeks. First, Edgar tricked her into going up there, and now this. "Someone bolted the door, and I could not open it."

"You made me promise not to go alone. How come you did? Cousin Lucius said not to." His mouth twisted. "I bet the rain scared you."

"The lightning scared me more. I believed you were up there, so I came to rescue you." She gazed into his large blue eyes, and her heart twisted. She would do anything for the child, and the evil little valet knew it.

"I promised Cousin Lucius not to, and now you must, too." Holding out his hand, he demanded a shake to seal the promise before propping his head in his hands again. "I am not supposed to tell you the earl asked to see you last night, but Ellen would not wake you. I do not like him because he is old and yelled at me when I showed him the admiral."

Rosalind closed her eyes, wishing for sweet oblivion

one more time. Oh Lord, Thomas introduced the admiral to the earl. "What else happened while I slept?"

"Nothing except more snow."

Snow, Christmas, her wedding, and the end of her freedom.

"Master Thomas, what are you doing in here?" Ellen entered the chamber and shooed the boy out, apologizing for allowing him to wake her.

Rosalind stared about her elegant chamber. Pale blue silk walls with gold and white furniture. A blue stuffed chair before the marble hearth with a pale blue and cream Persian rug on the floor. She stroked the delicate woven coverlet tugged up to her chin and sighed over the white and blue roses tied with golden ribbon in the design. Heavy pale blue velvet drapes tied back with golden ropes hung from the large picture window overlooking the flower gardens now dusted with snow.

Ellen closed the door behind her brother, sighing as she approached the bed. "Your mother wishes to have a word when ye are well enough to hear."

Rosalind had no doubt she would after being indisposed for four day. "Thank you, Mary. Please inform my mother she can come. I may as well get it over with."

Ellen nodded. "Right ye are. There is no sense in putting off the inevitable."

If she were very lucky or very blessed, the gods would send deliverance in her hour of need.

"I do have a request if you go to the village today." Telling Ellen about the locket in her pocket, she had her bring the item and showed her what she wanted the jeweler to do. "If you could drop this off, I would be so grateful. With Mama and the earl keeping such a close eye on me, I do not think I will have the time. Tell the shopkeeper I shall pick the locket up the week before Christmas."

"Very good, m'lady." Ellen took the locket and left to deliver Rosalind's message to her mother.

She spent the next hour listening to Mama vent her opinion on her recent behavior, threatening everything from being damned in hell to living her life as a spinster in a convent. Such a life grew more and more attractive by the minute. When her mother left to change for dinner, she sat up on the side of her bed. There must be a man out there somewhere, who could love her for her reasoning ability, but he would never find her unless she ventured out.

Ringing the bell for Ellen, she assured her she could withstand the strain of going down to dinner and chose a pale pink silk gown. Coming down the curved stairs on her own made her realize how weak her illness left her, and she gripped the rail for support. One minute she swayed, and the next, a warm male hand caught her elbow.

"Allow me to assist you, Rosalind." She knew him by the smell of his cologne before he stepped to her side.

"Cousin Lucius. You appear out of nowhere for the second time to rescue me." She smiled and tucked her arm in his, grateful for his support.

"Are you in need of rescuing?" Amusement laced his tone as he guided her down the corridor.

"Very much. My knees threaten to buckle whenever I take a step and your assistance is lifesaving." His nearness caused her cheeks to heat as she recalled her conversation with Thomas. "Thank you for coming to the tower and carrying me down."

"My pleasure, Rosalind. But the next time you plan to run away, inform me first so I know where to search if you do not return, agreed?"

"I did not run. A servant informed me Thomas climbed up the stairs. Terrified he would fall to his death, I followed. When I stepped into the tower room, some unseen person closed the door and bolted it. I could not get out and grew frightened I would die up there. How did you find me?"

"Ulysses. I sent for him when we could not find you, and he led us to the door, which I found bolted. We have not discovered who committed the act." A frown wrinkled his brow. "Edgar confessed to sending you to the tower, but who bolted you in?" His dark eyes bored into hers.

She shrugged. "The squeaky hinges made me turn in time to see the door close. The bolt slid into place right after. I saw nothing and no one."

Anger tightened his mouth. "Edgar stood in the door to the morning room all day and professes no knowledge of the situation other than informing you of Thomas. We have no evidence to tie him or anyone else to this. When I discover who is involved, they will be punished and banished from my castle. In the meantime, I will have your promise not to go off alone. Always take your maid or one of mine with you."

Rosalind agreed, and together, they strolled into the salon to greet the others before dinner.

Later as she tugged her bedclothes to her chin, she analyzed the situation. Edgar knew more than he said. A sinister air hung about the thin man, and he spoke to her with such haughty tones she wanted to throttle him. She may be a woman, and he a man, but he could learn his place. As a lady of noble birth, she held the upper hand. Whisperings among the servants spoke of a hierarchy in the earl's household, with Edgar at the top. He would soon learn his place if he plotted to dominate her.

Shivering as she remembered her time in the tower and tucking the blankets closer for warmth, Rosalind made the decision to deal with the rat on her own. If she did not, her life with the earl would be unbearable.

The valet professed to be allergic to dogs like his master, and she knew where to find a very shaggy-coated one. A few of Ulysses' hair in the valet's clothing should do the trick, and a smile tugged at her mouth as she envisioned his ugly face covered with hives. He would learn to walk a wide berth around her.

The next morning, Edgar stood behind the earl, covered in red bumps and inventing ingenious motions to hide his need to scratch. Frowning with ferocious intent, he informed the earl he could not stand the burn a moment longer and asked for a few hours of personal time.

His request upset the earl until the duke offered a manservant to do his bidding until Edgar could return to duty.

Afterward, the earl's valet glared but kept his distance, although she caught sight of him a few steps behind her several times. Her gut told her he reported her whereabouts to the earl, and she did not like the situation. Her life and decisions were her own, and if the sinister little man did not stop, she would have to consider more serious measures.

Thursday morning, Mary discussed the details of tomorrow's dinner for the local lords with her and Mama.

For once, her mother approved of the entire meal and did not offer a better opinion, to her surprise. When they finished, Mama left to sit in the teal salon, and Rosalind wandered into the hall, wondering what to do next.

A perplexing thought crossed her mind. Cousin Lucius showed no indication of indulging in a kiss nor of the other things she spoke of in her dream. So, did he, or did he not kiss her? Tossing and turning while she pondered the question the night before, she spent a sleepless night and now suffered the repercussions.

Drowsy and lost in thought, she walked into the library and came face to chest with the duke.

He caught her elbow to keep her from falling backward. "There you are. I have been searching for you and Thomas. I have something I want to show you. Thomas waits in the stable for us. Let us join him through here." Taking her elbow, he led her through to a panel on the back wall and pressed on the upper corner. The wall slid open to reveal the passageway behind, and after they stepped through, the panel slid shut behind them.

"Now I am curious. I climbed up the stairs to the nursery, searching for Thomas before Mary invited me to the morning room to go over tomorrow night's dinner. Nurse told me he left with you. What is this surprise?"

"Follow me and see." They walked down the long corridors until they arrived at the back door to the kitchen and out into the frosty air. Taking her hand, he escorted her to the stable.

Chapter Nine

She quivered at the first touch of his warm skin and tripped. No man had held her hand before and never her bare hand. Skin-against-skin contact made her knees weak and her breath quicken. She would follow him anywhere like this and focused on the way he held her, making a memory she could take out later in the dark and examine to her heart's content.

They arrived at the stable too soon for Rosalind, and she sighed with regret when he let her go.

Thomas stepped out of an open stall with a footman holding him by the hand. "Ruby, come see!"

His delighted squeal made her smile as she rushed forward to join him, stopping dead in her slippers when she spotted the tiny, perfect little foal.

"Come and meet, Isis, the mare I went to check on when I discovered you escaping from the morning room. This is her first foal and she gave us quite a time." He led her to a stall halfway down the inside wall.

The corral they stopped beside held a beautiful chestnut mare and beside her lay the tiniest, wobbliest little animal she had ever seen. Bay in color with a white star on his nose, the foal possessed three white stockings and big soft eyes she could drown in.

"Oh, my goodness! How darling." Rosalind sank to the clean straw beneath her and stroked the little velvet nose, murmuring with delight.

Thomas dropped down beside her and laughed aloud when the baby horse nudged him. "He likes me!"

For more than an hour, they fawned over the tiny animal with Cousin Lucius leaning on the gate, smiling.

"What are you going to name him?" Thomas munched on an apple one of the stable boys offered to him as he petted the young horse.

Rosalind took a bite of hers and sighed, relishing the sweet, crunchy texture as she chewed, listening with half an ear to the conversation. If she could stay like this forever, she would.

The duke shrugged. "What do you think he should be named?"

A name popped into her head, and she gazed up with a smile. "How about Eros? The foal is so beautiful. He must have a name to match."

The heat in the duke's gaze pinned her to the floor, making breathing difficult. "After the God of Love?" His gaze rested on her hair, her lips, her breasts, and back up to her eyes. "I am agreed. What about you, Thomas?"

"I think Eros is a good name if Ruby likes it." The boy scratched the baby horse on the nose without looking up.

Rosalind could not hear above the frenzied beat of her heart. She licked her lips and gazed back up at the duke, taking another bite of her apple.

The intensity of his gaze made her mouth dry as she lost her soul in his gorgeous blue eyes.

"Then it is settled. Eros he is. We must go now and change for dinner." He stepped toward Rosalind and held a hand down to help her to her feet.

The footman came to collect Thomas for Nurse and led him away after the child thanked the duke for letting him see the foal.

Lord, she would miss her brother when she married.

As she stood beside the duke gazing after Thomas, the evening grew quiet and intimate. The men left to go to dinner, and they were alone outside the stall. Conscious of the duke's tall, muscular body beside her, she sucked in a breath and froze. His heat and the scent of his cologne assaulted her sensitive nose, and she closed her eyes for the briefest second. Bugger, he smelled good.

Shaking her head over her sad state of her mind, she gazed at her hands, wondering what to do with them, and shifted her feet. Thomas had her swearing in her head like a street urchin, and if she were not careful, they might slip out in front of Mama or, worse, the earl.

The silence beside her caught her attention. Risking a quick glance at his face, she swallowed as her gaze met his. The air around them crackled with tension, and her mouth grew dry.

Heat flared from his eyes as he stared down at her. The intensity in his gaze made her heart beat faster, and fluttering filled her belly as she stared at his lips. Would he kiss her? Her knees buckled as she envisioned his mouth moving over hers, and anticipation broke out on her forehead. His arms would hold her against his powerful chest while his lips would slide against hers. Her breath quickened as she caught sight of a small smile tugging at his intoxicating mouth. Did he know her thoughts? Concerned he might, she took a hasty bite of apple, and a drop of juice clung to her lower lip.

Cousin Lucius froze and then leaned toward her, his gaze on her lips.

Rosalind forgot to breathe, and dizziness rushed

over her as he placed a hand under her chin and tilted her head up to his. She held her breath, not moving a muscle as he leaned close until his lips hovered right above hers.

God help her. She would remember this moment for the rest of her life and beyond. Excitement fluttered inside her as his gaze darkened, and the pad of his thumb rubbed along her lower lip, capturing the drop of juice and transferring it to his. She grew dizzy when he sucked the drop from his thumb and then returned his thumb to her lower lip tracing the shape with intense concentration.

Quivering with longing, she stared up at him with parted lips and wished for the unthinkable.

As if he knew, his mouth lowered in a slow, deliberate motion until his lips covered hers, and time stood still. His large arms closed around her, urging her closer to his lean chest and hips. A nameless fever took hold of her as she melted against him, allowing him to search her lips with his while she drowned in the heat and scent of his body. She remembered his touch from her dream and sighed with satisfaction.

The kiss continued while her blood turned to liquid desire and her knees buckled. Balls, he felt good. Wrapping her arms around his neck, she held on, mimicking his movements until she could no longer think but feel all the nuances of his hard hot length holding her close.

And then he lifted his head. Slumberous blue eyes claimed her soul while she stood in the circle of his arms, gazing up at him. Her lips parted, and her cheeks burned. Who knew kissing could be so desirable?

A noise outside the barn made her jump, and he dropped his arms, stepping back. His lids dropped over his eyes, shielding his expression. "We should not be here alone. Forgive me for taking advantage." His expression changed from heated desire to cool formality in a matter of seconds. Running a hand through his hair, he gave her a rueful smile. "You must go before the men return, and we are discovered."

Ten full seconds elapsed before his words made sense.

Her reputation and her engagement teetered in the back of her mind. The earl. Mama. She flushed and stepped back as well. "Yes, of course." Not knowing what else to say, she turned and ran out of the stable, coming to a full stop when she discovered Edgar lurking in the shadows.

"Who is in there with you?" The man's deep, suspicious voice lit her anger.

Lifting her chin high, she gave him her best glare. "How dare you seek me out and question me!" Scowling as her fury raged to full flame, she advanced with her hands on her hips. "Do not spy on me again, or you will wish you had not. Soon I will rule your master's household, and you will address me with respect."

He sneered in response. "My orders come from the earl, not you."

She scowled. "I do not care where they come from. You will keep your distance or accept the consequences." Her gut told her true. The thin sinister man reported her activities to the earl. She prayed he arrived too late to witness the scene in the stable, or her life would be over. Hurrying away into the darkness, she ran into the back door of the kitchen and all the way to her chamber, still trembling with the intensity of her emotions.

91

****

Another sleepless night passed. This one filled with heated remembrance of the duke's kiss, so like the one in her dream, she could not differentiate between the two.

The next morning, Rosalind exerted every ounce of control she possessed to hold still while Ellen helped her dress. Nervous and excited about her next meeting with Cousin Lucius, she played different scenarios in her head. How would he act? Would he find a way to be alone with her and kiss her again?

Every nuance of their kiss danced through her as she remembered the heat of his body, the strength of his arms, and the hardness of his length as he held her tight. Squirming on her velvet stool where she sat while Ellen dressed her hair, her cheeks burned, and her breathing accelerated as she relived the pleasure of his touch.

"Are ye ill, m'lady? Your face is flushed." Ellen held a hand to her forehead and clucked her tongue. "Yer cool to the touch." A sigh escaped her. "Thank the gods, ye are not fevering. His Grace will be disappointed if ye were too ill to join the party tonight."

Rosalind's heart jumped to her throat, threatening to choke her. Licking her lips, she peeked at Ellen. "Did his grace ask for me?"

The maid laughed. "No. Why would he? He wants to introduce you and the earl to his friends and neighbors in anticipation of the grand event. There has not been a wedding in the castle since the duke married his late wife, Lady Lucinda. God rest her soul. The entire village is a flutter with excitement, and his grace is no exception, although he does not show it."

Cousin Lucius expressed excitement over her

92

wedding? Rosalind snapped her mouth closed as her spirits plummeted to earth like a stone off a tall cliff. "Of course." Why would he mention her, the kiss, or the wonder and pleasure of their intimate moment in the stable? After all, it was not his first kiss but hers. He may not feel the same about the experience as she did. A frown furrowed her brow. Would he act differently now they touched lips? Or would he pretend nothing happened?

To her dissatisfaction and consternation, he proved the latter.

When she sailed into the breakfast room an hour later, Cousin Lucius glanced up, murmured, "Good morning," and left the room.

Staring at his retreating back, she took her seat and asked for a cup of tea. A frown wrinkled her brow as she digested his hasty retreat. How could he act as though the most magical thing she ever experienced did not happen?

Her fruit and muffin tasted like sawdust as she shuffled them around her plate and took a sip of tea.

"Good morning, my love." The earl breezed into the room and placed a damp, cigar-infused kiss on her cheek.

Edgar trailed him into the room and took up position behind his master. He must not have witnessed the kiss, or the earl would be livid.

Relief swept through her like a blaze on a chilly evening. "Good morning." Rosalind resisted the urge to scrub the spot where his withered old lips touched her skin and set her cup down on the matching porcelain saucer. Her earlier anticipation of meeting the duke dropped like a stone to the bottom of her stomach, and the earl's presence covered the stone with fast-growing mold.

"Did you sleep well?" The earl dropped down beside her and ordered a cup of coffee.

"Of course." She lied, dropping her chin to quell the nausea rising in her belly at the overladen plate of pork, ham, and fowl placed in front of the earl.

The scent of stale cigar and port clung to his clothes, making her want to gag. She shifted in her seat and shrugged off Edgar's ever-present, icy disdain.

The earl took a mouthful of sausage and wiped the juice from his chin, giving her a wink. "Better get rest while you can. Once we are wed, I plan to keep you awake the larger part of the night producing heirs." He nudged her with his elbow and laughed aloud, burping in the process. "Must be good food, eh, my dear?"

She made it down the corridor and into the lady's loo before losing the contents of her stomach. She retched and retched until she believed she would pass out. Now that she knew the pleasure of a real kiss, how could she bear to let the earl touch her when his presence made her sick to her stomach? Wiping her mouth with her kerchief, she leaned against the silk-covered wall behind her and closed her eyes. God, what she would give to marry a man more her age, one with teeth, hair, a fit body, and knowledge of appealing cologne. The earl's portly figure disgusted her. Though clothed in satin and fine broadcloth, he did not excite her or entice her to do anything but run away as fast as her legs would go. The problem arose with the parents. They would never forgive her if she broke the engagement. Mama's anger would arise from losing her coveted social position as mother-in-law to an earl, while Papa's disappointment would be more personal.

Shaking her head, she rose to her feet to go in search

of her brother. Walking out into the corridor, she bumped into the duke.

He murmured an apology, catching her by the shoulders to keep her from falling backward.

They both froze at the contact.

Staring up into his incredible blue eyes, she willed him to speak about their kiss, to give some indication he felt the same as she, but nothing happened. The heat of his hands on her shoulders sent thrills through her traitorous body as she resisted the urge to step closer.

He stared down at her for a full minute, his gaze wandering her face and resting on her parted lips. Time hung suspended in the air as she forced a breath into her lungs and held it there, hoping he would lean toward her as he did the night before.

Something flashed in his eyes, and then he straightened, clearing his throat. "Excuse me."

Setting her aside, he strode off in the direction of his study without glancing back, leaving her trembling like a newborn foal in the corridor.

She gazed after him, wondering how to get her racing heart under control. Kissing him in the stable may not have been her best idea because now she understood how pleasurable a kiss could be. Cousin Lucius must not feel the same for him to avoid her and put distance between them whenever they did meet.

Her gut told her the earl's kisses would not be the same, and somehow, she must survive the onslaught. Did the gods create the intimate occasion last night so she had something to think about when the earl took her to his bed? If so, Rosalind could not decide if she thanked the gods or cursed them for opening her eyes to the pleasure.

She did not see the duke again until she descended

the stairs for dinner dressed in her new navy-blue velvet gown. Sapphires adorned her throat, neck, wrist, and hair, sparkling in the light of the massive chandeliers overhead. Curls hung down her back from the elaborate style Ellen created for this occasion. Her breath caught in her throat when her gaze fell on the duke, resplendent in black evening clothes tailored to fit his body to perfection. The complicated knot in his cravat drew the eye to his royal blue vest and up to his amazing eyes. Her throat constricted as she stared at his full mouth and lean body.

"My dear."

Rosalind could smell the sicky-sweet scent of the earl's cologne before he appeared by her side. "You look quite passable tonight."

Quite passable. A wry smile curved her mouth. Of course. For a moment, she forgot about her ordinary hair and her ordinary figure. Lifting her chin, she took the earl's arm and allowed him to escort her into the dining room, ignoring Edgar's stiff form behind them.

She did not meet the duke's gaze when they stopped before him but curtsied with her gaze on the floor and into the distance. God help her. She sucked in a breath when he kissed her glove and got a whiff of his cologne. Her nose twitched with delight, and her mouth grew dry. She tripped as they walked away and prayed he would not guess the cause.

"I must hire a woman to teach you to walk in the proper fashion. We cannot have you tripping and falling once a year when the relatives come to call for the holidays. Your lack of training appalls me and causes me great embarrassment."

He said as much before and kept repeating the insult

as if she cared what he thought. Rosalind dropped her gaze to the floor, hoping no one caught the flash of anger in her eyes. She promised Papa earlier this afternoon when he asked for a private word that she would keep her temper under control until the vows were spoken. But God help her, if the earl spouted more nonsense, she would not be held responsible for the evil things her tongue planned to say.

Chapter Ten

The meal surpassed everything she had ever eaten before.

Sitting beside Papa and a young lord from the neighboring estate, Lord Edward Falcon, she delighted in every bite she took, closing her eyes in ecstasy as the moist tenderloin of beef fell apart in her mouth.

The duke sat at the head of the table with an alluring woman on his right and Mama on his left. Absorbed with the beauty by his side, Cousin Lucius did not gaze up once the whole meal, and Rosalind spent her time chatting with Lord Edward and avoiding the narrow gaze of the earl across from her. He did not like the attention the young lord gave her, and she did not care.

"You are enjoying your meal?" Lord Edward leaned closer and chuckled when her eyes flew open in alarm.

"I did not know you observed my appreciation so closely." She shifted in her chair and shot a quick glance at the earl, hoping he did not notice how close Lord Edward leaned.

A chuckle escaped her companion. "It is difficult not to when you make such enticing noises in your throat with each bite. I confess I have never been so jealous of tenderloin before this moment."

She swallowed and dropped her gaze, thinking about the proper way to answer such a statement. "The meat is excellent." Her defensive statement hung in the air between them.

In his twenties, with curly black hair and green eyes, the young lord must have many female admirers and she understood his appeal. For he gave her a seductive smile and murmured, "I agree."

Menservants cleared her dish and presented her with a glass of sherry and a slice of cream cake. Drawing her attention away from the young lord.

Rosalind took a bite of the cake and moaned aloud. The rich moistness danced on her tongue as the flavor exploded inside her mouth. She did not realize she expressed her satisfaction aloud until her companion gave another chuckle.

"Judging by your reaction, I better have a bite. Any cake worthy of a moan must be sampled."

She swallowed the delightful confection and risked a glance at her companion's face. "I believe you over-exaggerate my response."

"Perhaps, but I am not the only person to notice your delight." Lord Edward tilted his chin toward the head of the table, where she met the heated gaze of the duke. The blonde beauty on his right touched his arm and spoke close to his ear, but he did not turn his head. His blue eyes stared at her with raw hunger as his gaze darkened.

She swallowed the nervousness in her throat and held his gaze with her own. The air crackled with awareness down the length of the table between them, and her breath caught in her throat. He remembered their kiss with the same clarity and yearning she did. Her stomach twisted as the realization made her suck in a breath. She stared at his mouth and wanted more than anything in this world to be in his arms again. If God took every Christmas from here to eternity and gave her one gift for the entirety, the duke would be the gift. What would love be like with a man such as he?

"Rosalind?" Papa cleared his throat, dragging her attention away from the duke and the fire of desire blazing in his eyes.

"Yes?" She croaked the word from her stiff, dry throat and took a hasty sip of sherry.

"If you are finished, we shall make our way to the gold salon. Cousin Lucius has seating and refreshments set up with an entire array of entertainers." He rose and offered her his arm. "I shall escort you to keep the peace." He indicated the frowning earl and the bemused young lord to her right.

"Of course." Turning, she smiled at Lord Edward. "Thank you for a delightful conversation with dinner."

He bowed. "Thank you. Lady Rosalind, for such an amazing evening. I shall never gaze upon my food with indifference again without thinking of you. You have taught me this night to be more appreciative of my culinary experience."

Heat filled her cheeks. "My pleasure."

"Yes, it was." His comment brought a smile to her lips as they turned away, and she allowed Papa to lead her to the salon.

****

Mistletoe hung everywhere.

Less than five minutes and five kisses later, Rosalind gaped around the large room and discovered every floral arrangement contained the pesky plant as well as an infinite number of twigs dangling from the ornate ceiling above.

Turning on her heel, she hustled toward the door hoping for a quick escape when the earl made a straight line for her, elbowing guests out of his way. His left foot slowed him down, allowing her to escape.

With her head down, she walked into Lord Edward and froze. He glanced up with a smile, pointing at the offending plant above them, and chuckled. "Lady Rosalind. Tradition is tradition, and we must ever bow before her."

She risked a quick glance behind her to gauge her moments of freedom before capture and gave a cry of alarm when Lord Edward caught her against him, kissing her long and deep.

As his mouth slid over hers, she discovered the experience quite mechanical and boring. A little wet and pleasant, but nothing heart-pounding or breathless. Filing the information away, she thought of the earl hastening toward her and struggled against the young man. "I must go. Please release me."

The young lord lifted his head. "Of course. I offer one misgiving for this entire evening."

Rosalind spied the earl twenty feet away and closing the distance between them fast.

"Which is?" She smiled her regret and turned away.

"I regret I did not meet you first, or you would be betrothed to me. You are quite lovely, Lady Rosalind, and I am honored to meet you."

She gaped back at him. He believed her average face, average body, and average hair lovely?

"Rosalind!" The earl's demanding voice spurred her forward.

Edgar glowered behind his master's back. "Shall I fetch her, my lord?"

She dashed through the doors and into the corridor gazing back over her shoulder. The door closed behind her with a click. Sighing with relief, she turned and walked into the wide expanse of Cousin Lucius' broad chest, resplendent in his blue vest and impossible cravat.

"Excuse me." She meant to sidestep and run, but he caught her arm and turned her to face him.

"What is wrong? Is someone chasing you?" His gaze narrowed on her flushed face, and anger darkened his brow.

"I believe I mentioned I would avoid the mistake of mistletoe at all costs should the plant appear. My very forward and determined fiancé is two steps behind and has ordered his manservant to collect me. If you do not mind, I must make haste." She leaned back to ascertain if Edgar stood on the other side of the closed door. "I must go."

The duke's gaze swiveled behind her and back to her face. "In here." Placing a palm against the wall, a panel slid back, and they entered the back corridor.

No sooner did the panel slide back than Edgar's voice rang out. "Lady Rosalind? Where did you go?"

She held her breath and dropped her gaze to the ground for fear the man would hear her breath and guess her location behind the wall.

The duke tugged her forward, and together they walked along toward her chamber. When they arrived at the panel outside her chamber corridor, the duke turned her to face him. "Why do you run with such haste? Has the earl or his man offended you? I have no report of them mistreating you." His gaze pierced her soul, and she swallowed hard.

"What difference would it make? In less than three weeks, I shall be the earl's wife to do with as he pleases, and there shall be no escape."

Silence followed her outburst. "If he hurts you in any way, I will kill him."

"And how shall you know? How shall anyone know? I shall be secreted away to his castle and locked within his walls where no one will be allowed to see or visit me. Once a year, I shall be allowed to have visitors—his relatives, I am informed—if I am not with child."

Surprise flashed in his dark gaze. "He said this to you?"

"Yes, in one of our morning sessions." Lifting her chin, she met his searching gaze. "I run while I can, but soon, my time will be over. There is nothing you or anyone can do to stop what is."

He nodded. "I have given your plight considerable thought and can think of no way out of your marriage contract except by breaking it. The fine and scandal shall be significant, but I have faith a local lord will take on the task. Let us return to the salon and see what the universe delivers."

Another man thought marriage to her a task. Rosalind shook her head. "A few kisses will not convince someone of my worth or cause them to fall in love with me."

"How do you know? How many kisses have you had to base this statement on?" He gripped her shoulders and stared down at her face.

Truth can be hard to speak at times. This happened to be one of those times. "Six. Yours the other night and five just now before I made my escape. I do not see how any of them made a difference to the man I shared them with." She smiled a sad smile and opened the panel, disappearing down the corridor into her own chamber.

****

When her chamber door bolted behind her, the duke sighed from the bottom of his soul. "I do." Her kiss seared his mind and made him hungry for more. He never should have taken her in his arms and drank from her sweet lips, but he did. He would not be so desperate to save her if he did not know how enticing she tasted. Thinking of her with the earl filled him with disgust.

Such beauty and zest for life should not be wasted on an old man. He relived the moment at dinner when he glanced down the table as she took a bite of her food and closed her eyes. The passion and pleasure in her expression made him freeze in place as he envisioned her in his bed. Fascinated with her uninhibited response to pleasure, he had not taken his gaze from her all evening to the dissatisfaction of Lucinda's younger sister, Lady Abigail, who sat on his right. God, what must such passion be like in a loving wife? He could not fathom the depth of such a relationship, for Lucinda had been the opposite of passionate. Cold and disapproving, she allowed him in her bed when trying to conceive but rejected him the rest of the time. His busy life kept him from taking a lover following her death. Now, for the first time, he wondered what he missed. If he were given one Christmas wish for the rest of his life, his wish would be to share his life and love with a woman like Rosalind.

But wishing did not create reality, and as head of the family, he must shoulder the responsibility and act with honor. Christmas and all the magical anticipation which accompanied the holiday had always been his favorite time of year. Until now. He had no desire to see Rosalind gift-wrapped and handed over to the earl. Something must be done to prevent disaster, but what?

Lord Edward appeared quite smitten with Rosalind. Such a match would relieve her of the future her parents planned and give her a modicum of freedom. But while she would be better off, he would be under the necessity of witnessing her live with another man beneath his nose and in his village. His lips twisted with self-derision. Better Lord Edward than the withered-up Earl of Gloucester.

While he worked the problem out in his mind, he would keep his distance. The first time he kissed her, he could not resist the pleading in her eyes, and once he tasted the sweetness of her lips, he wanted more. The second time he kissed her, he did so because he could not get the taste of her out of his mind. He remembered the softness of her body and the noises she made at the back of her throat. Passion and longing burned in his blood as he drank the nectar of her mouth, and he knew he must stop before he did something reprehensible. As last night taught him, if he got too close, he would not be able to resist temptation, for her kiss teased him with promise, passion, lust, and a host of other things he dared not think about. The price he would pay for acting on the desire pounding through his body would be too high, and he could not afford the price.

****

Ever the perfect host, the Duke of Weston provided lavish food and impeccable entertainment as the days to Rosalind's Christmas wedding counted down.

Hopeful to get a moment alone with Cousin Lucius, she dawdled after dinner and rose an hour earlier in the morning to catch him alone, but to no avail. Polite, distant, and kind, the duke had another meeting to attend to or an overseer who demanded his attention and hurried away every time she stopped to speak to him.

And every time she turned around, she met Edgar's disapproving glare.

Disheartened, she sat through every hour and a half reading on etiquette and deportment in the morning room, staring with unseeing eyes out the frosted window at the glistening white landscape and biting her lip to contain her sigh of longing. Freedom beckoned a few hundred feet and one keenly observant fiancé away. Edgar stood at attention inside the closed door, frowning at her. His job? To prevent any more premature disappearances, should the earl drift off to sleep again.

Everyone followed an unspoken command to keep her alienated from both the duke and Thomas. And she did not like it the least bit.

Mama changed Thomas' schedule, so his free time coincided with tea, making it difficult to speak to the boy, and three whole days passed without a word between them. Her lips twisted as she imagined the marriage noose tightening around her neck and the preacher's hand on the lever.

Christmas had always been her favorite time of year, and every season her spirits soared with the wonder and excitement the holiday created. Until now. As high as her expectations flew in previous years, they now plummeted.

Lord Edward called twice the following week on some pretext of borrowing a specific book from Weston's library, and although Rosalind searched the numerous shelves and bookcases both times, the mysterious volume never appeared. Ellen joined her in her search on both occasions while the earl frowned from the depths of the leather armchair before the fire keeping his gaze on them while they wandered through the library's extensive collection.

Lord Edward gave her a wry smile following his second foray into the library, leaning close as he gathered his cloak and hat. "Would you care to meet me by the front gates after dark? I have something urgent to discuss with you." His whispered words surprised her, and she drew back as he kissed her hand farewell. What could be so important he required a clandestine meeting? With her heart in her throat, she gave a slight nod as Edgar's stealthy footsteps approached.

His frown and the speed with which he shot from behind the earl's armchair did not bode well for her. Dipping her curtsy and murmuring an excuse, she hurried away before her ancient husband-to-be's man could corner her.

Of late, Edgar appeared out of nowhere at least twice a day, demanding she follow him to speak to the earl, who sat in his armchair holding a sprig of mistletoe and a nauseating gleam in his eye. She had no intention of being caught and kissed. Thoughts of his flabby lips and groping hands filled her with disgust. Soon enough, she would have no choice but to suffer his advances in silence. Ever sensitive to the area around her, the hair on her neck would stand on end when Edgar got within twenty feet, and she took the opportunity to escape with all possible haste.

Bolting the door to her chamber, Rosalind retrieved a tunic from the bottom of her wardrobe and sank down in the chair before the fire. Ellen made the article for Thomas at her request for a Christmas present. In her spare time, Rosalind stitched around the neck and hem so the child would have something to remember her by.

She bought a fur muff for Mama and a new pipe for Papa in the village at home. Sometime this next week, she planned to go to the village with John and pick up the locket for Cousin Lucius.

Mama bought an expensive dressing gown for her to give to the earl, and though expertly tailored and soft to the touch, her stomach lurched when she thought of giving it to the man because of the intimacy the article implied. He would no doubt make a suggestive remark and comment on the color in her cheeks as if she swooned at the idea of him so attired. As she knotted her thread, Rosalind wondered if the earl knew blushes turned the cheeks pink, not a sickly shade of gray. For he often suggested she flushed with shyness at the thought of being intimate with him when in truth, she struggled with nausea. Her silence did not depict a shy nature but grim determination to keep her word to Papa and not let loose the rebellion running rampant in her head.

Chapter Eleven

The chamber door opened, and Ellen appeared to help her change for tea. She touched the silk embroidery with work-worn hands and sighed. "Ye do beautiful work, and young Thomas will be delighted with the design. I do worry yer mother will take exception to frogs and spiders on the lad's tunic and take it from him."

Rosalind frowned. "Frogs and spiders hurt no one when they are stitched and not real. Thomas does not like the flowers she has the maids sew around his cuffs and neck. So, I made him something he will like."

"So ye did. If ye do not mind the suggestion. What if ye stitched a vine down the middle? Yer mother might not notice the spiders and such if she believes the design is a vine."

A smile tugged at Rosalind's mouth as she jumped up to kiss Ellen's leathery cheek. "You are such a dear. A vine will be just the thing. I will start one tomorrow after my deportment sermon in the morning room."

Ellen clucked her tongue as she unlaced the rose morning gown the girl wore. "A sermon? Do ye blaspheme God? He has nothing to with the reason yer in the morning room."

"Nay, but the devil does. No one could sit still for so long listening to such drivel unless possessed. And I do not blaspheme God. I blaspheme the earl for expecting me to remember so many rules and behaviors. What difference does it make if you hold your cake with your left or right hand? Or if you turn to the right when you sit with your knees clenched together? Have you ever clenched your knees in such a position? 'Tis not possible to do so while maintaining a pleasant expression and a soft tone. I think the earl should try it out and see how pleasant he is before requiring such a thing of me."

Ellen chuckled as she slipped the bodice of an apricot lace tea gown over Rosalind's shoulders and tugged on the laces up the back. "And there lies the problem betwixt men and women." The two stood in silence until Ellen pronounced her done. "Now, off ye go or yer mother will send a footman to see why yer late. The duke asked her to pour, and she will not like ye being late."

Rosalind strolled to the door. "Thank you, Ellen. I shall miss your wisdom when I am gone." Blinking back emotion as she unbolted the door and lifted the latch, she flashed a smile over her shoulder. "I owe you much."

No good would come of lurking in the corners crying over something she could not stop. Squaring her shoulders, she marched down the corridor and down the stairs, making her way to the gold salon for tea.

Taking her seat, she sat in silence while Mama poured tea and passed out cake, smiling with satisfaction. A superior gleam shone from her eyes as she gazed at the other occupants of the salon as if she were queen and they her loyal servants.

The earl plopped down beside Rosalind and misted his foul breath all over the side of her face. Swallowing her revulsion, she shivered and scooted away, plastering her hip against the padded arm of the satin settee.

"Why did you run from Edgar earlier? I wanted to

have a word with you." His sicky sweet cologne assaulted her senses, making her want to gag.

"I had an important errand and could not stop." She leaned away from him as she lied, taking a desperate sip of tea as she sucked in the scent of orange, hibiscus, and lemon and thanked the gods for fragrant tea leaves. With the steam of the tea in her face, she could not inhale the foul odor of her fiancé.

"What important errand?" He leaned against her and sniffed her hair. "You smell of roses. A scent I dislike." He tapped the floor with the head of his cane and nodded at her. "We shall have to replace your soap with lilies. I will have my man order some for our return to Gloucester."

Rosalind choked on her tea. He planned to dictate the scent of her soap? She swallowed the angry words rising to her tongue and took a vicious bite of her cake. The earl could go to the devil and take Edgar with him. He could dictate and order whatever he liked, but she would decide her own destiny and the scent of her soap.

"I like roses. They remind me of home. And lilies give me hives." Cringing inside over her lie, she lifted her teacup and took a hasty sip before her tongue could say more.

"Your home is with me." He narrowed his gaze on her face. "In my home, I am master, and you have no choice but to obey. Your duty is to please me."

"And if I do not marry you? What then?" The words slipped out before she could stop them. Damn, she should have taken another sip.

A hush fell over the salon.

Mama stared at her as if she had gone crazy. "Why would you ask such a thing? Have you taken leave of your senses?"

Papa set his cup down and folded his hands in his lap. "Do not be ridiculous, Rosalind. His lordship does you an honor by making you his countess."

Ridiculous? Hardly. Monumentally nauseating and plain old wrong. The earl should be happily wed to a woman Mama's age, not hers. "In my visit to the village, the townspeople spoke of a lady running away to Scotland on the day of her wedding, leaving the groom waiting for her in church. I think the story is romantic."

The earl's lips thinned. "Such a creature is not worthy of the sanctity of marriage. To leave a man waiting is unthinkable. I, for one, will not tolerate such disrespect. I have faith you are not such a fool as to listen to this kind of nonsense with any form of consideration. You are well favored by me to receive a proposal from my hand, as your stepfather mentioned. Most maidens would be pleased to be in your shoes."

Edgar nodded his head in agreement.

She doubted the earl's statement with all her heart. If so, many would. Why had no one else jumped at the chance?

The anger flashing in Mama's eyes stopped her from making another observation. "If you do something so foolish, I am afraid we would have no choice but to cast you out, and you would never be allowed to speak to Thomas again." Mama's lip curved in a cruel, satisfied smile, calculated to hit Rosalind in her most vulnerable area for maximum results.

Mama found her mark with remarkable accuracy.

Anxiety gripped her with a closed fist as she considered her mother's threat. She would never accept defeat when the matter involved her little brother. To use him as a pawn against her had to be the most vicious thing her mother threatened yet.

Papa sealed the ache in her heart with his next words. "A woman in your position has no choice but to accept the sanctity of marriage with a grateful heart. We have done all we can to aid you in procuring your future. Do not waste the opportunity, for there will not be another one." Mama could say things of this nature to her, but when Papa did, they cut deep.

Jumping to her feet, she made her escape. "Thank you for tea." Dipping a curtsy, she hastened from the room, ignoring Mama and the earl's protests. They could all go to the devil and burn there for all she cared. Except Papa. Angry tears blurred her vision as she rounded the corner and collided into the solid wall of Cousin Lucius' chest.

"Excuse me." Her mumbled apology lingered in the air as she sped past him and up the stairs to the security of her chamber.

She made it inside before her tears erupted in a rampage of anger. Tossing pillows and kicking chair legs while she swore did not make her feel any better. Mama meant every poison-laced word she fired at her, but Papa's caught her off guard. Whatever she did to make him so stern with her escaped her. The wound his sharp words created would have to be bound up for now and set aside until she had time to unravel her emotions and deal with them.

Staring down at her bruised and shaking hands, she plopped down on her soft feather bed and ignored the throbbing. After several deep, calming breaths, her temper dissipated, and she stared into the dancing flames on the hearth, swearing a solemn vow. Never again would she allow anyone to control every facet of her life as Mama did. If the earl tried, one of them would die the first week, preferably him.

And may God have mercy on the souls of anyone who entertained the idea of keeping her from Thomas, for she would not allow such a thing to happen. Coming to terms with the fact she would live in Gloucester, a four-hour drive away from the village and Thomas, had been difficult enough. But she would never accept not seeing him again. The child needed her to champion his cause, and the gods above knew she needed him, too. For there were times he alone understood her thoughts and feelings. And his chatter, with all the hundreds of questions, gave her joy.

Long minutes passed as she stared into the fire, wondering how best to proceed. The more she knew of the earl, the less confidence she had in her ability to follow through with the plans made for her.

There had to be a way to escape and keep Thomas in her life, as well.

A log settled on the hearth, making her jump. Noting the shadows lengthening in her chamber, she glanced out the window. The shadows grew thicker by the second, and soon darkness would cover the landscape. The footman would call them to dinner soon, and if she planned to meet Lord Edward, she must do so now.

Tying a black cloak beneath her chin, Rosalind drew the hood over her head and hastened down the back stairs. The servants were busy with their evening preparations, and she ran into no one, not even Edgar, as she made it to the kitchen and slipped out the back door.

With a sigh of relief, she sucked in the cool air of the evening and hurried around front, setting off at a brisk pace for the front gate. Ten minutes later, she stopped, peering into the shadow for signs of Lord Edward. No sound could be heard but the murmur of wind in the trees and the hoot of an owl. She waited five minutes before turning and hurrying back the other way. What Lord Edward had to say must not be as important as he suggested.

As she neared the castle, a man stepped from the shadows scaring her, and she gave a cry of alarm.

"It is I, Lady Rosalind." Lord Edward's face popped into view, and she let out a shaky breath of relief.

For a moment, she wondered if the evil Edgar discovered her.

"I believe you said to meet at the front gate. Why are you here? You frightened me." She stopped a few feet in front of him, gazing up into his emerald eyes.

"I waited the better part of an hour by the gate before drawing near the castle. The boy told me you take a walk in the gardens most evenings before dinner." He took a step toward her, his warm breath caressing her cheeks as his hands settled on her shoulders. "I hoped for a private word with you."

She stared at his lopsided grin, and compassion twisted her stomach. Glancing around, she frowned. "What is so important you risk being caught alone with me? If the duke or Papa finds us here, there will be severe consequences."

He dragged a hand through his dark wavy hair and shrugged as if unconcerned about discovery. "I have thought of this moment and what I would say for days. But now you are here, I do not know where to begin."

An odd feeling twisted in her stomach at the intensity of his stare, and uncertainty made her hesitate.

Squeezing her shoulders, he leaned closer, dropping his voice. "I am afraid, dear Rosalind. I cannot get your kisses from my mind and fear I have fallen in love with you. I must know, my darling, do you feel the same?"

Her jaw sagged open, and she tilted her head up at him as shock waves rocked her being. Of all the things she anticipated him to say, this one did not enter her mind. Men did not meet and fall in love with ordinary her. What happened to Lord Edward to make him so different from other young men of her acquaintance? Did his wet nurse drop him as a babe?

"Please do not keep me waiting for your answer. The uncertainty is hard to bear. Tell me, Rosalind, my darling. Do you love me?" His green eyes pleaded with hers, twisting her up inside.

She had been on the other side of this situation more times than she could count. Rosalind sighed as she studied his face, not wanting to hurt him the way she had been hurt so many times before.

Her feelings for him stopped far short of the loathing she entertained for the earl but also a great deal shy of the dizzy, tantalizing excitement she experienced with the duke. But how did one say, I find you mediocre?

Clearing her throat, she shrugged. "I do not know what I feel." The lie seemed easier than the truth, and she waited for his reaction before deciding her next course of action.

"Then let me convince you we were meant for each other." Sweeping her against him, his mouth covered hers in a deep, passionate kiss.

Rosalind felt nothing but warm damp lips and gripping hands. She stood still as a statue while he slid his lips over hers, moaning and caressing her back.

"God, you taste good. Kiss me back, my darling, and we will plan our escape. I wish to take you to Gretna Green tonight, where we will be married and spend the rest of our lives together. I have a carriage waiting down the road for us, and paradise is around the corner. Tell me you love me as much as I love you."

For long moments she allowed her mind to dwell on the blessed escape he offered, but then Mama's words in the salon floated back to haunt her.

"I thank you for the offer, but I must ask for time to think on my answer. This is a big decision for me. My parents will be upset with the scandal such a decision will create." She put her hands on his shoulders to push him away, but he captured her lips again and tightened his hold. While he kissed her, her thoughts drifted off to her question on how many true loves she had at one time, and sighed. Lord Edward did not qualify. If he were one of them, her heart should be pounding in her chest, should it not? Her knees should be weak and her stomach full of fluttering. None of the above-mentioned experiences occurred, and she gave a sigh of disappointment. She wanted to ache for him the way she did the duke and not the freedom his offer presented. Escape did not qualify as a replacement for desire.

When he lifted his head, he gave her a tender smile. "I shall give you one week to think my offer over. I cannot give you more time, for I know I shall not sleep or eat while I wait. And if you are to escape, it must be soon. Christmas shall be upon us before we know it. You must choose me, and I have every confidence you shall." He brushed his lips over hers and whispered. "What I offer is far superior to anything the Earl of Gloucester promises you. Until we meet again, my dearest, I bid you good night."

A door closed behind them, and Rosalind stiffened, searching the area. "You must go before we are discovered."

"There you are. I have searched everywhere and wish to speak to you." The deep voice behind her made her jump and turn as the duke strolled into view.

In dark breeches, and a topcoat, he looked as though he stepped from the salon a moment earlier. His gaze narrowed on her face, and he gazed past her into the shadows. "Is someone here with you?"

Lord Edward must not be behind her, or the duke would not ask. "Nay. I required some fresh air. So, I stepped outside for a brisk walk." First, Edgar trailed her around, now the duke. Although she much preferred the latter.

"I see." His expression suggested he did not believe her, and she ignored the guilt nagging at her.

Rosalind shivered in the cold beneath the cool surveillance of the duke, grateful he did not come out a few minutes earlier and catch her with Lord Edward. "Shall we go in? I believe I have enough air now."

One eyebrow arched as his gaze swept behind her one more time. "Of course. My arm, Rosalind." He tucked her hand into the crook of his elbow and led her back to the front door of the castle.

Chapter Twelve

Their footsteps crunched on the crusty snow, and their breath hung in the air around them as they walked. The air smelled of wood smoke, pine, and snow.

Another thought interrupted her. The duke's presence created fluttering in her chest and the breathless excitement she anticipated a true love would but never experienced with anyone but he, not even Baron Richard Carruthers from her youth.

"Lord Edward has not called at the castle this many times in a week before. I think he fancies you." The duke's quiet comment made her cheeks flush with embarrassment. Had he seen?

Her gaze shot to his, and she tripped, gripping his arm hard to keep upright. "Where could such an interest lead but disaster? And were such the case, he is too late. My fate is sealed."

"Oft times, we keep our gaze on the distance and do not see what lies at our feet." The heat of his length beside hers made her shiver, and she resisted the urge to lean closer. Did he speak of the path beneath their feet or Lord Edward? Did he overhear her conversation with the lord a few moments earlier?

An awkward silence ensued.

"I shall watch where I am going after this. Thank you for keeping me steady." She gave her back a mental pat of approval for keeping her voice even.

He escorted her through the entry hall and down the corridor to the stairs in silence as if deep in thought. "Your parents worry for your wellbeing. They have your best interests at heart, and though this marriage seems…odd, they do care." He turned at the bottom step and gazed into her eyes.

She shook her head in denial. "You must understand. This is less about me and more about Mama. Every girl in the village near my age married into a higher station this last year, but I. Social standing is more important than my welfare, and Papa will not stop her if she is determined. "

He did not answer for a moment but continued to gaze at her. "My cousin would be quite heartbroken if anything happened to you. When I met him in the corridor earlier, he expressed true concern. One cannot fake the heartache lurking in his eyes."

She nodded. Papa and Thomas would both miss her. Turning, she changed the subject, hopeful for a more pleasant conversation. "What did you want to speak to me about?" Her breath sped up as she remembered asking the same question minutes earlier and her then companion's answer. What she would give to have the duke give the same response.

A frown wrinkled his brow. "I would like to invite you to join me early in the morning. I plan to get our Christmas tree tomorrow and get it set up so we can plan the other activities around it." He took a step back and nodded toward the stairs. "Be ready to leave at first light and tell no one of our plans, or we shall not be able to leave without an army of chaperones. See you at dinner."

****

The sled crunched over the glistening snow as they

sailed into the thick forest of Weston Castle. The duke held the reins with a firm grip and clucked to the massive black beasts harnessed before them. The heavy fur tucked around them kept the chill away as clumps of snow flew from the horses' hooves and the crisp early morning air blew against their faces. Sleigh bells jingled with every step the horses took as they sped over the frozen terrain.

Thomas sat between her and the duke, clutching the fur tight beneath his chin. "It is cold out here." His red nose and cheeks peeked out at their surroundings, and snow clung to his black eyelashes.

"It will warm up as soon as the sun rises." The duke guided the horses through the thick forest with ease. He did not glance down at the boy but kept his gaze on the trees before them.

"How do we know when we find the right tree? How long will it take to cut it down? Are you going to cut it alone, or is Ruby going to help you? Are we going to tie the tree to the sled?" The boy's questions flew out one on top of another until the duke laughed aloud, asking for mercy.

"Give me a chance to answer, Thomas, or I will fall too far behind. The answer to the first question is we will know the perfect tree when we see it. I do not know how long it will take to cut down. I do not plan to cut at all. We have John and several woodsmen behind us. They cut trees for a living and will know how long it takes and how best to go about it. They will also ensure the tree makes the journey back to the castle and gets set up in the ballroom."

He slid a glance sideways at Rosalind. "I plan for your sister to decide which tree she wants and watch as the men chop it down from the safety of the sled. Nothing more. She has a busy schedule with plans for her wedding, and I do not want to tire her out."

Rosalind stared at him. "I have cut firewood on occasion at home. So, I know which end of the ax to use, and I do not tire out easy."

He drew the sled to a stop and turned to gaze into her eyes, his voice firm. "I have no control over what transpires in my cousin's home. I do in mine. I invited you to join us so you could pick the tree you desire and perhaps get a moment of respite from the others. I have workmen to see to the rest. My request from you is to allow my woodsmen to show off their skill while you relax and enjoy the day."

Several sleighs drew to a stop behind them, and the duke stepped out to speak to John. The men cleared an area of snow and built a fire with dry wood from the castle. A few minutes later, they sipped cups of hot cocoa and coffee while the sun peeked over the trees sending rays of orange, yellow, and red across the sky in vibrant waves of color.

Rosalind gloried in the pleasure of the moment. No Mama, no lecture on etiquette or deportment, no fiancé, and no Edgar. Pure bliss filled her soul with delight as she sucked in the much-needed scent of freedom.

The men set up an awning with tables and chairs while they waited. When Rosalind questioned the duke about their activities, he smiled.

"Cook and the others will arrive soon and prepare breakfast for us. If our search takes until lunch, she will also serve lunch here." He laughed at her exclamation of surprise. "Finding a Christmas tree is serious work, and we cannot be expected to find the perfect one if we are uncomfortable, can we?"

"I suppose not." She never would have guessed tree hunting required such extravagance. "What about the people back at the castle. How will they get breakfast if Cook is here?"

"Are you worried about the earl?" His brows drew together in a frown. "Because I assure you, Cook left ample food laid out and an army of footmen to take care of my guests."

She flushed with embarrassment. "I did not mean to question your hospitality or your thoroughness. I worried about Papa. I would not like him to go without so I could pick out a tree."

"Ahhh, I see." He gave her a quick smile. "All is forgiven." He strode away to speak with John, and Rosalind studied his retreating form. The rumors about Cousin Lucius were false. Cold, aloof, forbidding, and a wealthy snob, too good to help his fellowmen were words often circulated about their host. And every one of them was false. A kinder, more caring man did not exist. If he were all the villagers said of him, they would not be here now. Why had he never remarried? A handsome man such as he resided on many an unmarried lady's list, hers included, she discovered with a start.

Cousin Lucius made all other men pale by comparison. Her feelings for him were the real reason she could not accept Lord Edward's proposal. She swallowed the tightness in her throat and dropped her gaze so no one could read her expression.

Good lord! She had fallen in love with him and did not realize it until this moment. What on earth could she do?

Thomas wiggled out of the furs beside her and ran

to the duke, slipping his hand into their host's larger one and making a comment.

All the men laughed, and Cousin Lucius ruffled her brother's red-brown hair, answering in his deep voice.

Rosalind sucked in a breath at the tender smile he bestowed upon the child before lifting his gaze to meet hers. She could not hide the yearning in her eyes and knew he recognized her emotions by the way he stiffened and stared back at her.

Warmth flooded her face as his heated gaze traveled over her. Desire simmered beneath the surface, and her lips parted. She remembered being held tight against his chest as his lips slid against hers, filling her with wonder at his touch.

Everything stood still as she drowned in the depths of his blue eyes. The air crackled with awareness, and she sucked in a breath, trembling with emotion. Did he feel the same about her?

John spoke beside him, and the duke turned away, moving off into the trees with several of the others, and Rosalind slumped back in her seat.

What in the name of hades could she do now? Falling for the duke complicated her life in a million and one ways. Even if he did return her feelings, he would not interfere, for the scandal alone would be life-shattering. Not to mention, disruptive to his relationship with Papa. Mama would create a scene more dramatic than any the world had ever known, and she would be sent to a nunnery in Switzerland and the map to her location burned.

God, what a mess.

If they had been invited last year, she could have fallen in love without a hitch. But if wishes were angels, they would have a heavenly choir.

Ten minutes later, they sped over the snow, deeper into the wood and circled back around to a section of the forest the duke said she must see. "There is a tree twenty feet high if an inch, and I think it perfect. What is your opinion?"

He turned and pointed at perfection. Twenty feet tall with sweeping limbs covered in dark green pine needles, the tree before her made her gasp in surprise.

"It is perfect. In my mind, I envision the ballroom with this tree rising to the ceiling between the two sets of stairs, and I cannot breathe. There never will be another Christmas tree such as this again. I cannot believe you knew where to find the exact tree I imagined in my mind."

"Can I climb it? I want to see what the ground looks like from the top." Thomas stood on tiptoes beside her pointing up at the top of the magnificent tree, his eyes glowing with excitement.

"Why must you want to go up every time you see something tall? Think what a fall from such a height would do." She hugged the boy to soften the harshness of her words while concern wrinkled her brow.

"You must promise not—"

"I cannot promise not to climb to the top. But someone must put a star on top, and I am small enough to do so." The child's chin rose in defiance, and she sighed.

"The lad makes a good point, and there is a platform behind where the tree will be mounted for him to stand on. I will help him." The duke ruffled the boy's hair and shook his head at Rosalind. "If we do not help him, he will go when he is alone, and who knows what will happen?"

The longer they stayed at the castle, the more the duke understood the boy and his mind. "If you help him, I will say nothing more." She capitulated with a shake of her head, knowing she would worry nonetheless.

The duke laughed and whistled for the men while he drove around the object of her desire so she could view it from every angle.

And then the men arrived with their saws and Ulysses.

The duke took Rosalind and Thomas back to the fire while he left to oversee the chopping.

An hour later, they sat at a table under the tarp and ate a hot, hearty breakfast, and sipped more cups of hot cocoa.

The duke appeared a few minutes later and joined them at the table. "The men should be done soon. Do you want to watch the tree fall?"

Thomas grinned and nodded, setting his cup down on the linen-covered table. "Will there be a loud noise?"

"Come and see." Cousin Lucius tucked Rosalind's arm in his and led her to the sleigh. As they neared the cutting activity, the tree creaked and groaned while the men hacked away at the massive trunk.

The duke drew the sleigh to a stop several feet away. "We can see from here. I do not want to get too close."

As the men worked their blades and the creaking grew louder, Thomas jumped to his feet, pointing. "Look! There's a snow hare over there."

Ulysses growled from his perch at their feet.

Rosalind took her gaze from the magnificent tree in time to see a white object hop from under a tree in the distance and run across the open area into a pile of shrubs. "Why would the hare run into the open with so many people around?"

The duke shrugged. "She might have a burrow and babies she wants to protect, or she might feel threatened in her former position."

As he spoke, the giant tree gave an ear-splitting crack, teetered, and fell forward, looming over the bush the rabbit hid in.

"No! The tree is going to smash the hare to bits!" Thomas' wail of protest sent fear racing down her spine.

Before she could stop him, he threw back the furs in the sleigh and jumped out, running toward the bush as fast as he could, with the dog hot on his heels.

Rosalind did think about the situation but jumped from the sleigh to go after Thomas running with all her might across the frozen ground. The duke's voice rang in her ears, but she did not hesitate in her determination to catch her brother before the tree smashed him along with the hare.

Another loud boom split the silence as she caught Thomas by the tunic and tugged him backward. A menacing shadow fell over her and glancing up, she gave a cry of terror. The massive tree hung suspended right above them, and she gulped, knowing they would not make it to safety.

A powerful arm caught her and Thomas against a large warm chest as the duke catapulted them across the open area and under a massive oak. Ulysses beat them by the smallest fraction of time. Bushes faced them, and the duke gave a giant leap, tucking them tight with both arms. They hit the top of a small swell and rolled head over heels down the other side as a loud boom split the area behind them. Branches and twigs flew everywhere as they rolled to an abrupt halt in a drift of snow.

Rosalind lay still, blinking, not sure if she dared search for injuries. Every part of her body ached, and snow covered her lashes, making it difficult to see. Thomas wiggled beside her, and with a start, she discovered she lay sprawled on top of the duke.

Ulysses appeared beside her head, licking her cheek, and she shook the dizziness off.

Lifting her head, she gazed down into blurry blue eyes.

"Are you injured?" He felt along her ribs and over her arms before dropping to her hips.

She sucked in a breath as his warmth penetrated the haze clouding her mind. The intimate contact of their bodies made breathing difficult. "Thomas." She licked her lips and rubbed a hand over her eyes, trying to focus.

Her brother's voice sounded on her left side. "Can we go down the hill again?" He rolled to his feet and stood over them, brushing snow from his woolen jacket. "I want to roll faster next time. The snow stopped us before we got very far."

"Thank God." She did not know she said the words aloud until the duke's rumble beneath her chest answered with the same fervency.

"I hear John calling. Can I go to the top and wave so he knows where we are?" The boy bent down at eye level.

"Take Ulysses with you." The duke's deep voice rumbled beneath her.

With an excited cry, the boy ran off with the dog, leaving them alone in the silence.

Rosalind dropped her head against the duke's shoulder, too spent to do more. She feared Thomas would die, and the emotion of their brush with disaster filled her eyes and threatened to run down her cheeks.

Chapter Thirteen

A sob escaped as she considered how close she came to losing Thomas, and all the days she must do without him from now on were as numerous as the stars in the sky or the flakes of snow all around her.

Loneliness, terror, and longing for a different future filled her chest. How could she face time ahead of her with what she knew of the earl and his objectives for her?

"I cannot do this. I must escape before it is too late." Pushing against the duke's chest, she levered her body up.

He followed her, drawing her around to cradle her in his lap as he lifted her chin to gaze into her eyes. "I meant to protect you, not entrap you. Forgive me." He stroked the side of her face, brushing snow from her hair and shoulders.

His tenderness brought tears as she struggled to explain her remark. "I spoke of escaping my life, not this situation. You saved Thomas and me from certain death, and for this, I am grateful. My brother has much to live for, and I cannot think of how I shall repay you for rescuing us."

"I can." His gaze dropped to her mouth, and he leaned close.

Rosalind stared at him, trembling with emotion. She yearned to feel his lips on hers and his arms holding her close. Her eyes closed as she lifted her face in anticipation. Warm lips brushed across hers, once and then twice before settling against her own.

He held her tight as his mouth covered her lips, tasting and caressing every contour like a man starved of thirst. He drank from her mouth in slow tantalizing motions creating a myriad of emotions within her.

Warm, safe, and alive, she returned his kiss with all the pent-up frustration, anger, and relief of the past few days, willing the moment to go on forever, so she never had to face the future, the earl, or her Christmas wedding.

"Rosalind. You make me forget all else but the taste of your kiss. You intoxicate me like the finest wine and make me hunger as if this were my last meal." His deep voice made her quiver against him.

Liquid fire raced through her veins, and she moaned as he caressed her back and deepened his kiss. For long moments they gave in to the pleasure of the moment, forgetting their surroundings and the others up in the trees until the earl's whiny voice spoke from right above their heads, "Where did she go?"

"I believe the girl disappeared in this direction, my lord." Edgar's deep voice made her freeze.

"Good God, what a miserable waste of a good day. I cannot think why Rosalind participated in this outing without my permission or consent. Cutting trees is a man's job."

Reality crashed down on her head, interrupting her perfect world with a reminder of the present, and she sighed. With regret, she removed her arms from around the duke's neck and rose to her feet, crying out with pain as she put weight on her left ankle.

The duke caught her about the waist, steadying her. "What is it? Where does it hurt?"

She could not put her foot down, and tears streamed down her cheeks. "My ankle. I think I may have broken it."

"What is this?" The earl's gray head popped into view, followed by Papa, John, and Edgar. "I will thank you to remove your hands from my bride's body. What are the two of you doing here all alone?" His gaze narrowed on the duke's hand at her waist and the debris sticking to her woolen coat.

"I fell. His grace caught me, or I would have been smashed by the falling tree. He saved my life." She stood on her right foot and clung to the duke's arm for fear she would slip.

The earl snorted. "You fell again? I have never met a more bumbling woman in my life. This is what comes of seeking to put your nose where it does not belong. The men should have dealt with the tree while you did needlework beside the hearth. This is not the place for you."

"Did you twist your ankle?" Papa hurried to her side and knelt, taking her foot in his hand. "Show me where it hurts. Can you stand on it?"

The earl glared. "I say she deserves whatever she gets. Quit making such a fuss, Timothy, and send the girl back to the castle. If she steps out of line, she can expect a difficult life."

Rosalind did not want to think about what he meant. "I am here to choose the tree for my wedding ball. If I desire to go on an outing, I shall." Her gaze held his as she squared her shoulders.

The earl's gaze narrowed on her face, promising retribution in the future, but he said nothing.

Papa pressed against the side of her foot, and she

winced. "We need to get you to bed and call the doctor."

"You spoil her, Timothy, making her unappetizing to possible suitors. As her husband, I shall rectify your omissions and pray God she turns out to be worth a damn."

Rosalind had enough. Turning to gaze at her fiancé with every ounce of dislike she possessed, she gave her mouth free reign. "There is nothing wrong with me, and I am worth much more than a swear word. The problem is you. I dislike the way you smell, the way you look, the way you talk, and your archaic notions about women. You are not my superior, and I shall never submit to your tyrannical ideas and demands. Nor shall I obey the commands of your over important manservant. The book on etiquette you delight to torment me with has a section for men as well. And yet, you do not adhere to those suggestions and teachings, so why should I? Do you bend from the knee as described on page forty-four? Or hold out a lady's chair as suggested on page forty? Your idea of marriage is nothing more than slavery, and I do not accept the terms. If you do not like my opinions and temperament, I suggest you look elsewhere for a broodmare. For I have no plan to change. Ever. And for your information, I can walk just fine. 'Tis my dislike of you which causes me to trip."

Unnatural silence thickened the air around them as the earl's face turned pale and then beet red with anger. He said nothing and would not until they were far away. She knew it in her gut and shivered.

"Rosalind. It is not like you to be so unkind." Papa squeezed her shoulder. "The pain must have loosened your tongue, for in ordinary circumstances you are careful to not be so sharp. I am sure the earl meant no offense. You must apologize, daughter."

The earl's gaze swiveled between the duke and Papa before he glanced away. He took a deep breath, and when he gazed back at her, raw fury burned beneath a forced smile. "The fault is mine, and I apologize, my dear. Of course, I am concerned with your injury. We shall get you back to the castle, where you may rest for a couple of hours. With any luck, you shall be well enough tomorrow to join me in the morning room. I quite enjoy our time together when we do our reading."

Rosalind gaped. The earl never apologized to anyone, but in front of Papa and the duke, he pretended to be docile. How frightening.

"All right." She stifled a moan as pain throbbed through her ankle.

The earl held out his arm, but Papa shook his head. "She cannot put weight on her foot. Lucius and I will help her to the sleigh. As soon as she is settled, I will send for the doctor. You may see her afterward."

The earl nodded his agreement but not before a flash of rage shot toward her. "Of course."

She swallowed, knowing the earl planned to have his revenge for speaking her mind after they wed when no one could interfere. The duke's arm about her waist offered little comfort as Thomas kept pace with Papa on her other side. The going up proved more difficult than she imagined, and with an exclamation, Cousin Lucius swung her up in his arms, to the earl's dissatisfaction, and carried her the rest of the way.

He sat her on the velvet seat and covered her shivering body with the heavy furs. Taking a seat beside her, he picked up the reigns. "Would you like to accompany us to the castle?" He directed the question at the earl with an arched brow.

The earl sniffed. "If Lady Rosalind does not mind my smell." His words dripped with sarcasm and the need for retribution.

She swallowed and nodded, aware her hour of reckoning would come soon.

Later the same day, the doctor tucked the blanket back over her swollen ankle and pronounced her fine. "'Tis a sprain. I recommend ice or snow for the swelling and to keep off her foot as much as possible the next few days."

The earl frowned from his position on the landing outside the corridor and, with an exclamation, stalked off, murmuring to Edgar in a quiet voice.

Ellen tucked the covers around Rosalind and ordered everyone from the room.

Papa nodded and left, taking Thomas by the hand. "We must not disturb Rosalind while she rests. We want her to be well so when Christmas comes, she can walk down the aisle and marry the earl as we planned. Come along now."

Thomas gave a dramatic groan. His voice carried up and down the corridor as he responded. "I do not want Ruby to marry the earl! I want her to marry Cousin Lucius so we can stay at the castle."

From her position on her soft feather bed, Rosalind noticed the duke stop mid-stride as the child spoke his piece. He appeared frozen in place for long minutes before he walked away without a backward glance.

She closed her eyes and sank beneath her covers, wishing the bed would swallow her whole. She knew he heard Thomas, and she had no way of knowing what he thought about the boy's statement. Cousin Lucius possessed wealth, power, and influence in court. He hailed from an elite family among the highest echelons of society. While she sprang from a normal, genteel family with no great claim to wealth or glory.

Why would he wish to marry plain, simple her? If she could evaporate into thin air, she would do so. The prospect of gazing into his eyes after Thomas' declaration made her queasy. And thank the gods the earl did not overhear, for she knew how unhappy he was with her already. Ellen carried in her dinner on a tray, and for the next two days, she lay with her foot elevated on pillows to help the swelling go down.

On the third day, Ellen bustled into the room to help her dress. "His grace requires your presence in the garden."

When Rosalind questioned her, she shook her head. "He has a plan to help your foot get well. 'Tis the first of December, and we have a tree to decorate. He wants you well enough to oversee the project."

Of course. Christmas and the tree. There would be another dinner next week for friends and family. And Lord Edward! In her situation, how could she get word to him? He told her he gave her a week and her time would run out in a couple of days. She knew in her heart she could not accept, and yet, she enjoyed the idea of an escape. Just in case things got worse. And they would if she read the look in the earl's eyes the correct way.

The servants carried a chair out of doors for her to sit in and provided a pan filled with snow. Cousin Lucius instructed Ellen to leave her foot bare so she could place it on the snow-filled basin.

No sooner did she settle in the chair than Edgar appeared in the courtyard with a frown of disapproval.

He studied them for a few minutes and then stalked off.

"How have you been?" Keen blue eyes gazed into hers from the duke's position at her feet, where he piled snow on her ankle.

The heat in his gaze made her swallow. "Fine. A bit alone, but in good spirits." The lie stuck in her throat, and she coughed to dislodge it.

"I see. If we carry you downstairs and provide a chair for you, we could garnish the tree with your direction." He slipped his hand into the snow and rubbed the side of her foot, sending shivers of awareness through her. His hand burned her cold skin and made her knees weak. Thank God no one required her to stand now.

"I accept." She stammered the words as his thumbs rubbed circles on both sides of her foot. The snow numbed the pain while his touch heightened her senses. She remembered his hands rubbing her back the day of her injury, and her hands shook. Stuffing them beneath the fur covering her, she leaned back and closed her eyes, giving in to the pleasure of his touch.

"We put the tree by the stairs, and the men made a box at the bottom so it does not tip over." Thomas leaned against the side of her chair and gave a detailed account of the setting up process. "And now, the tree is ready for us to put candy and cranberries on it. We are waiting for your foot to feel better." Peering into the basin of snow, he stared for a minute and then gazed into her eyes. "Are you better now? That's a lot of snow."

She chuckled despite her decision to focus on the duke's hand and nothing else. "I feel much better when you are here." She gave the boy a smile and closed her eyes again.

"What about me?" Cousin Lucius' deep voice filled

her belly with flutters, and her heart pounded in her chest as she contemplated an answer.

"She feels better with you, too, but she likes me best." Thomas saved her from having to answer, and she laughed again. How did one argue with his logic?

"I am sure you are right." The duke rubbed a hand up to her calf beneath her skirt and caressed her, making her suck in a deep breath of disbelief and pleasure.

She could not speak but stared at him, wondering what to do.

"Does this hurt, here?" His silky soft voice drew her to a realm of infinite desire and heart-pounding lust.

She licked her dry lips and adopted a neutral expression. Fearful, her face would give her thoughts away. If this moment could last forever, heaven could be no better than his gentle hands on her flesh.

"Are we done? Can we go hang things on the tree?" When neither answered, Thomas leaned over by the duke. "Can I rub her foot, too? Maybe if I help, Ruby will feel better faster."

The earl appeared behind Cousin Lucius with a frown on his face, and Edgar two paces behind as always. "What is going on here? And why is Rosalind here without a chaperone?"

The earl's response time had improved, for she figured he would be another five to ten minutes before he made his appearance.

"We are putting snow on Ruby's foot. She does not need a 'rone for snow, she has me." Thomas stood up and faced the earl. "Cousin Lucius and I are rubbing her foot to make it better."

The duke continued his massage, ignoring the irate older man and his disapproving servant.

The earl's eye twitched. "Are you indeed? This is an outrage, Weston. This is the second time I have discovered you alone with Rosalind. I have half a mind to call you out. Get your hands off my property before I send Edgar for my revolver."

Rosalind sat upright, gripping the arm of her chair. "Nothing happened." He could not challenge the duke to a duel because of her. What if Cousin Lucius got shot?

"I will decide. Well, Weston? Have you ruined the girl?"

The duke rose to his full height, anger flashing in his blue eyes. "Your question does not deserve an answer, Gloucester. Lady Rosalind is my relative and my responsibility while she is a guest in my home. As head of the family, her security and welfare are my greatest concern. Dare you question me when your man skulks behind doors and sneaks along passageways, following the lady everywhere she goes? I tend her injury nothing more, nothing less. Never challenge me again unless you wish to accept the consequences."

The earl glared before turning his attention to her. "We will discuss your behavior at length, Rosalind. First, I find you alone in the woods with Weston. And now I find you out here with your skirts up and his hand on your leg. I have half a mind to call off the wedding and claim a broken contract."

Hope flickered before her like a candle in the wind before he snuffed it out with his next sentence. A sneer crossed his face. "I am good-natured, by choice, and give you one final chance, Rosalind. Behave as a proper lady or all promises are off. I shall keep the generous dowry your father gave me as payment for default of contract." With his thin nose in the air, and his cane tapping his disapproval, the earl sauntered off out of sight.

The generous dowry your father gave me... She knew of no dowry, and now, so much made sense. Papa could not afford to give much, and he did so to see her wed. His sacrifice sprang from his desire for her happiness, while Mama hoped for a leg up in society with her marriage to an earl.

God, what a mess.

Chapter Fourteen

The duke rose to his feet. "What say we retire to the ballroom and string cranberries for the tree until time for tea?"

Her dry mouth refused to form the words, and they burst forth in a croak. "Of course. I am delighted to."

Ellen appeared as if by magic and rolled a woolen stocking over her left foot before the duke carried her into the ballroom to decorate the enormous tree.

They spent every possible moment during the week and the first part of the next stringing fruits, candies, and paper before draping them on the majestic branches of their twenty-foot tree.

Workmen carried in scaffolds to stand on while they worked the ropes of sweets to Rosalind's satisfaction. Mama entered the ballroom once for a half hour and left when her daughter did not submit to her demands. Papa joined them quite often and sat beside Rosalind while the men worked. His opinions carried wisdom, and she accepted them with gratefulness.

Thomas stood beside her or climbed the scaffolds when the duke allowed draping strings of sweets to his heart's content.

When the last string hung from the branches, and only the angel for the treetop remained, the duke ordered everyone from the ballroom. When Thomas complained, Cousin Lucius dropped to his haunches so he could gaze into Thomas' eyes. "We want to wait until Rosalind can stand. She has not put anything on the tree because of her foot. She should do the angel. Do you not agree?"

The boy gazed from the wonderful tree to Rosalind and back to the duke. "Aye. Ruby should put the angel up."

He said not a word about the matter again, and Rosalind believed the matter settled until the day after the family dinner when all hell broke loose.

The snow did wonders for her foot, and Rosalind could put weight on it and walk around with a slight limp. So, when the day of the dinner rolled around, she could enjoy the occasion without aid.

The evening turned out well, with everyone exhibiting their best manners and behavior. Rosalind met several relatives she knew nothing about, and a few she did.

Then she turned and met the blonde who whispered to Cousin Lucius at dinner when the local nobility dined with them.

"Hello." Rosalind held out her hand in greeting.

The other woman assessed her from head to toe and gave her an icy smile. "I am Lucius' sister-in-law, Lady Abigail. His late wife Lucinda is my sister." She made no effort to take Rosalind's hand.

"How nice to meet you." Rosalind dropped her hand, not at all pleased to meet the sour-faced woman with the narrow calculating eyes. She turned to go, but the other woman's words stopped her in the act.

"You cannot have Lucius. I promised Lucinda I would look after him, and so I shall. Lucius is a man of discriminating taste. He prefers women with…age and experience. I do hope you have not set your cap for him, for you will be disappointed. He is too important a man to risk his all for a simple girl like you. The price is too high, and the scandal too big. I suggest you marry your ancient earl and leave Lucius to me. If you continue to draw his attention, you will be hurt. So, take my advice and leave him alone."

Rosalind snapped her gaping mouth shut as the blonde slithered away to stand beside the duke and toss her a winning smile.

Not knowing what to make of the conversation, she put the matter out of her mind and turned away. She had more important things to worry about, like how to avoid the earl and his groping hands.

Lord Edward kept popping up in the back of her head and she groaned. She had not had the chance to speak to him again and avoided the subject whenever thoughts of him floated across her mind.

Her foot kept her from making her trip to the village to get the locket. The morning after the family dinner following breakfast, she sent a note to John, ordering a carriage for the village and another note informing Mama of her plan to leave the castle before tea. Making her escape with Ellen sitting stiff and quiet beside her, they traveled to the village in silence.

Stepping from the carriage in front of the jewelers, she entered the shop and paid the man what he required. The proprietor had restored the piece to perfection, and Rosalind left feeling quite satisfied with the transaction.

Turning, she stopped short when she came face-to-face with Lord Edward. Swallowing, she held out her hand. "Lord Edward, how delightful to see you today."

He kissed her glove, smiling into her eyes and caressing her knuckles as he stepped closer. A twinge of guilt twisted her stomach as she met his hopeful gaze, with Mama's threat about Thomas blazing across her mind like wildfire.

"Lady Rosalind." His deep voice caressed her name like a lover's hand and her anxiety increased. "Is there somewhere we can talk in private?"

She preferred they do this in public and shifted her feet to hide her nervousness. "I do not believe meeting in private wise. The earl's man reports everything I do, and if he discovers me alone with you, I will be ruined. I cannot disappoint my parents. I am sorry, Lord Edward, but I must decline your offer."

His gaze sharpened on her face. "Why? What happened? The other night you were amenable to my suit, and I have not been able to sleep for dreaming of you. I know you feel the same for me because I tasted desire in your kiss. Let us go to Gretna Green today. Do not go back to the castle but come with me. I will prove to you for the rest of my life you made the right choice if you come now." His pleading gaze twisted her stomach in a knot. She could not and told him so.

"Tell me what or who has frightened you away?" Taking a step closer, he caught her by the shoulders and gazed down at her face.

Losing Thomas. "There is nothing but my principles. I cannot hurt my family by creating a scandal, and I want to apologize for giving you a different impression. My desire is to please my parents and do my duty." She kept her gaze steady to hide the lie. Glancing toward the sky, she searched for lightning in case God planned to strike her down for telling so many untruths while Ellen stiffened beside her.

Pleading turned to rage, tightening the lord's jaw.

"If you felt this way, you should not have left me dangling for the past two weeks." His gaze swept her from head to toe. "No wonder you are not wed, and your one prospect is a decrepit old earl with one foot in the grave."

Heat filled her face as she inwardly acknowledged the truth of his words. Turning around, she jerked free and took one step before the irate young man caught her in his arms, tugging her back against him.

She gasped as he twisted her face up to his and planted his lips on hers for all to see. His kiss robbed her of her breath, punishing her with hard bruising pressure while he held her body hostage against him.

"Let my lady go, or I will wallop you!" Ellen yelled at the top of her voice, brandishing her umbrella like a sword.

Rosalind grimaced as Lord Edward ground his lips against hers, and she shoved against his chest with all her might. Lord, help her if word of this encounter reached her mother or the earl. "Let me go!" Kicking him in the shins, she lunged for the carriage and tripped up the step to sink down on the seat. God, what a day!

Lord Edward hurried off down the street without glancing back, his anger evident in the stiffness of his stride.

Ellen bustled in behind her and took a seat, blustering with threats and evil promises should she meet Lord Edward again.

"Do you need my assistance?" Edgar's head appeared at the door of the carriage with a frown, scaring the life out of Rosalind. "Nothing good can come of two women alone. I shall join you for the return trip, and I must say, the earl will be upset when he learns of your activities this day." His eyes glinted with relish as if anticipating the moment.

With a sinking heart, she stared with unseeing eyes as the thin man stepped into the carriage and took his seat opposite, glaring with disapproval.

They stopped at the milliner despite Edgar's numerous opinions on the subject, and Rosalind stepped out of the carriage with a breath of relief. The stuffy, critical haze in the carriage threatened to choke her, and she had to get out. On impulse, she entered the shop and snuck out the back, walked around to the cobblestones in front, and hurried in the opposite direction. She wondered how long it would be before the haughty servant discovered she disappeared.

Several shops down, the crunch of carriage wheels hurried up the cobblestone road behind her, and she turned to enter the closest shop door and froze.

The Duke of Weston sat against the opposite wall on a velvet chair, gazing at Lady Abigail, who stood before him draped in red velvet before an enormous mirror. He stared at her while the woman turned around in a circle to model the daring gown she wore. The bodice dipped low in the front and in the back with short cap sleeves dripping with diamonds. Her hair glistened in the afternoon light, and pink touched her cheeks. Her blue eyes lit up with excitement as she gazed down at her companion with a slight smile on her delicate lips.

Rosalind's heart jumped to her throat. How she longed for Cousin Lucius to gaze at her the way he did the woman before him, and jealousy filled her bosom. Shoving the emotion aside, she left as quickly as she arrived, coming to a dead stop in front of the carriage waiting outside the door. Her carriage.

How did Edgar know which shop she entered and exited? So much for independence and a day away from her problems. Her marriage and the earl's evil valet tethered her like an anchor dragging her down.

After informing the driver she would return to the castle, she dropped her gaze to her lap while she grappled with her feelings over the fact the duke loved another woman. Her situation would be quite amusing if it were not so serious. Here she sat after declining an offer of marriage from an attractive young lord who she did not love while engaged to a fat ancient gentleman old enough to be her grandfather whom she would never love, let alone like, and in love with a powerful duke who loved another.

Shaking her head, she gazed out the window, ignoring the icy conversation between her companions as they challenged each other on their authority.

She yearned to find one of her true loves, and when she believed she had, he did not return her affection. At all. How could he when he gazed with such longing at Lady Abigail?

The realization her first true love passed her like a dream in the night hit her like a load of stones. How could her life be so complicated when she was so mediocre? Forcing her feelings to the bottom of her stomach, she stared out the carriage window as they trotted back to the castle.

Numb with emotion, she accepted the footman's hand when they wheeled into the cobblestone drive in front of the castle. The nip in the air and the scent of the trees filled her with sadness. Christmas would come in two weeks, and she would be married, ready or nay. With trembling hands, she gathered her purchases and climbed the steps to the entrance door.

No sooner did she step inside than her mother hurried into the room. "Where have you been? Do you have Thomas?"

Her brows drew together. "Nay. I sent word of my trip to the village so you knew of my whereabouts. Thomas and his nurse were eating breakfast in the nursery when I checked on him before leaving."

Mama placed a hand over her chest, breathing hard. "His nurse let him out to play, but she has not seen him for the past hour. I cannot think where he would go. He might have gone to the tower."

She doubted Thomas would after her ordeal and told Mama so.

"But how do you know? He could be up there. I think you should go search for him."

And she would, but not up there. She fell for such a statement once and would not again. If Thomas gave his word to her, he would keep it. "Let me hang up my cloak and put my packages down, and I will go search for him."

Ten minutes later, Rosalind walked the main level, searching every room and calling his name. No one answered, and the silence made her cringe. Where could he be? For an hour and a half, she searched until she arrived outside the ballroom. Swinging the door open, she stopped and froze with fear.

Her little brother clung to the top of the twenty-foot tree clutching an angel in his hand.

She dared not say a word for fear of startling him. His precarious position scared the life out of her, and she must be careful, or he would fall. Crossing the ingrain parquet floor, she climbed the stairs on the left and walked across the platform until she stood behind her brother's position in the tree.

Tilting her head all the way back, she gazed up in dismay at the distance between him and her. She would have to climb up to help him down. Many times, at home, she had the same view and, as a result, ascended trees with remarkable agility. Mama's punishment for such a situation resulted in her brother going without his evening meal. Something Rosalind did not agree with and learned to deal with the situation on her own. She did not want to think what Mama's reaction would be here in the castle where she wanted to impress both the duke and the earl.

Thomas turned his head to gaze down at her with a concerned look on his face. "Oh, hello, Ruby. I wanted to put the angel on top and surprise you."

"You got your wish and surprised me, but the top is too high for you. If you climb back down, we will ask Cousin Lucius for help. I think the men plan to set up scaffolds so we can climb to the top without falling." If she remained calm, the child would also. But Lord, she wished the duke were here.

Her brother's other foot slipped on the branch he stood on, and he gave a squeal of fear. "I am going to fall, Ruby. You must help me!"

"Keep your gaze on the tree, and do not look down. I will be there in a moment." Gazing around to be sure they were alone and she did not miss a silent footman or guard, she lifted her skirt and untied her numerous petticoats, allowing them to fall to the floor. Catching the hem of her voluminous skirt, she tied it into a knot to keep the fabric free of her feet. Then, slipping off her satin slippers, she climbed on top of the rail, holding the sides to catch her balance before rising to her feet. She clutched a branch with both hands for support and studied the limbs for possibilities. Thinking once she stood on the rail, she could touch his feet, Rosalind discovered her calculations amiss. "Hold tight to the tree, and I will help you down." Her calm tone did not betray the anxiety holding her captive. Frozen with fear, Thomas needed her to climb up and show him how to get down.

With careful motion, she placed one foot on a hefty branch in front of her and prayed the duke's men anchored the trunk well in the massive wooden box on the ballroom floor. Catching a branch above her head, she rose to place her other foot beside its twin and held her breath. The tree swayed just a little with her added weight, and she glanced up to see how far she must climb. One more branch up, and she would be able to touch his feet. From there, she could guide him back down to safety. Ice-cold fear clung to her like mist in the forest as she took the next step up. Swaying in the air, she sucked in a deep breath and whispered words of encouragement to them both.

Chapter Fifteen

Taking hold of her brother's foot, she coaxed him to step down to the next lower branch. "Now, the other foot. I am here, Thomas. You will be all right."

"I am scared, Ruby. It is too high. I cannot hold the tree when I have the angel. I think I am going to fall."

Rosalind swallowed hard. Her brother would die if he fell from this height. And she might as well, for she would not let him fall without catching him.

"Hold on, Thomas. Drop the angel and clutch the branch beside you for balance." She slipped on the branch, and the tree swayed. Praying harder than she had since her parents signed her marriage contract, Rosalind gripped the limb beside her with one hand and her brother with the other.

"If I drop the angel, she will break." Her brother's voice shivered with fear. "And she is too pretty to drop."

"And you are too important to fall. Drop the angel. We can get a new angel, but I do not want a different brother." Her hand inched up her brother's leg as he took another step down.

She did not know they had an audience until Ulysses gave a short bark beneath her.

"Hold on, Thomas."

The duke's deep voice broke her concentration, but she dared not glance down for fear she would lose her balance.

"There is a sturdy branch to your right. Rosalind. Take a step down."

She appreciated his guidance, worrying she would lose her balance if she twisted to gaze behind her. "Everything will be fine, Thomas. Cousin Lucius is here, and so is Ulysses. Hand me the angel, and I will give her to the duke for safekeeping. Then you and I can focus on getting down."

"All right." He handed the angel down, and she let go of her brother to take it.

"Please take the angel, your grace. I cannot bend over, or I will lose my grip on the tree."

He took the angel without comment. No doubt tongue-tied by her unladylike appearance. Rosalind did not want to know what their host thought or what his view of her might be at this moment in time. She could not be much of a shock. After all, he had a view of her backside once before.

The duke's hand caught her left ankle and guided her foot down to the next lower branch. "Step there. You are doing a fine job of climbing down. A bit more, and you will both be on the platform beside me."

Rosalind breathed a sigh of relief too soon, for the admiral leaped from Thomas' jacket pocket at the same moment.

Her brother let go of the tree to catch his pet, tumbling onto her and knocking the breath from her.

Her feet slipped on the thick branch, and she lost her grip on the tree as Thomas crashed into her. Crying out in terror, she tumbled backward, clutching tight to her brother's lower half.

Everything happened in slow motion. So many thoughts, fears, and desires raced through her mind while they were suspended in the air. Rosalind knew they had died together and closed her eyes in defeat, wishing Thomas had the chance to grow up and she the chance to kiss the duke one more time.

Strong arms closed around her the next moment. They landed with a thud against the broad expanse of Cousin Lucius' chest, and together they fell to the floor, using him as a cushion.

The breath left her lungs with impact, and she closed her eyes in gratitude for the second chance at life, clutching a wiggling, protesting Thomas to her chest. This made the second time she used the duke to break her fall and moaned with pain.

"There you are, Admiral. I thought you were going to die." He made a dive for the amphibian as it jumped over her and landed on the other side of the duke. Ulysses followed, clawing at the wooden floor in his haste to change direction.

Rosalind leaped forward, catching the wriggling creature as the dog's jaws snapped on empty space. Turning, she handed the frog to Thomas, who tucked the amphibian back inside his pocket and buttoned the flap.

Shooting Rosalind a sheepish glance, he muttered. "I am sorry I fell on you, but I had to catch the admiral. He got scared when he looked down and jumped out."

Rosalind shook her head, bracing her hands on either side of the duke's head and unable to answer past the lump in her throat. "Next time, leave the admiral in his cage if you plan to climb a tree. Just like the angel, we can replace the admiral, but you, we cannot."

The boy dropped his chin. "He wanted to see what the top of the tree looked like. He knows what is on the ground around a lake but not what happens in a tree."

"And I have no wish to find out what happens without you." She meant every word with a wealth of meaning the boy would not understand. "So, leave the frog in his cage."

Ulysses interrupted their conversation by whining and licking Thomas' face and then hers. When he licked Cousin Lucius' head, the duke made no response, and Rosalind frowned, disconcerted to discover her bosom planted over his face.

The duke's arms held them tight, though he made no sound, and she wondered for a minute if they killed him.

Levering her body backward, she met his heated gaze. "I am sorry for landing on you once more."

His gaze dropped to her breasts and back up. "I am not." The sensual grin he gave made her stomach flutter with awareness.

Caught up in the moment, she jumped when the door opened behind them, and shuffling footsteps approached. She knew who had arrived by the sound of his dragging foot and the stench of his toilette water. She sighed.

Of course, the earl would appear at this very moment.

Rosalind rolled to her knees and levered her body up. But her trembling arms gave out, and she fell against the duke's chest with a groan.

They gazed at each other for several heart-pounding seconds before the earl's dry tone brought her to her feet.

"What have we here?" Clasping a hand over his nose, the earl took a hasty step back when Ulysses turned toward him and gave a low growl.

The duke commanded the dog to heel and called for a footman.

Rosalind had no strength left but forced her trembling arms and legs to hold her up as she faced her irate ancient fiancé.

In the corner of her eye, the duke rose to his feet and turned his attention to Thomas. Running his hands over the boy to make sure there were no broken bones before summoning a footman to take him to the nursery.

She kept her gaze forward as the earl's dark eyes traveled over her with disgust before moving to the pile of discarded petticoats against the rail.

"So, after kissing a ruffian in the village, I come in search of an explanation and find you half-naked in the arms of our host. You undress and cuckold me in the ballroom, the very place we are to celebrate our union? What have you to say, Rosalind? Shall I find you are not a virgin on our wedding night? Or did I stop you in time? If I knew you were so wanton, I would have accommodated you, but the duke made his views clear. Now I understand he protected you from me to save you for himself. I have a good mind to file a broken marriage contract with the local magistrate listing Weston as offender."

The duke faced the earl. "Lady Rosalind and the boy fell from the tree. Once again, I broke their fall, nothing more. Had I not, there would be no ceremony to celebrate. There is nothing between the lady and me, and I resent the accusation. To become romantically involved with Lady Rosalind would be extreme folly and not worth the price or the scandal such a situation would create for someone of my wealth, importance, and position. She is yours, and the wedding will proceed as planned. You have nothing to fear as far as I am concerned." Without a glance in her direction, the duke turned on his heel and left, closing the door behind him.

Devastated by his damning words, tremors shook her body. Lady Abigail said much the same, and the coincidence crossed her mind like a chill before a toasty fire.

Rosalind shoved her broken heart to the bottom of her stocking feet to examine later and in private. With a mask of indifference on her face, her gaze rose to the earl's. "I did not invite or instigate the kiss in the village. As for the duke, he caught us, as he said. Good day, my lord."

With a swoop of her arms, she gathered up her discarded clothing and fled for the comfort of her chamber, where she could cry in private.

Two hours passed while she dealt with the jagged shards of her heart, refusing to answer any of the knocks on her chamber door. With the latch secured, she harbored no fear of interruption and let her emotions come out in force.

Terror for their near-death experience took precedence until she calmed her racing heart with gratitude to be alive. Sorrow replaced her gratitude as she probed the possibility of losing Thomas and all his loss would mean now and in the future. Although thankfulness filled her heart for his safety today, knowledge of their parting in the near future overshadowed it. A fresh wave of tears accompanied the worrisome thoughts until she remembered the earl.

Anger and resentment followed as she relived his assumptions and accusations, although parts of them were true. She *did* kiss the duke twice, but according to his word, they were not romantic in the least. Pain such as she never knew ripped through her as she considered his lack of emotion for what to her were unparalleled moments of indescribable bliss. How could he be so callous over experiences she would cherish for the rest of her life? Now she knew what passion and desire tasted like. She wanted more and knew she would never experience the same with the earl. Or anybody else.

Her heart ached, and she swallowed the lump in her throat. Self-pity had never been part of her personality, and her pride rescued her.

Sitting up, she squared her shoulders and hardened her heart. If the duke did not experience the same delight she did in their kisses, so be it. He would never know her feelings or how he changed her view of the world.

The shattered fragments of her feelings would be tucked away out of sight for the rest of her stay here. After her marriage and departure, she would deal with her broken organ, and not before. Placing a mental wall around her heart, she piled the stones high and threw the key into the accompanying moat noting with detachment its drop to the silt below. Numbness settled around her, and ice flowed into her bloodstream.

Christmas lost its fascination, and she no longer experienced the brilliant magic and wonder which accompanied the season. Stark and alone, she rose to her feet and stared out her chamber window at the frozen gardens and landscape. From now on, she would wear her numbness like a suit of armor to shield her from the arrows of desire and want.

Footsteps approached, and another knock sounded on the door. With a sigh, Rosalind straightened her spine and unlatched the door.

"Your father would like a word with you in the private sitting area adjacent your parents' suite." Ellen's compassionate gaze swept over her face. "Do not worry, m'lady. We will figure a way out of this mess."

Rosalind gave her a small smile. "There is one way out, and we both know it. And although I appreciate your concern and offer to help, I accept my fate, and you must do the same. Tell my father I will come as soon as I have righted my clothing. Thank you, Ellen."

Rosalind refused her offer to help, and the maid hurried away with a frown of concern furrowing her brow.

With her petticoats and slippers once more where they belonged, she walked down the corridor and turned left to her parents' suite.

Papa answered the first knock and ushered her inside the elegant cream and wine sitting area, empty of occupants other than the two of them.

She sat on the edge of a wine velvet settee before the marble fireplace and crossed her feet beneath her skirt. With hands folded in her lap, she glanced up at him and waited for his lecture to begin. Mama's disapproval was one thing, Papa's another.

Papa's gray peppered hair glinted in the afternoon sunlight as he stood before the large window overlooking the rose garden. He wore black trousers and a light blue shirt accompanied by a darker blue vest embroidered with black leaves and garlands. Folding his hands behind his back, he turned to give her a small smile. "The earl paid me a visit an hour ago."

She did not doubt it for a second and waited for him to proceed.

"He requires more dowry to proceed with the marriage due to recent events. I offered a thousand gold coins, but he refused saying I must give him ten thousand more for offering damaged goods. He warned if I do not give him what he asks, the wedding is off, and he will file charges against Cousin Lucius as the offender."

Her stone-cold heart did not twitch as she said the first words which popped into her mind. "Then let him. You have done nothing wrong, and neither have I." Ignoring the slight twinge of conscience as she said the words, she lifted her chin and continued. "I refuse to allow such an odious man to use my mishaps to bleed you for more money. He touts his importance and the throngs of women envious of my position. While he is no prize with his age, foul breath, and haughty manner. I say, put him to the test. Refuse to accommodate his demand. My guess is he will bluster, spout a few more threats, and concede to give me another chance. I would rather perish in a convent than let such a man make a pauper of you." She meant the words with every icicle in her frozen heart.

Papa studied her face for long minutes. "Under the circumstances, I think it wise to placate the man, not offend him. We have no other options, Rosalind. I have done all I can to protect you and save you from a miserable life. I may not have the coin, but I could ask Cousin Lucius to make me a loan." His quiet offer wrenched the last vestige of feeling she harbored in the barren wasteland of her chest.

"No. I will not allow you to do such a thing. Your cousin has extended his kindness above the call of duty, and I will not be beholden to him or allow you to be. I am serious, Papa. Refuse the earl, and if the conversation goes sideways, I will go to the nuns without complaint and spend my life behind stone walls as Mama threatened. I will not bow to the horrible man you paid to marry me. And if you give in now, he will continue to make demands of you after the vows are spoken for offenses, real or imagined. You should know I do not plan to be a humble, obedient wife, content to bear offspring I cannot speak to or play with. My life is my own, and I cannot defend my position if I worry. He will tax you with every non-compliant act on my part."

Papa's brown eyes were sad as he smiled down at her. "Had you been born a man, we could take over the world and would not be in the position we are today. I think the world unjust to accuse the woman and allow the man to run free. But here we are." He crossed the room to stand before her and helped her to her feet. "I love you, daughter, and shall do as you suggest. While I agree with your decision to not bow before him, you must understand my mission is to see to your happiness the best I can, and I will adjust as needed. The earl is old but a good man. You must do your part to show him appreciation for rescuing you from a life of pain. A humble, obedient wife can be forgiven of much."

She nodded, not sure what he thought she needed forgiveness for, but keeping her fingers crossed behind her back for future situations should they arise. Papa could believe whatever he chose, but she would never concede to the level of humility the earl envisioned.

Papa escorted her back to her chamber, suggesting she stay out of sight until dinner while he worked out the details with the earl. She agreed and spent the better part of two hours finishing the stitching around Thomas' tunic before the need for freedom and fresh air filled her soul.

Tucking the tunic back in her wardrobe, she checked the corridor outside her chamber for occupants. Finding the area empty, she walked on whisper-quiet feet to the opening in the corridor leading to the secret passageway.

On impulse, she turned left instead of right and walked around to the back of what she figured would be her chamber. Searching for a lever or latch, she pressed, and the wall slid open to the side of her wardrobe. Cousin Lucius did not mention her chamber possessed an opening and frowned. The use of this secret door would have saved her a great deal of trouble had she known about it beforehand. Although to be fair, she had not asked, either. Turning around, she made her way down the long passageway to the stairs leading to the kitchen doors and freedom.

Chapter Sixteen

Edgar stepped from the shadows as Lady Rosalind swept past and escaped through the large kitchen doors with a cry of satisfaction. Anger tightened his fists as he stared after her. The stupid girl needed to learn her place and acquire some humility. His lordship's other wives took less than a week to learn subservience. One little lesson on the correct person to fear forced them to their knees before him and kept them there.

The earl's second wife grew so frightened of Edgar's power that she cowered when he walked into the room and scurried away when he turned his attention elsewhere. This lasted for months before the woman announced she carried the earl's child, and his master fell into a drunken stupor in celebration. But when the countess delivered a stillborn child, she threw her body from the tower rather than face the valet's wrath for failing to produce a son for his master. Those were fond memories Edgar often revisited when he had a bad day, like the one when Lady Rosalind escaped the morning room.

He frowned. The earl's tongue stung like the bite of a viper when riled, and the valet would never forget the punishment he received when the earl discovered the girl left while he slept. Lady Rosalind had to pay for the pain he suffered at his master's hands.

Gloucester servants knew Edgar ruled as undisputed

king in their master's household. So, ordering one of their footmen to bolt the lady in after he sent her to the tower in search of her brother held no risks for either of them. Though the duke questioned every servant, Gloucester and Weston alike with intensity, Edgar harbored no fear of discovery, for the earl's footman knew better than to talk.

He believed the experience in the tower would temper Lady Rosalind's unruly disposition, but it did not. Quite the opposite occurred, in fact. Somehow, she guessed who orchestrated the situation though he covered his tracks with care and stuffed animal hair in his small clothes causing him to suffer a horrible episode of hives. How she placed the hair there occupied his mind for days. He never suspected a thing until the itching and burning took over, and in desperation, he returned to his chambers to discover the cause. When he fished the long white and gray hairs from his under drawers, rage surged through his blood with such speed, he thought he might explode.

Searching for the culprit took him less than an hour. A small, satisfied smile on Lady Rosalind's lips as she sailed past on her way to dinner spoke volumes, and he waited for the right opportunity to get even.

Twice, Lady Rosalind's maid returned pots of tea containing Saint John's Wart to give the lady runny stools and Calamus to irritate her skin and give her stomach upset. How her lady's maid knew when he laced Lady Rosalind's tea confused and angered him. Ellen had to go.

In a strange household, one must discern the servant's attitude before speaking or asking anything out of the normal. Most noble households possessed a handful of servants willing to look through locks, slip notes in and out, or reveal their master's secrets with no twinge of conscience. But not at Weston Castle. As far as Edgar could ascertain, every person who worked for the duke loved him and maintained their loyalty, making any further attempts to force Lady Rosalind into submission out of the question. Until they returned home, and the servants were loyal to him alone.

The gentry often overlooked the ones who served them as if they were obsolete, making subterfuge and mutinous acts easy to orchestrate. One too-hot kettle of water added to a bath, one spilled cup of tea in the right lap, or one well-placed puddle on a treacherous walkway could cause havoc. A loose saddle strap, wrong dosage of herb, or accidental addition of tainted meat to the family soup could devastate the lives of those they served.

The valet had every confidence he could humble the lady in a short span of time once they arrived at Gloucester Manor, where he ruled the earl's domain.

A calculating gleam entered his eye as he stared after Lady Rosalind. He long suspected the castle of having hidden corridors after the morning room incident and Lady Rosalind's sudden disappearance following the first public dinner but had not been able to get any of the servants to reveal the passageway's location or how to access them.

Strolling over to the wall the lady emerged from, he ran his hands over the wood, searching for the mechanism which opened the panel. When he pressed the upper right corner, the panel slid open, revealing a lighted, narrow corridor and steps leading up.

Huzzah! An evil plan formed in his mind as he

inspected each narrow corridor and the prospective rooms of the castle.

The earl's bad temper following his failed attempt to lever more money from Lord Weston after the Christmas tree incident hung like a thundercloud over his master. Once Edgar figured the passageways out, he would present a plan to his master sure to entice him out of his bad mood. And give him pleasure. The valet chuckled at his own pun and continued down the corridor, content with the knowledge he had found a way to restore his master's good humor and return to grace.

****

"You were right, Rosalind. The earl capitulated after several threats and a lot of bluster. I opened my mouth to recant my decision, but he beat me to the draw. How did you know he would back down?"

When she returned to her chamber, Papa invited her back to his sitting room to talk after he confronted the earl. Now, leaning back against the softness of the settee, she shrugged.

"He threatens to file a breach of contract every time something does not go according to his wishes. For instance, informing me he plans to keep the dowry even if he calls the whole thing off and then demanding more for something so stupid as my landing on the duke. His attitude tells me he is in debt. He does not want to lose you as his father-in-law in case he needs to borrow money from you in the future. Besides, I know enough desperate women in London to know if they wanted to marry him, they would have by now. No one wants the earl for the same reason I do not."

Papa smiled where he sat beside her on the wine-velvet settee. "I would pay any price to see you happy. I am sorry all I can offer under the circumstances is an old earl, but I believe marriage to him is a better life for you than living in a convent. I am grateful we have him and wish there were more options for you."

The devil took hold. "There are. Lord Edward Falcon asked me to run away to Gretna Green today in the village." She clutched her hands together in her lap and waited for his reaction.

"He is the man the earl claims you kissed in public?" Papa frowned. "I believed the earl made the situation up to use against you."

Rosalind shook her head. "I declined Lord Edward, and he forced a kiss on me before I could evade him."

Papa remained silent for a long moment as if turning this new information around in his head. "If he will take you as you are and marry you, I will go have a word with him. Your mother need not know until the deed is done."

She loved Papa more in that moment than her whole life beforehand because by offering, he proved she did mean more to him than his reputation, good name, or any scandal they created.

The ice around her heart cracked a little. "Thank you, Papa, for the offer. I know how much it costs you to say it, and I love you for doing so, but Lord Edward is not the man for me. He could never make me happy."

"Are you suggesting the earl can?" Surprise lifted Papa's eyebrows into his hairline. "I understood you struggled with the idea."

Struggle did not describe the loathing she entertained for the man and his servant. "I harbor no delusions about the earl, but the deal is done. I cannot go back without causing a scandal and dragging your name through the mire. I would never hurt you, Papa. And the hope exits he will give me my freedom once I produce his heir. Many lords do."

Papa sighed from a place deep inside. "I accepted his offer to provide a reasonable future for you, daughter. I believe he will provide a good home and the honor of his distinguished name. One cannot hope for much more in the best of circumstances. Your mother and I are one of the few who found love but this was after previous arranged marriages. Though your plight seems harsh to you, the earl is quite advanced in age, and you may be free before you know. After he passes, you will be given a house and a stipend for life. You need never marry again if you do not desire. I made sure the earl added this condition to his will, and a signed copy resides in my safe at home."

She understood now. All this time, she wondered how Papa, of all the people in her life, could agree to give her away to the Earl of Gloucester. Her dear father did so to secure her future and for no other reason.

Throwing her arms around Papa's neck, she kissed his cheek. "Thank you. I must go now, or I will not be ready for dinner, and Ellen shall be upset with me."

He nodded his agreement. "Off you go then."

A note appeared under her door while she dressed, informing her his grace placed the angel on top of the tree to prevent further mishaps, and all décor not hung had now been taken care of.

A wry smile touched her lips. They should tell Thomas, not her, for he instigated the tree-climbing adventure and would do so again if he got the chance.

She passed the note along to the nursery as a precaution and settled onto the stool for Ellen to brush her hair.

Two days later, Rosalind descended the stairs in her glorious red silk dress created for this special occasion, her Christmas Ball. Shimmering in the light of the candles overhead, she stepped down to the main floor and sucked in a huge breath of courage. Mama did not know she changed the color of tonight's gown at the dressmakers. Busy with her own ball gown, she left Rosalind to her musing, and her daughter took advantage of her distraction.

Somehow as she stood there, she knew tonight would be the end of so many things and the beginning of others. The night spoke to her soul of momentous things on the horizon, and she did not know if they were good or bad but that they would come.

****

The main corridor of the castle smelled of hothouse flowers and pine boughs. For the side tables held massive bouquets of fresh-cut blossoms, vying for attention with the heavy boughs draped along the stairs and down each side of the corridor. The boughs were adorned with pinecones, strings of crimson cranberries, and caught up with red velvet bows creating a festive atmosphere.

The delicate strains of the orchestra filled the air along with the murmur of guests in the massive ballroom. Rosalind turned her head when a blast of cold air brushed over her, followed by the murmur of new guests coming to join the celebration.

Lifting her chin in the air, she turned and came face to head with the earl, and she froze. For once, his sweet toilette water did not give his presence away, and she wished it had for surprise at his appearance must show in her expression.

"My lord." Dipping a curtsy, she resisted the urge to

gag when he leaned forward to see down the neck of her gown.

"Rosalind. In future, save the wanton display of bosom for the pleasures of our bedchamber." He licked his fat lips and offered her his plump arm. "Come, my dear. Our guests await."

Swallowing her nausea, she gave a nod of her head to indicate her compliance while she battled with the rocks in her stomach created by the touch of the ancient slobbering man at her side. "Of course."

They strolled and limped their way down the corridor at a snail's pace, stopping every few feet for the earl to catch his breath. When he caught the frown on her brow, he patted her hand. "Do not worry, my dear. Walking is tiresome, and I must rest, but in bed, I have fantastic stamina. You shall not be disappointed with my performance. I suspect we shall have you with child the first week of our honeymoon."

Oh God! The honeymoon. Her food did come up then and gasping out her apology, she ran for the lady's loo before disaster occurred. She made it in the nick of time. Retching and gagging until she could do so no more. How in God's name would she survive the honeymoon? Thoughts of him touching her and being intimate with her had her bending over the seat again, dry heaving.

Leaning against the silk-covered wall, Rosalind took a linen towel and wiped her mouth. She shook like a newborn lamb from the force of her purging and strove to catch her breath.

Voices echoed in the corridor outside, reminding her of her duty, and she straightened with a grimace doubting the earl made it more than a few feet since the time she left.

His slowness gave her hope once they were wed, for he would never catch her should she choose to elude him. Which she did with every thump of her frozen heart.

Entering the corridor, she met the duke, resplendent in black evening clothes, a white cravat, and a gold vest. His windswept hair glistened in the light of the candles overhead, and his gaze pierced her soul.

"Good evening." Whispering the words, she dipped a curtsy and turned on her heel, anxious to put as much space as possible between them before her heart caught a whiff of his cologne and discovered how close he stood.

"Rosalind." His deep voice sliced across her panic and made her pause.

Swallowing, she lifted her chin, locked an extra chain around her heart, and turned to meet his gaze. "Your grace?"

His gaze flickered at her distant manner as he strode toward her. "You look quite stunning this evening, as I am sure every man you met has told you. Allow me to add my admiration as well. May I escort you to the ballroom?"

No one said anything of the sort, and she planned to keep her distance. "Thank you, your grace, I appreciate your offer, but I believe I can make it on my own."

Turning, she ignored the flash of surprise in his eyes and fled before he could stop her. To her surprise, the earl did not hover in the corridor as she feared, for once she stood in the open doorway, she spied him sitting beside her mother, deep in conversation.

The scene made her flinch. If Mama liked him so much, her chances of living without her constant supervision dwindled like a candle in the wind.

And then the duke stood beside her. "Give me your arm, Rosalind. As my guest, you will accept my escort." His tone suggested he would not accept anything less than he asked.

She kept her gaze forward as she placed her arm on his, ignoring the tingling in her body at his presence. His nearness made her crazy. The heat of his body next to hers took her breath away and made her heart jump around in its cell.

"Why did you run from me?" His deep voice made her weak in the knees, and her stomach flutter with nervousness.

"I would hate for the scandal and price of my company to be more than you can afford, your grace. You have eight days more of my presence, and then you shall be free of me forever. Thank you for the escort." Dipping her curtsy, she turned away and hurried over to the refreshment table for a cup of punch. Anything to distract her mind from the duke's intoxicating presence and the scent of his cologne.

The footman in attendance handed her a cup of punch, and she took a sip to calm her nerves. Her breath came fast, and her chest heaved with emotion.

You can do this because you are strong. Do not let them beat you. Keep your chin up and your heart locked. If you do, everything will turn out for the best.

Even she did not believe the words running through her head and took another sip of punch. She would never be fine again. Of this fact, certainty grew.

"This is our dance, my dear." Somehow the earl dragged his fat body over to stand beside her without her knowledge.

Swallowing the rest of her punch, she wished it were laced with liquor for the ordeal ahead. "Of course." Her sweet tone gave no indication of the turmoil, resentment, and loathing in her bosom.

He clasped her to him, burying his face in her neck as he twirled her around in snail-slow motion. His hot hands at her waist made her sick to her stomach, as did the soft fluffy skin of his abdomen and chest. She focused on keeping the punch in her belly as his hands squeezed her back.

"Can you feel me? I am hard with wanting you and cannot wait to take you. Every man in this ballroom is jealous of me right now and what I can do to you." His voice dropped to a low, evil chuckle. "The time is closer than you think, and I am ready."

The music stopped, and she offered up a fervent prayer of gratitude for her deliverance.

"If you will excuse me, my lord. I must greet my parents." He caught her arm, protesting, but she broke free and hurried away before he could catch her again.

Chapter Seventeen

Papa stood beside the massive Christmas tree gazing up at the gossamer angel high on top. He held a cup of rum and a slice of cake.

Rosalind stopped at his side, closing her eyes and wishing she were not about to marry the awful little earl whose touch made her skin crawl.

"You climbed this tree to rescue Thomas?" Papa's gaze remained on the top of the tree.

"Yes. He could not get down and froze, too frightened to move. I climbed up to help him down like I do at home." She did not see why her father appeared surprised by the information.

"You both could have fallen to your deaths and should have called for help." His voice rasped with emotion as he turned to gaze at her.

"I did not have time, and I have helped Thomas down from taller trees more often than you think. We were quite safe." Her matter-of-fact tone created a flash of surprise in his eyes.

"How many times did this happen at home?" His voice broke off in a wheeze as his gaze returned to run the length of the tree.

"At least once a week in the summer. Less in the spring and fall. The last time it happened, Mama's dance instructor stopped on his way out to offer his assistance. Why do you ask?" She turned her head as Mama appeared by her other side.

"Amelia, why did I not know Rosalind scaled trees to assist our son down and not the servants?" His tone remained even as he studied Mama's face.

"I do not see what it matters." Her mother shrugged as if discussing the type of soap she used for her hands.

"You informed me one time and spoke of servants helping the boy down. I knew nothing of the regularity nor of Rosalind's help. They both could have fallen and perished. And who is this dance instructor Rosalind speaks of? I should have received the details. They are my children, as well." Papa's concern warmed her heart.

While Mama shrugged. "Why do you care about the foolish things *my* daughter does? I do not understand." She gazed out over the crowd as if searching for someone and ill at ease with the conversation.

"Rosalind is as much mine as yours, Amelia, and I care very much." Papa's eyes gleamed with the intensity of his emotions. Then he grew still as if a sudden thought struck him. "What else have you misled me on? I note you did not answer my question, Amelia. Who is this dance instructor?"

Her mother did not answer but picked up her skirt in preparation to leave. "Oh, look. There is lovely Lady Abigail. I think I will go say hello." She sailed away without looking back, leaving Papa staring after her with a thoughtful look.

"Mama's instructor is Lord James Danbury. He proved a great help with Thomas."

Papa paled and stared at her as if she were a stranger. "Who?" The quiet question took her off guard.

She frowned, wishing she had not mentioned the man after the way he reacted. The intensity of his words and the look in his eye made her swallow. "Mama's dancing instructor. I met him twice on his way out of the house when I returned from going out calling. Why do you ask?"

A curious expression crossed Papa's face as he stared at her. "You know nothing else? You had no other…connection?" His voice cracked with emotion as he awaited her answer.

"Mama hired him to teach her the latest dances while you were in London. The second time I met him, I spotted Thomas clinging to the tallest tree in the drive as I returned home. Lord Danbury offered his assistance, and I accepted. When we discovered the boy frozen with fear, I asked Lord Danbury to return and fetch James. Which he did, and then assisted the stable master in carrying him down."

James tended to the household affairs in Papa's absence and sent ladders and menservants to retrieve Thomas.

Papa stared at her as a mixture of emotions crossed his face, surprise, enlightenment, grief, and then anger. "We will speak more of this later."

The hair on the back of her neck picked up the earl's approach, and she whispered an excuse before fleeing to the other side of the ballroom, forgetting the conversation in her haste to escape.

Making small talk came naturally to most women, she supposed, but not to her. Blundering her way through several one-sided conversations, she gave up and wandered back to the refreshment table to regroup and decide what to do with her hands. Did one hold them in front? Let them hang by their side, or tuck them behind their back? Her stomach swirled along with the music, and she paused, turning toward the table when a gruff noise reminded her of Ulysses.

The dog made her think of her brother.

She wished Thomas could see the ballroom with all the beautiful swirling skirts of the ladies in every color of the rainbow and beside them, the elegant, dashing gentlemen in their black evening wear. The scent of pine tree, roasted chestnuts, and apple tarts wafted in the air with hot apple cider and hot cocoa. Green pine boughs draped the entire ballroom, adorned with cranberry strands and red velvet bows replicated by the corridors outside. The ornate hearth burned with massive logs from the forest outside and filled the room with a pleasant, comforting warmth.

The strain of the orchestra drifted through her along with the delightful scents and sights around her to create the perfect Christmas Ball. If she married one of her true loves, she would be in his arms right now, swirling to music and so in love she would know nothing but him.

"Lady Rosalind, will you favor me with a dance?" The duke's deep voice jerked her from her musings with a start.

"You wish to dance with me?" She stared at him and searched the area around him for Lady Abigail and her sneering contempt. "I do not think it would be proper, and Lady Abigail will not like it."

He frowned at her refusal. "What has this to do with Lady Abigail? What could be more proper than dancing with your host?"

Closing her eyes and damning her wayward mouth for speaking her thoughts, she lifted her chin and met his questioning gaze. "Nothing whatsoever, your grace. Although I thank you for the kind offer, I do not wish to ruin your reputation." She turned, but he caught her elbow.

"Rosalind."

The way he said her name made shivers race down her spine. Swallowing, she gazed up at his hypnotic blue eyes, mentally locking her heart away, out of harm's way.

"People have participated in this activity for years, and consider the exercise most appropriate. I would very much like to dance with you." Stepping closer, he picked up her hand and laced his fingers between hers. "Say yes." His breath blew against her cheek, smelling of brandy, cigar, and desire. The lure of his heat drew her like a blazing fire on a cold frosty night, and with a moan, she gave in, allowing him to lead her onto the floor. One more time. She would allow his closeness once more. Quivering to the tips of her toes, she lifted her gaze to his and answered. "Yes."

Satisfaction glimmered in his eyes as he turned her in his arms and slid his hand behind her back. His touch sent heat waves pulsing through her body, and butterflies took flight in her belly.

Squeezing her waist, he drew her close against the hard length of his body and smiled into her trembling eyes.

She held her breath as he tilted her back over his arm and then straightened, gazing into her soul as no one had before. She knew nothing but him as they swirled around the room, clasped tight in each other's embrace. His arms filled her with the most delightful sense of security, warmth, and unexplored delight. Clinging to his shoulder and hand, her fingers still laced with his, she allowed her heart and soul to savor this one moment in time, hoping the joy, desire, and happiness of being in his arms this last time would bolster her against the horror to come too soon.

Another couple whirled past, too close, and would have collided with them, but the duke whirled her in the other direction, keeping her safe in the circle of his embrace. Her lips parted as she smiled up at him, content to let him guide her wherever he desired, and prayed this moment would last forever and beyond, a memory to relive again and again when the present became too much to endure.

Their bodies molded together in perfect synchrony as the music enveloped them in a golden bubble of intimacy. Her slight form complimented his as if made for him while they performed the steps of the romantic dance, lost in a world of their own.

She quivered against him as she gazed into the intense blue of his eyes. The heat of his hands on her waist, the strength of his arms, and the fluid movements of his powerful body made her breath come fast. She sucked in the scent of his cologne and the heady essence of pure male and trembled with longing.

Leaning close as if to whisper in her ear, he tightened his grip around her, as all hell broke loose.

Ulysses' excited bark and the screams of several women guests penetrated the sensual haze of her mind, alerting her to the disturbance on the other side of the ballroom. Turning her head toward the refreshment table, she gasped in dismay, for chaos reigned.

They stopped in the middle of the floor and took in the scene.

Thomas appeared from under the heavy red damask linen of the refreshment table with the admiral held high above his head. Ulysses jumped and barked, running from side to side to get closer to the admiral while Thomas yelled for him to heel.

Lady guests close to the boy screamed and ran in every direction when they got a glimpse of the fat amphibian in the boy's hand. Menservants rushed around the table to help, and in the excitement, one guest knocked Thomas over, sending the admiral flying into the punchbowl with a loud splash.

The dog, seeing his opportunity, jumped onto the table, tipping the other end into the air and sending a wave of cake, apple tarts, cider, and roasted chestnuts hurtling through the air and splattering guests in a veritable tidal wave of sugary stickiness.

Rosalind stared, unable to breathe as her Christmas Ball dissolved around her.

Cousin Lucius squeezed her fingers and gave a short whistle. "We will speak later."

Ulysses whirled around and ran to his master, sending a wave of ladies running in the opposite direction to avoid the excited, galloping beast.

Commanding him to heel, the duke left with the dripping, frosting-covered dog and disappeared up the stairs.

Mama appeared at her side spewing accusations and "I told you so's" in a steady stream of chatter until Rosalind rounded on her.

"Stop, Mama. I will hear no more. This—" She waved her arms at the disaster around them— "is no more my fault than a too early frost. 'Tis not my lack of planning, my clumsiness, nor the fact I made decisions you did not approve of which caused this situation. Had you been in charge, all this would still have come to pass."

Mama's lips pinched together in disapproval. "I disagree. The fault is yours. If you kept a better eye on Thomas and allowed me to preside over the ball, the boy would be in the nursery and the ball a grand success. Mark my words. This ball shall be listed at the top of the entertainment disasters of the season."

She sighed from the deepest part of her soul. "I shall be wed in four days' time and shall no longer be available to see to my brother or be the reason for every failure. What are your plans then?"

Her mother's mouth dropped open in disbelief, and she spluttered with anger. "How dare you speak to me in such a manner?"

Rosalind ignored her and hurried over to rescue Thomas and the admiral from the army of menservants, intent on catching the jumping creature and subduing him. Her steps quickened when the earl appeared in front of her brother and yelled at him.

She could not make out what Thomas answered, but when the earl lifted his cane to strike the boy, she broke into a run, throwing her body in front of her brother's.

"If you strike him, so help me, I will knock you on your ass. Do not ever raise your hand to my brother again, or by God, I will make you wish you were never born." Anger pulsed through her with such force she wanted to hit the puffed-up old man.

Shocked silence filled the area around them as the guests gaped at her in surprise. She knew such language would get her into trouble, but she did not care. Her hands fisted at her sides as she waited for his response.

Everyone stilled except the servants.

Menservants righted the table and whisked the

broken dishes and splattered remains away as fast as they could, their gazes darting to the scene taking place.

Edgar sneered and stepped from his usual place behind the earl to confront her. "Raise a hand to my master, and you will have me to deal with." His menacing gaze slid over her slight form with contempt. "I outweigh you by several stone. Do not be foolish."

She did not stop to think. Too much animosity toward the sneering, domineering valet ran in her blood to stay her hand. Swinging her fist with all her might, she flattened his uplifted nose and knocked him to the floor with one blow. Blood pooled on the floor from his nose as he howled with pain.

Rounding on the earl, she took a step forward. "If your servants, any of them, raise their voice to me or threaten me again, they shall receive the same."

The earl dropped his cane, his gaze darting from her to the guests around them before dropping to the valet at his feet. "You will apologize, or the wedding is off. I cannot make a countess of a sow's ear, though the good Lord knows I have tried."

Her chin lifted a notch. "God has nothing to do with any of this, and I will not apologize for defending my brother. Ever. You can call the wedding off if you choose, but make no mistake, I will never marry you. *I* break the contract to end this *first* because *I* refuse *you*, and not the other way around."

The earl's face turned purple as he sputtered with rage. "No woman speaks to me in such a manner. This marks the end of our volatile engagement. Tell your father I am through." Tapping the wood floor with his cane to emphasize his words, he glared back. "I am not giving the dowry back. I have suffered too much."

She did not care. "Then do not. I am well rid of you." Turning, she wrapped her arm around her brother's shoulders. "Let us get the admiral back to his cage, so he does not frighten any more guests."

In the corner of her eye, Edgar rose to his feet, holding his bleeding nose, and together with the earl, they left the ballroom.

The boy kept his head down, refusing to meet her gaze. "I am sorry, Ruby. I did not mean to ruin your ball. The admiral wanted to see the pretty tree and watch the dance. So did Ulysses. We climbed down the stairs and waited under the table where no one could see us. We watched for a while before the admiral got hungry and jumped out of my pocket."

When he lifted his head, his big sad eyes tugged at her heart. "I did not mean to let him get into the punch bowl."

Ruffling the boy's sticky hair, she laughed. "No harm done, Thomas. The ball means nothing to me. Very little does at the moment, but you. Off we go."

"I beg to differ. This ball is a disaster, as I predicted." Having found her voice, Mama's angry words carried across the ballroom, and the rest of the guests stopped to listen. Her mother's gaze swept over them with satisfaction as if they were a jury in a murder trial and she the accused.

Rosalind lifted her chin and met Mama's gaze, unwilling to be the subject of her scorn anymore. "I will not air our disagreement before our guests. Good night, Mama."

Several of the guests nodded their heads in agreement and turned away from the scene.

Mama's gaze turned glacial. "Go to the nursery,

Thomas. We will discuss this later, Rosalind, when you are calm and ready to listen to reason."

Her mouth twisted at the irony of her mother's comment. Mama believed having the last word and issuing commands made her right.

"May I have your attention?" The duke's deep voice broke through the clatter of dishes, the murmur of the guest, and the thumping of Rosalind's heart.

She turned when he spoke, unaware Cousin Lucius returned until his deep voice rang out.

Strolling toward the two of them, the duke stopped beside Thomas and laid a hand on the boy's shoulder. "We apologize for the disruption of your evening, but if you will indulge me, I would like to introduce you to the newest member of my family and the source of the chaos here this evening."

Rosalind studied him with surprise. Most hosts would be angry at the child for the mess his antics created, but not the duke. Warmth crept around her heart as she waited to see what he planned.

Bending down, the duke held his hand out to Thomas. "May I hold the admiral?"

The boy plucked the amphibian from his jacket pocket and placed him in the duke's hand, not meeting his gaze.

"Thank you. I shall give him back to you in a moment." Holding the frog high, the duke announced, "I am pleased to announce the presence of Admiral Georgeous Frederick Alexander Junior the Third Weston, the youngest member of my household. I wish to apologize for not preparing a place for his cage so he could join the festivities and for not introducing him at the start of tonight's entertainment. My omission forced the boy to sneak him in under the Christmas tarts where he could see unobserved. I hope you will forgive me for my oversight."

The crowd twittered with curiosity, and Rosalind gaped. The duke took responsibility for the entire mess, relieving the boy of any wrongdoing. If she were not in love with the man before this, she would be now. How could he be so wonderful? Those who called this man cold did not know him as she did.

"Now we are introduced, if you will allow my servants to help, we will get you cleaned up and comfortable for your journey home. Housemaids wait in the corridors with linen and water. If you have a specific need, let them know, and we will accommodate you. Baths can be arranged as well as clean clothing. I offer accommodations for those who wish to stay. Thank you all for coming."

Several ladies hurried out into the corridor holding their sweet-splattered gowns by the tips of their fingers, followed by their equally garnished husbands.

As the guests dispersed, Rosalind glimpsed Mama in deep conversation with Lady Abigail, casting glares in her daughter's direction. Something about the way they glanced her way made her shiver with trepidation as if a storm cloud brewed above their heads.

Shrugging the feeling away, she smiled at the guests around her, hoping she adopted a successful air of unconcern. Little could be done now the duke had made his speech and accepted the blame in front of the entire ballroom.

Glancing toward the exit, she glimpsed Papa on his way back inside and frowned, not realizing he had left. His stony expression and simmering anger made her pause as she thought hard about when he left and why.

As he strolled down the stairs, his gaze never left Mama's face until he stopped in front of her. "Come with me, Amelia. I believe a conversation is in order."

To Rosalind's surprise, her mother wilted on the spot, stuttering in her attempt to find a valid excuse to refuse his request. But Papa would have none of it. Tucking her arm in his, he escorted her from the ballroom with a determined expression on his face.

She stared after them, wondering if this had to do with the earl and her breaking her engagement to him or something else. Now she thought on the subject, Papa had not been in the ballroom during all the excitement, and she frowned with concern. Her father wore the same face and walked with the same stiffness he did on one other occasion, the night Mama lost a newborn son. A knot formed in her belly, and an uneasy feeling shivered over her.

Turning to make her excuse to the duke, Rosalind found him speaking with a group of guests, so she took Thomas' hand in hers. "I will go with you to the nursery and see you to bed."

For once, the child made no protests and allowed her to lead him along, slipping away without notice.

All the long way up the stairs and down the long corridors, Rosalind returned to the moment she danced in the duke's arms and sighed. Heaven could not be any better.

"I am glad the fat old man left. I do not like him. I want you to marry Cousin Lucius and stay here forever." Her brother's quiet comment echoed in the empty corridor.

"I do, too, Thomas. But we do not get what we want

and must accept what we are given." The words fell flat to the wooden floor with her lack of belief in them, and she sighed.

"No, we do not. It is Christmas, Ruby, and I know what to do to make everything better. Come and see." Running across the floor of the nursery, he pushed open the window and pointed up at the brightest star. "The big one is the Christmas star. Make a wish, and it will come true."

Rosalind dismissed the nurse and wandered over to stand beside her brother.

Frigid air blew against her heated face as she lifted her gaze to the heavens. The black night sky sparkled with shiny dots of light, and one large one outshone them all.

"Make a wish, Ruby. I made mine before I snuck away to see the ball." Thomas slipped his hand into hers, and when she gazed down at him, he smiled. "I wished the old man would go away, and he did." Standing on his toes beside her with his red-brown head tipped all the way back so he could stare at the largest star, he glanced at her. "I am ready to help you if you need me." His childish trust in the age-old tradition warmed her heart.

"I have all I need with you here beside me." And she did. Closing her eyes, she wished for the impossible with every ounce of belief she had left. If dreams came true, the earl would leave for good and give Papa back his money. The duke would sweep her into his arms and profess his love, dropping to his knee to ask for her hand in marriage. Christmas morning, she would don beautiful lace gown and wed her one true love in a glorious ceremony the guests would speak about for decades. Their love would last for eternity, growing deeper and more profound by the year as they raised children, enjoyed countless adventures, and grew old together, content to be in each other's arms.

When the last scene of her imagination drifted away, she opened her eyes to see Thomas gazing at her with satisfaction.

"I know what you wished, but I will not tell because I want it to come true." Padding over to his bed, he removed his tunic and breeches before climbing beneath the mountain of soft blankets. "I am ready for my story." Tucking his arms beneath the bedclothes, he smiled up at her and waited.

After telling him his favorite one involving Christmas and the magic of wishes, she kissed his forehead and wandered back to her chamber, deep in thought.

Uncertain whether the earl planned to leave and accepted she broke the marriage contract, she stopped mid-corridor and sighed. Anything and everything could be changed according to the parent's decision. The earl might be all bluster like every other time, in which case, she would have to convince Papa she meant every word she said. She would never marry a man capable of hurting a child. A life in the convent held more and more appeal.

Turning around, Rosalind retraced her steps to her parent's chamber. If they were awake, they should have the unpleasant conversation tonight and get it over with.

"I am serious. Amelia. I will not tolerate being made a fool of. Despite what you have done to me, think of Rosalind. I would have challenged Danbury to a duel, except you convinced me the scandal would not be good. Rosalind's name and reputation would be ruined if word of the affair got out. No man would ever want her, and she would die a spinster. I could not demand the man marry her when he already had a wife. So, I let the matter drop. Your argument is the one reason I let Danbury go and accepted the earl's offer of marriage. Even threatening Rosalind with life in the convent if she did not agree. God, when I think of the lengths I extended for her, gathering a generous dowry we could not afford and begging the earl to take her as his wife to hide her shame, it sickens me."

She turned to stone with one hand raised to knock on the wooden door. Her breath sped up, and her heart thumped in her ear. *He begged the earl to marry her?*

"And all because *you lied to me*! Danbury is not Rosalind's lover but *yours*! I want to throttle you with my bare hands. How can you do this to her? To me? To us? How can you accuse your own daughter of such a vile act and all the while hide your guilt behind a façade of caring mother? Forcing her to marry a man twice her age? And the threats of the convent. My God, I have spent half the night walking, coming to terms with the fact you betrayed me, you betrayed Rosalind, and you betrayed our vows to each other. I believed I found true love when I met you, but it appears I am mistaken."

Rosalind closed her eyes and slumped against the wall, shaking with reaction. So much made sense. Different conversations floated through her head as phrases and things Papa said to her now held a different meaning. All the times he referred to her situation, he meant her alleged lover, not her clumsiness and outspokenness like she assumed. And Mama. To accuse her daughter of being intimate with her lover to shift the blame and avoid detection made her speechless with the pain of betrayal. She knew Mama had a hard time with her but *this?* Rosalind could not decide what hurt most, Mama's evil deception or Papa's belief she could do such a thing outside the marriage covenant.

Swallowing the pain in her throat, Rosalind turned on her heel and ran for her chamber. Her vision blurred and she fought back tears as she raced down the west wing corridor.

Chapter Eighteen

Another thought stopped her mid-way. Did Cousin Lucius know? Is her alleged affair the reason he spoke of the price being too high to pay?

Oh, God. What little food she had in her stomach threatened to come up, and she fled down the corridor. The duke thought she allowed a man into her bed without being married. No wonder Lady Abigail looked down her nose and refused to shake her hand. God! Who else knew? Every conversation and meeting for the past two months danced in her head as countless comments she did not understand now made sense. Anger burned bright in her chest as she considered the deviousness of Mama's plan. Scenario after scenario swept through her mind as she played out what she wanted to say to her mother and how she wanted to say it. After all the criticism, harshness, and put-downs, Mama's secret lay at the bottom of her forced marriage and threatened to ruin her life. How *could* she? Hurt such as she never experienced swept through her. If the woman who bore her could not love her, who would?

And then she stilled, for in her heart, she knew Mama cared nothing for her or anyone but her own selfish whims.

Rosalind undressed and laid her beautiful ball gown across a chair. Tugging a night rail over her head, she climbed between the silken sheets and closed her eyes.

Tossing and turning as the agony of the past replayed in her head, she spent the next two hours sorting through her feelings before rising to get a drink from the glass on the table in her chamber.

A log settled on the hearth as she stood close to the warmth sipping her water.

A slight noise caught her attention. Shuffling of feet and whispered voices spoke in the passageway on the *other* side of the wall. A frown furrowed her brow. The moon's place in the night sky said the time to be well past midnight. On silent feet, she crept to the secret panel. The servants should all be in bed, not roaming the castle corridor.

A shuffle and a drag made her stomach tighten into a knot. The earl. His foot made the same noise as he traversed the corridor on the main floor. Nausea and terror both clawed at her throat. How did he know about the secret passage? Tying her dressing robe around her shivering body, she slipped her feet into the soft fur-lined slippers beside her bed and stepped back into the shadows, waiting to see what happened.

A soft click came from her left, and the panel in the wall slid back, allowing the cool air of the secret passageway to fill her chamber, followed by the musty scent. Rosalind held her breath as the bulky form of the earl shuffled into her chamber, followed by Edgar.

"Her bed is right in front of you, my lord." The men advanced, and she stared in disbelief as they approached her bed.

The panel slid back into place as *the earl dropped his nightshirt and climbed into her bed.* The sight of his bulky naked body would give her nightmares for years, she knew and closed her eyes, wishing to erase the image forever. She could live to be old and wrinkled without seeing such a thing ever again and be just fine.

Sinking into the heavy velvet drapes, she prayed they could not hear the frantic beat of her heart and the nervous flutter of her belly. Gauging the distance to the door, she shifted her feet a little to get the blood flowing and then remembered latching the door when she retired. *Bugger!*

Precious moments would be lost when she stopped to unlatch the door to make her escape.

Perhaps waiting to see what they intended had not been her best idea. After the rumors about her and her morals, this situation could be very damaging to what remained of her tattered reputation.

"The girl is not here." The earl's angry voice filled the emptiness of the chamber. "Did you lead me to the wrong room? Dammit, Edgar! After all the insults I endured at the shrew's hands, I wanted to fadoodle her good before I told Lord Timothy of my decision to break the marriage contract. My shaft aches to show her the meaning of submission. I had my heart set on taking her virginity, and now I find she is not innocent; I want what is due me. Damn Lord Timothy and the wording in the contract. He knew the girl did not come to me as an innocent, and had you not overheard his argument with Lady Amelia, I would not know now. When I think of all the nights I could have been riding her and did not, I get angry. Find the lady for me, or you are out of my employ."

His menacing words sent a shiver down Rosalind's back, and she stifled her gasp of outrage. She had to get out of here before she gave her presence away.

"This is her room, my lord. I cannot imagine where

she would be unless she fell asleep in the nursery while reading to the tiresome brat. Wait here, and I will go see if she is there. If not, I am sure the child can be persuaded to tell me her location." The threat spurred her to action.

Caring not what anyone might say or what might happen to her, she stepped into the light of the fire, catching the poker up with both hands for a weapon. "How dare you sneak into my chamber like you have a right! Get up and get out, or I will strike you both to the ground. Think what the duke and Papa will do when they discover what you were about this eve." Bracing for an attack, she stared at the valet for, of the two, he posed the larger threat.

Edgar turned his haughty face toward her and gave her a thin smile. "Your heavy breathing gave your hiding place away the second I stepped into the chamber. Lord Timothy offered spoiled goods to my master and has no legitimate reason to take offense over what happens here. Drop the weapon, lady, and remove your clothing. Your lord and master desires to take you, and I am here to see he does. After you showed your lack of breeding by striking me in the ballroom, I find I have no patience for your shenanigans."

The audacity of the man stunned her, and she shook her head in denial. Unafraid of the haughty valet, she lifted her chin. "If you want the poker, come and get it. One scream and every footman in the castle will descend to defend me, and either way, the toad in my bed shall be thrown from the castle. And you, along with him. You chose."

Edgar's face grew more sinister. "But will they come? After the rumors circulating about you, they might not, and then where will you be? Submit to his lordship, and all will be over soon. The last thing you want to do is anger him when he is feeling…amorous."

She snorted, tucking his comment about rumors to her slipper where they would be flattened as they deserved. Right now, she had to escape before either man stopped her. For the evil valet inched forward the longer they talked, and the earl slid from the bed and advanced, his fat, white, naked body gleaming in the light of the fire. Relaxing her shoulders, she dropped the tip of the poker as if in defeat and then swung from the ground, hitting a pouncing Edgar in the face. He let out a curse and hit the floor, holding the two-inch gash on his head, now pouring blood all over her clean, wooden chamber floor.

Turning back, she discovered she underestimated the earl's ability to cover the space between them and found him too close for a good punch. Diving toward her, he threw both arms wide, pinning her arms to her sides as they fell to the floor with a loud thud.

The earl's rotund body knocked the breath from her, and she blinked, sucking in little bits of air before struggling to get free of his groping hands. His fat, sweaty body pinned her in place, and his shaft pressed against her belly, filling her with disgust.

When she could take a deep breath, she screamed with every ounce of strength she possessed.

"My lady, are you well?" The soldier outside her door knocked and rattled the locked latch and called again.

The earl slapped her hard across the face, dazing her. "Be silent. No more screaming." Ripping her dressing gown open, he shoved her legs apart with his knees while he gripped both her hands above her head in one of his.

Dazed, she blinked when his other hand tugged her night rail up.

He gave an evil chuckle in her ear. "You believed you could challenge my superiority and get away with it, did you? Consider this your first lesson in humility."

Shaking off her dizziness, she sucked in a breath, she screamed the second time. "Get off of me, you pompous old fool."

Bucking with all her might, she ripped her hands from the earl's weaker one and tugged her night rail back down. Jerking her arm free, she expressed her opinion about him by punching him in the face, sending him grunting onto the floor. Rolling to her knees, she jumped to her feet as Edgar clambered to his. "I shall never, ever submit to any man who thinks he is superior. If you imagined differently, you have the wrong lady."

The valet stared at her for two long seconds before he lunged forward to grab her.

Sidestepping, she sent him sprawling onto the floor at her feet. "If you were smart, you would stay away from me." Turning toward the secret panel, she took one step when the earl caught the bottom of her night rail and tugged.

"Not so fast. I intend to collect what Lord Timothy promised me." He may have thought to stop her, but the thin silk ripped leaving her standing there in her chemise and pantalets.

"What in God's name is going on in here?" The duke's deep voice penetrated the haze of anger inside her head. Turning, she met his icy glare where he stood in front of the secret panel as he took in the earl, naked, at her feet, clutching what remained of her night rail to his loins.

Edgar must have risen to his feet, for the duke's gaze shifted to an object behind her head. Blood poured from his wound and dripped onto the floor behind her.

"Lady Rosalind, what happens here? My footman awoke me informing me of screaming and a latched door. Under normal conditions, I do not interfere with my guests and what they do in the privacy of their chambers. As you are a relative and I have a responsibility toward you, I offer you my assistance. As the door is latched from within, I apologize if I interrupt a mutual…tete-a-tete."

Her jaw sagged. He wondered if she *invited* the earl to her chamber. His question answered hers on whether he knew the story involving her and her supposed lover, Danbury.

Amid the cracking of her heart, she dug to the bottom of her soul and found strength. Lifting her chin, she met his intense blue eyes and straightened her shoulders. "I *did not* invite the earl or his man to my chamber. They entered through the panel behind you, thinking to force their way into my bed. I latched the door, as is my custom *every* night when I retire. Thank you for your kind offer of help, but as you can see, I have no need for your assistance. I would be most grateful, however, if *every* man in this chamber would leave at once. I grow weary."

The duke's gaze swept over her shivering form clad in her thin undergarments, and anger tightened his mouth. His glare swept over the earl and Edgar. "Get out. Now. We will have a discussion with Timothy when he rises in the morning to see what he wishes to do about this affair. Were she my wife or daughter, I would shoot you where you stand and shall inform my cousin I am happy to stand in for him if he chooses to challenge you to a duel. There are laws about this sort of thing, and you have crossed the line. Stay in your chamber until Timothy and I have a chance to speak."

"I have every right to be here. We have a marriage contract." The earl's face flushed red as he rose to his feet with her night rail still clutched in front of him.

"Every one of the guests tonight will testify both parties renounced your contract, making it null and void. Without a contract or a priest's blessing, you are guilty of attempted rape. Now, get out before I send for my pistol." The duke speared the earl with an icy glare which spurred both men to action.

Retrieving the earl's nightshirt from the floor, Edgar dropped the article over his master's head as they skirted the duke.

"Not through the passageway. Go down the main corridor to your chamber. I gave orders if any of my servants witness you outside your chamber before the constables arrive, they are to subdue you and inform me at once." Anger vibrated from every part of his taut body as he glared at the two men.

Grumbling, they turned and walked a wide path around her on their way out.

When the chamber door closed behind them, Rosalind turned to face him with her arms folded in front of her chest and met his unreadable expression.

"If you have need of me—"

"I do not." She cut him off before he could offer the second time. Now she knew what he thought about her, she no longer entertained feelings of love and wanted him to leave so she could think of what to do next. Her tender heart deserved to grieve alone and in private.

He stared at her for a moment and inclined his head. The panel slid open the second he touched the hidden latch. "We will speak of this after you have rested. I will post a footman in the passage outside this panel so you are not disturbed."

Turning away, she nodded as the first tears slid down her cheek. The soft slide of the panel and the click of the latch told her he had left, and she drew in a shuddering breath of relief. Retrieving a new night rail from the wardrobe, she slipped it on and sat beside the hearth to warm her trembling fingers. Not wanting to go near her soft bed where the earl put his naked body not so long ago, she removed the warm coverlet and wrapped it around her shoulders.

Her alleged affair appeared to be common knowledge, for even Edgar knew. And if so, she had no life and no prospect of any sort for the future. The earl had one thing right, this world allowed men to dally to their heart's content while women were required to be as pure as the first snowfall. Tugging the coverlet closer, she closed her eyes, weary of the whole business to the core of her soul. Who would have guessed the earl's intent, and if she had not woken, he would have overpowered her with Edgar's help. A shiver of terror raced down her back.

Papa would not be pleased when he learned of the incident, and under normal circumstances…

Rosalind sat up straight. *Papa would force the marriage to go through as planned, for the earl would be her one chance at a normal life.* He said as much when discussing her alleged affair with Danbury. If the earl spoke of the story of being in her bedchamber, she *would* be ruined.

Fear pumped through her hard and fast. If Papa forced the marriage anyway, the earl would follow through with what he planned this night, and no one could stop him. She envisioned the hell her life would be if bound to him as wife and jumped to her feet.

All her dreams of love and happy ever after fell to her feet like ashes when she glimpsed the coldness in the duke's eyes. What had he said about her?

"To become romantically involved with Lady Rosalind would be extreme folly and not worth the price nor the scandal such a situation would create for someone of my wealth, importance, and position."

His words cut her to ribbons as she played them over again in her head. Mistaking his kindness for something more would be fatal to her, and she danced with disaster tonight at the ball as he twirled her around the floor.

Making a mental list of her options, she ticked them off on her finger. If she waited for Papa to hear about tonight's activities, he could well force her marriage to the earl despite any arguments the earl might offer. And life with the earl would never be an option.

She could not stay with Papa and Mama. For one, she doubted either one would allow her to if she refused the marriage. And she could not stay with Ellen, for hers would be the first place they searched.

Staring at her third finger, she shook her head. Life in a convent constituted the third and only option. If she sent to the stables and ordered Papa's carriage, she could be at her destination by nightfall. The Church of the Holy Virgin lay a day's ride to the north.

On second thought, if she took the carriage, they could catch up to her and prevent her from seeking asylum from the good sisters. Then she would be right back here, facing an impossible situation with a horror wedding looming over her.

A glimmer of light in her window roused her attention. Rising, she drew back the drapes and discovered she had sat in front of the hearth the entire night. The first pink and purple fingers of the sun lit the sky above the forest, telling her she had no more time to think. Once Papa awoke and made his decision, she had no more choices.

Taking a valise from the wardrobe, she chose two dark gowns of linen and added two sets of undergarments and two night rails. Dressing as fast as her frozen fingers could work the laces, she made quick work of her hair and selected a heavy velvet cloak. Her oldest satin slippers were added to the valise along with her hairbrush. Lacing up her riding boots, she dropped her skirts and took a last look around the chamber.

Thomas. Risking a glance out the window at the sun, she pressed the latch and faced the footman outside the passage. "I wonder if you could order one of Papa's horses made ready for me. After my…experience last night, I find I cannot sleep and think a brisk ride will tire me out enough to get some rest."

The footman bowed. "Of course, my lady. Do you wish to be escorted to the stables?" His dark gaze met hers, and he smiled.

"No, thank you. I plan to wake my brother and let him know I am riding so he does not come searching for me and find me gone." She planned to kiss him goodbye and go before the pain of her decision overcame her will to depart. Leaving him would be the hardest of all.

The footman gave a nod and disappeared, leaving her free to make her way to the nursery.

When she opened the nursery door, she stopped and stared inside. The duke ordered Ulysses kenneled during the earl's stay, and yet, here he lay asleep on the floor beside her brother's bed. The little scamp snuck the dog into his room once everyone left.

Her gaze rose to Thomas. His sweet little face, fast asleep in the large bed, tugged at her heartstrings, and she sped across the room to sit beside him, skirting the dog, who lifted his head when she approached.

"Thomas, dear. I must go away for a little while, and I do not want you to worry. I shall be close and will come visit when I get the chance." Stroking his silken hair, she bent and kissed his forehead. Tears misted her sight as she stared down at him.

"Are you marrying the old earl today?" The boy's eyes flickered in the dim light and opened. "I thought you wed on Christmas."

"I do not marry the earl. Something happened, and I find I cannot go through with the ceremony. Papa will be angry, and so will Mama, but I cannot do what they ask."

Thomas' eyes blinked and then closed. "I wished on the star for the earl to go away, and he shall. I made another wish, too, but it is a secret." His words trailed off, and his breath came even and slow.

So did she, and look what happened.

Stroking his cheek, she told him of the church. "There is the one place I can live and be allowed to visit you. I shall be safe there. I love you, brother, and shall find a way to see you. I promise."

"I love you too…Ruby." Turning, he tucked a hand beneath his cheek and drifted off to sleep once more.

Closing her eyes against the pain of separating from the one person in her life she loved with no restrictions, she rose to her feet. Time to go before they discovered her plans.

Ulysses lifted his head and yawned, his eyes on her.

"Take care of my brother. Stay." Patting his white and gray head, she rose to her feet, tucked her valise back under her cloak, and left the nursery, keeping to the shadows as she descended the secret passage to the kitchen doors.

Chapter Nineteen

Ulysses barked in his dreams, jumping at the bed and urging him to wake. Once he discovered the commotion not part of his slumber, Lucius opened his eyes and came face to face with Thomas. And the dog.

The boy lay on his bed with his chin propped in his hands, not a foot from his face staring at him with big round blue eyes while the dog jumped and barked beside them.

He smiled at the child. "Good morning, Thomas. To what do I owe the pleasure of this early morning visit?" Brushing the hair from his forehead, he stretched as he waited for the boy to reply.

"I made a wish last night on the Christmas star, and Ruby did too. I told her to because Christmas wishes always come true. They must." His tone suggested Lucius agree or he lacked knowledge on the subject.

"I see. And what did you wish for, or is it a secret?" He enjoyed the child and his penchant for mischief more than he liked to admit. Wondering why the boy chose to wake him with his thoughts on wishes, he rolled to his side to be more comfortable and stacked his pillow beneath his head.

"Some of the wish has not happened yet, so I must not talk about it. But I wanted the earl to go, and he did. I saw him out my window." The child smiled. "Christmas wishes are the best kind."

Lucius snapped his finger, and the footman outside his door entered. "Yes, your grace?"

"Find out what time the Earl of Gloucester left and report back."

The footman bowed and disappeared.

Turning back to the child, he studied the boy's face. "Why are you awake so early? I should think you would be tired after your adventure at the ball last night."

"I slept 'til Ruby woke me up." Rolling to his back, the boy stacked his hands under his head and stared at the ceiling. "You must go find her. I think she is scared because she cried when she kissed me goodbye."

Alert in an instant, the duke stared at the boy. "Tell me all you know. Ruby came to the nursery early this morning and woke you up crying?" His mind whirled with the information. What else happened in the night? If he discovered the earl hurt her in any way, he would not be responsible for what happened to the man. Gazing into Rosalind's pain-filled eyes the night before as she stood alone and proud in nothing but her undergarments tore at his heart like nothing before. At first, he wondered what he interrupted, and jealousy lit his blood on fire when he thought of her giving her luscious body to the earl while he slept a few chambers down.

But then her chin lifted, and the defiance in her gaze turned the jealousy into pure blinding rage as she explained the situation and what nearly happened. Nothing would please him more than to rip the old bastard's throat out.

Thomas shook his head. "Ruby did not cry until she thought I fell back to sleep."

Panic gripped his chest, and he took a deep breath to get control of his racing heart. Visions of her in her red silk dress dancing in his arms made him groan in agony. If anything happened to her, he did not know what he would do. "Start at the beginning when your sister woke you and tell me everything."

The child sighed. "Ruby wished for the earl to go away. I know because she told me. Then she cried and said she must go to church."

Lucius' mind raced. "Did she mention becoming a nun or a convent or something along those lines?" The Church of the Holy Virgin sat a good day's ride to the north. Anxious to get to her before something happened, he lifted the blanket to slide from the bed and changed his mind. He slept naked, and the task must wait until the boy left. But first, he required more information.

"What else did she say? Think hard, Thomas. Anything you can remember will help us find her faster." Tugging on the cord beside his bed, the duke ordered clothes and his valet before turning back to the child.

"She said she would come see me, and Papa and Mama would be mad because she left and did not marry the earl. Ulysses growled when she left, and I think he wanted to find her because he kept running to the door. So, I woke you up."

Anxiety gripped Lucius' chest. This could not be happening again. Not to him and not to Rosalind. He refused to let it. Lucinda ran away in the wee hours of the morning following a terrific fight to join her lover as a storm descended on the castle. He did not know of her absence until sometime later when her lady's maid gave him the news. When he found her, he arrived too late. Stiff, dead, and frozen, he discovered her body hours later curled against a tree where she huddled to escape the fierce winds of the blizzard sweeping the countryside. She died four years ago to the day, and he shoved the memory aside, unwilling to do the comparison of then to now.

"There is a good lad. I am happy you woke me." The valet appeared, and Lucius patted the boy.

"Run up to the nursery now, Thomas, and tell nurse to get you ready for the day. I ordered a new sword for you, and one of the footmen volunteered to give you sword lessons. As soon as I find Ruby, I will send word. I believe I can convince her to come back. What do you think?"

Thomas slid from the bed and stared at him. "I think you should marry Ruby because she likes you. I made a Christmas wish for you to kiss her. I think if you did, she would come back." After imparting his opinion, the boy ran for the door and disappeared down the corridor whooping with excitement.

Lucius stared after him as visions of Ruby and their time together floated through his mind. Her kisses intoxicated him, and if they did the same for her, Thomas could be right. For now, finding her took precedence over anything else. "Send for Lord Timothy as soon as I am ready. We have much to discuss."

The valet shook his head. "There is no need, your grace. Lord Timothy waits in the teal salon and sent word Lady Rosalind has disappeared. He sent for her this morning and discovered her chamber empty, whereupon he asked for you."

"Then let us get to it, Vickers."

Half an hour later, Lucius strolled into the teal salon clothed in woolen riding breeches and a linen shirt. "Speak fast, cousin. A blizzard rages to the north. The groundskeeper just sent word, and Rosalind rides right for the storm. I must make haste if I am to have any chance of finding her or bringing her home alive." The lump in his throat threatened to choke him as he said the words, and visions of Lucinda's purple face swirled before his mind's eye.

Timothy nodded, turning pale with concern. "I wished to discuss the earl, but Rosalind takes precedence. Let me change to riding breeches, and I will join you."

Lucius shook his head. "Your wife and son have need of you here. I shall travel faster if I travel alone. I have two of my hunters accompanying me, and Ulysses. I shall send word when I have news."

The dog danced in the corridor beside the kitchens as if anxious to show him the way to Rosalind, and the duke related to the urgency of his bark.

Striding from the room, he ran for the stable and the riders waiting for him.

****

At first, Rosalind did not see the darkening sky for the tears blurring her vision. The dappled mare she rode plodded with certainty along the forest road to the north, tossing her head and sidestepping whenever a gust of wind hit them. Lost in thought, as she considered her situation and all the events leading to their arrival at the castle, she missed the signs of the storm. The wind picked up, and the air grew frigid, smelling of snow and freezing temperatures.

As the storm darkened the sky, Rosalind glanced up and froze as the first snowflakes swirled around her in a mist. A blizzard. Glancing to the left and then to the right, she bit her lip, considering her options. She calculated her departure from the castle at least four hours prior and shivered. The unknown forest and terrain frightened her as she assessed her predicament. Too far from the church and too far to make a run for the castle, she would be caught in the blizzard. Where could she find shelter? Weston Village lay to the south of the castle and would do her no good. She did not know if there were other villages to the north. On her journey here, her mind had been consumed with thoughts of her marriage and Thomas' chatter to pay much attention. And now she wished she would have paid more attention. Nudging the mare into a trot, she leaned forward and stared through the trees. Oft times, woodcutters kept cottages in the forest for harvesting trees. If she were more familiar with the area, she knew she could find one, but here? Perhaps the gods would direct her on the right path, and she would locate one through the thick trees. Forcing her mare into a gallop, she raced up the forest road, searching for signs of smoke or human inhabitants. The wind knocked the hood of her cape from her head and blasted her chest and legs with freezing temperatures making her grit her teeth. And then she slowed, drawing the mare to a walk. The wind blew against her from the north, telling her she rode for the storm, not away from it. Fear tightened a band around her chest as she drew the horse to a stop and glanced back behind her.

How could she go back when she knew what awaited her? Even if, by some miracle, Papa and Mama did not force her to go through with the marriage, she could not bear to remain at home, listening to news of the duke and knowing his feelings about her. No man would ever touch her heart the way he did, and she could not bear the thought of him marrying another and making a life without her in it.

Nor could she bear the knowledge of Mama's lies and what others said of her, for she had no way of knowing who knew about Lord Danbury. Life in the village would be brutal. No. The convent would provide sweet oblivion from the outside world and the answer to her dilemma.

But first, she must weather the storm and arrive at the convent alive.

The snow fell faster and faster, and the wind howled with the force of the gale, making it impossible to see two feet in front of her face. When her mare snorted and tossed her head, threatening to dump Rosalind into the bushes, she stopped and slid from the saddle. The horse's breath froze over her nostrils, making her unable to breathe.

Tugging her glove off, she held the mare's head by the bridle and cupped her other hand over the horse's nose until her warm breath melted the ice around her nose.

The mare tossed her head and whinnied, side-stepping as the storm blew around them.

Rosalind had no idea where they were and could no longer make out the road in front or behind their position. If she kept going, she could wander off the road by mistake and become lost in the vast forest, too far for anyone to find her. One option remained, to seek shelter beneath one of the nearby trees and pray for the storm to blow over before she froze to death. Without the ability to discern the road, her choices were limited.

Leading her mare to a nearby tree, she scooped the snow away from the tree trunk and sank down on the southern side, away from the fierce winds. She forced the mare down beside her for warmth and snuggled against the beast. Petting the mare's nose, she sighed. "There is just the two of us, now. With any luck, the storm will be gone in an hour or so, and then we will be on our way again." The mare nudged her hand as if to say she understood.

The warmth of the horse and her sleepless night took their toll, and before Rosalind realized the danger, she drifted off to sleep, still clinging to the mare's bridle.

In her dream, she gazed down at her body, snuggled beside the mare, and noted her blue lips and skin. The thought jerked her from her slumber with the realization if she stayed, she would freeze and die.

Rising to her feet, she stamped the feeling back into her frozen limbs and roused the mare. "We cannot stay here, girl." As she stared into the thick swirling snow, Papa's voice played in her head.

"If you are in trouble, let your mount have its head. Animals have a sixth sense and will find the path easier in a dangerous situation than if you guide them." Her father spoke the words following a perilous ride across a floundering bridge in a thunderstorm, and she nodded now in agreement.

Patting the mare's neck, she dropped the reins. "There you are. Take your freedom and guide us to shelter."

The horse tossed her head and walked into the storm as if she knew where to go.

Rosalind hugged her cloak tight to her chest and bowed her head to keep the snow from entering her hood. She rode for what seemed like an hour or so, and the horse stopped. She nudged the mare forward, patting her sides. "Come on, girl. We must keep going." But the animal did not budge an inch. When Rosalind lifted her head, she discovered they stood in a small clearing in front of a little cottage and could have wept with relief.

No smoke blew from the chimney and no sign of life existed. She wondered if the cottage were one of the ones the woodcutters left in various places for situations such as this. Papa told her this happened on larger estates.

A small stable behind the cottage contained a stall, hay, straw, and a frozen bucket of water. Breaking the ice, she let the mare have a few swallows before taking her saddle off and rubbing the horse down with a piece of wool folded on a shelf beside the single stall. Resting her head against the mare's neck, she whispered her gratitude for rescuing them both from an unpleasant situation. Tossing some hay into the feeding trough, Rosalind shut the stall door. "I will be back in a while to check on you. Get some well-deserved rest."

Latching the stable door against any beasts roaming the forest, she stumbled to the cottage and knocked. When no one answered, she stepped inside. Roughhewn wood made up the interior, but the small cottage contained enough to keep her alive, and she thanked God for the bounty before her.

A small bed with straw ticking and a colorful patchwork quilt stood opposite the hearth. One table and two chairs stood in the center of the room, drawing her attention to the shutter behind it and the rough shelves filled with pots, trenchers, and mugs. Stepping into the room, she latched the door and walked to the hearth. A pile of dry kindling ready for lighting sat on the grate, and a stack of logs stood to the side. With a smile of gratitude for whoever owned the cottage, she lit the fire and drew one of the chairs over to sit before the blaze. She had no way of knowing if she remained on Weston land or some other lord's. Either way, their foresight saved her life.

Soon the little cottage warmed enough she removed her wet cloak and hung the article over the other chair before the fire to dry.

Gazing out the shutter at the swirling snow, she sighed. With nothing to do but wait for the storm to blow over, she glanced at the bed and walked over to remove her boots. Soon her wet gown, petticoats, and stockings hung across both chairs before the fire, and she crawled beneath the pretty coverlet to rest. Shivering as the warmth of the fire settled over her, her eyes drifted closed for the second time.

****

The duke found her four hours later, guided by Ulysses' frantic barking as he leaped from the sleigh. His woodsmen knew this forest well and kept them on the road, although every sign of its existence disappeared beneath a frozen blanket of white. Unsure if she remained on the main road or took a side road, they trudged along behind the dog, who followed a hidden path he alone could sense by sniffing everything around him.

Terror of what he would discover when he found her pounded in his veins like a soldier's drum leading men to battle. Déjà vu of Lucinda's tragic death kept him on the edge of the sleigh's seat as he scoured the blinding whiteness for signs of life. And then Ulysses bounded away from the main road and raced between the trees in a frenzy of excitement.

Lucius died a million times as he jumped from the sled and raced after the dog, coming to a dead stop outside a little cottage. His men followed.

Ulysses lunged at the door, barking and wagging his tail until the duke told him to heel.

"There's a stable in the back, your grace." Tucker, one of his men, disappeared behind the cottage while Lucius approached the heavy wooden door and tapped. "Hello? Is anybody home?"

Ulysses barked at the door and turned to stare at the duke as if asking him to hurry. Lifting the latch, Lucius swung the door in, praying Rosalind would be there. And there she lay, cuddled beneath a colorful quilt while her clothing dried before the fire.

She found a woodcutter's cottage filled with supplies judging from the interior of the cabin, and he thanked the gods for keeping her safe.

Ulysses bounded into the room to lick her face, barking and wagging his tail while he nudged her with his nose.

Rosalind murmured, smiled and turned her back to the dog, drifting off to sleep once more. The duke snapped his finger for the dog to heel and sighed with relief. He would remember this moment for the rest of his. The solace of finding her alive and asleep in the little cottage overwhelmed him as he sank to his knees beside the small bed. Unwilling to accept the consequences of what he might encounter, and the terror he experienced while searching for her replayed in his mind as he gazed at her.

To have her gone now would be too much to bear, and in his heart, he knew he would never recover from her death. Touching her cheek, he smiled over the warmth of her skin and rose to his feet. Turning to his men, he directed them to take the mare back to the castle and inform Lord Weston they found Lady Rosalind alive and well. The sleigh and his horse would remain for the return trip once Lady Rosalind rested from her ordeal.

Bending forward, he patted the dog's head. "Good boy, Ulysses. Now, find Thomas and protect him." The dog gave a short bark and trotted to the door, turning to gaze back at his master with a whine.

"Rosalind will be fine, thanks to you. Thomas is the one who requires your attention now. You must keep him out of trouble until we return." The dog gave another short bark in answer.

The men nodded and left, taking Ulysses and leaving the two of them alone in the small cottage.

Lucius latched the door and removed his wet cloak and boots, setting them beside hers to dry, and shook his head over the intimacy of the sight. If life were so simple, how happy they would be. One man and one woman, alone in a tiny cabin in the woods, away from the predators of society and the influx of relatives. The difference between Rosalind and Lucinda surprised him even yet. His first wife came from a noble family and reigned as the darling of society, sought after by both princes and lords. She loved the pleasure and entertainment of London, yearning for the drawing rooms and balls of the elite. Thriving on the gossip and scandals, she lived to pass the rumors around and compare notes with the other hostesses of the Ton.

Vying for her attention amid a swarm of suitors, he thanked the stars when she agreed to be his, and they were married. Once he took her home, he discovered his mistake. Like a flower before the sun, Lucinda blossomed under the scrutiny of society and wilted in the privacy of their home, turning from his advances with coldness and criticism.

When he withdrew to the country at the death of his grandfather and made his home in the castle as head of the family, she sulked and threatened to leave him. Overcome with the duties of the family and the responsibilities upon him, he did not take her threats seriously until the morning he discovered her gone. A blizzard blew in from the north, and she rode toward it. As the storm approached, he made inquiries into her disappearance. He discovered his cold, dispassionate wife had taken a lover to the north, Lord Granbury, and was riding to meet him at the crossroads in the forest.

Saddling his favorite stallion, he raced after her, determined to catch her before the storm. But he arrived too late. Once the wind started and the snow fell, Lucinda climbed from her horse and sat down under a tree to wait. There she died, frozen by the blinding snow, still frowning at the road as she waited for her lover. They recovered the mare the next day when she trotted up to the castle gate, still saddled with Lucinda's sidesaddle.

Rosalind proved the exact opposite from the passionate way she played with Thomas to the uninhibited enjoyment of her food. She spoke her mind and threw her heart into everything she did. He could still see her pantalete-covered legs dangling from his morning room window and remember the sweet nectar of her kiss the night in the stable. The earl's disappearance saved his life, for the more Lucius thought about his appearance in her chamber the night before, the angrier he got. Shooting a man in a duel never appealed as much as now. He once believed the price too high to break her marriage contract but now discovered the price meant nothing when compared to the cost of losing her. Glancing down, he drew the coverlet higher and tucked the edges around her before bending to kiss her flaming red hair.

Chapter Twenty

Rosalind awoke to the smell of something delicious. Had there been a dog? She yawned and then remembered the blizzard. Sitting up, she gazed around the room and stopped when she discovered the pot of food bubbling over the fire. Her heart rate increased as she swung her legs over the side of the cot. The door opened, and she made a dive for the fire poker just in case and hit the floor with a thud.

"Ruby? You are awake." The duke appeared in a swirl of snow, closing the door behind him.

She stared. "How did you get here? How did you find me?" Sitting up, she slipped the poker behind her and folded her arms over her chest. Her chin lifted as she met his searching gaze. "I am not going back, and there is nothing you can say to convince me."

"Nothing? Are you certain?" A glint entered his eye as he stacked his armload of wood beside the fire and swung his cloak from his shoulders to hang it on the peg beside the door. "I hope you are incorrect because I have a great deal to say to you."

"Nothing you say matters. I refuse to marry the earl, and my mind is set on joining the church." Rising to her feet, she put a hand on the back of the chair beside her for balance. Her legs wobbled and threatened to buckle as she addressed him.

Stepping into her personal space, he tucked an errant

strand of hair behind her ear and stroked her cheek. "The earl left an hour after I sent him from your chamber. So you have nothing to fear from him."

Rosalind quivered to the bottom of her bare feet and stiffened her knees to keep upright. "Even so. I cannot go back. The sisters will take me in once I explain my situation. I have made up my mind." His breath blew across her cheeks, and the heat of his body beside her reminded her why she should keep distance between them. "Why are you here?"

His hands closed on her upper arms, and she discovered them bare. Her bodice hung beside her petticoats, and she wore only her chemise and pantalets. Stepping back, she tripped on the poker behind her and fell forward into his arms.

"To rescue you." His arms closed around her as she held onto him to regain her balance.

When the heat of his body enticed her to lean closer, she shot back to the bed, tugging the coverlet to her chin. The aroma wafting from the pot above the fire made her stomach growl. "As you can see, I have no need of rescue. I am fine."

"When I discovered you asleep in this cottage, I stayed to watch over you until you woke. Now you have, I imagine you are hungry. Would you like some stew?"

She gulped. They were alone in a little cottage in the middle of the wood, and she wore nothing but her underwear. "If Papa discovers us alone…after the story about Lord Danbury…I cannot be here. I must ask you to leave so I can dress and be on my way."

The duke ladled thick stew into a dish and added a spoon ignoring her comment. "Here. This should make you feel better." He stepped to the bed and held the dish toward her. "It is hot and will warm you up."

She shook her head. "Did you not hear me? I cannot be here alone with you...especially not after..."

He sat on the bed and studied her face. "I know of this tale your mother told of Lord Danbury and knew it to be false. Timothy is aware of your location and my presence here with you. We wanted you to rest until the storm blew over before escorting you back to the castle. You have nothing to fear. Now, have something to eat."

Rosalind wanted to shake him. "But if someone finds out I am here, alone with you, and unchaperoned, I will be ruined!" Why could he not see the seriousness of the situation?

"And what could come of such tidings? The usual occurrence is the couple marries and lives happily ever after. I, for one, am willing to accept the consequences." His gaze slid over her and rested on her lips.

She gaped at him. "Since when? The last I knew, you believed such a thing too high a price to pay and commended me to the earl."

The duke rose and set the dish on the table before retaking his seat. Catching her hands in his, he leaned close. "I wanted to do the right thing and support the wishes of your parents though the thought of you married to the earl filled me with jealousy and disgust. I lay awake at night and considered all the ramifications of claiming you as my own. You see, you enchanted me from the first moment the admiral jumped from your pocket, and you scolded Thomas for saying 'bugger' in my presence. No other woman of my acquaintance sneaks out of morning room windows to play in the snow with a child or eats their dinner with such relish every man at the dinner table cannot keep their eyes off her.

You laugh out loud and curse when the mood takes you with no thought as to your location or who might be listening. You use the wrong fork and climb trees in your stocking feet with your skirts tied in a knot. How could I not be enchanted with the loveliness of your spirit when you live each moment to the fullest? You intoxicate me with your flaming hair and sparkling eyes while the purity of your soul enchants me. Your luscious body calls to mine like a siren seeking a mate, and I find I cannot get you out of my mind. When I believed I lost you in the storm, I feared living this dreary life without you and found the thought intolerable."

Rosalind could not breathe. Every cell in her body waited for him to continue, not believing this could be happening to her, the average girl of average height. As she gazed into his vivid blue eyes, her heart thumped so loud in her chest she feared he could hear. "How can you say this to me?" The wonder of his words filled her with hope as though the sun burst forth through the winter of her life, promising a glorious spring.

"I can because the words are true. I love you, my darling, and cannot live without you. You are everything I never knew I wanted in a woman, but once I met you, I discovered I did. Tell me you feel the same way." The intensity of his gaze took her breath away.

He loved her? Trembling, she slid her hand from his and stroked his cheek, shivering when she encountered the heat of his skin. "I do love you. I ran away because I thought you believed the story Mama spread about me. I have no wish to marry any other man but you, and the thought of you moving on in your life and, at some point, marrying another is something I could not endure. The convent seemed the safest place to be in the circumstances. You have no idea how the thought of you believing Mama's story hurt me, and I could not bear to stay."

He laced his fingers with hers, his eye darkening as he gazed down at her. "Timothy mentioned the situation, and once I listened to the tale, I knew it to be false. Your kisses are too innocent, and you have too pure a heart to do such a thing. You would never hurt someone to the extent Danbury's wife will be when she discovers her husband's dalliance. After our dance the night of the ball, I planned to go to the magistrate and pay the fine for breaking your marriage contract. Holding you close as we danced made me aware of my deep feelings for you and how much I desire you in my life and in my bed."

Her lips parted as she gazed up at him, unable to believe this had happened. "I desire you as well." The words were smothered as he leaned down and kissed her thoroughly, holding her tight against his chest until they both drew back for breath. Trembling in his arms, she gazed into his eyes and whispered. "I cannot believe you love me. How does a powerful duke fall in love with an ordinary girl with ordinary hair and an ordinary body? I talk too much, trip on things, and make so many mistakes. I am frightened you will discover your error and beg Papa to take me home."

He laughed and shook his head. "There is nothing ordinary about you, darling. I dream of your hair on my pillow when I wake, of your body in my arms as I sleep, and your presence in my life as a thirsty man dreams of drink. Come." Standing, he retrieved the bowl of stew. "Have something to eat so you regain your strength. I have a great many surprises planned for the next few days, and you must be healthy and well to enjoy them.

So, eat up."

And she did. The stew warmed her insides while the duke's words warmed her heart. When she finished, she lay back with a groan and closed her eyes. "How long have I been here? You mentioned the night of the ball as if it were days ago."

"You slept all yesterday and most of today. We leave for the castle tomorrow. I have word from my staff. Thomas waits for your return with an eager heart. The boy woke me the morning you left, or I would not have been able to find you so fast. He misses you." His fingers rubbed circles on the inside of her wrist, driving her crazy.

"And I miss him." A lone tear escaped before she could stop it, and she stilled when the duke's thumb brushed the wetness from her cheek. Her eyes flew up to his, and she encountered his searching gaze.

"Do not cry, my love. We shall have the boy to visit as often as you like once we are wed. You shall not have to do without him in your life as I know you would have if you married the earl. In our home, he will be welcome." A gentle smile teased his lips. "The boy injects such life into the castle I could not turn him away under any circumstances."

Wed. In our home. His words filled her soul with happiness. "You have not asked, and I have not answered. How can you be so sure we will be married?"

"Because we belong together. You are the other half of me, and I, you. To not be together is a crime against everything good in this world. And our wedding is Thomas' Christmas wish. So, we have no other choice because Christmas wishes always come true."

"You *know* he wants us to wed?" She gazed at him

in surprise. "Thomas would not tell me about his other wish."

The duke chuckled. "What else could it be? The boy mentioned his wish for us to marry often over the past few weeks. I am surprised you did not hear him since you were closer than I when he spoke the words."

She flushed several colors of red. So, the duke *did* hear Thomas all those times. "He speaks his mind quite often and not in a quiet manner."

"As I have discovered. I hope he never changes." Brushing her lips with his, the duke rose to his feet. "Get some rest, Ruby. We leave at first light."

As she drifted off, she gazed at the pile of furs on the floor before the hearth where the duke slept. He called her *Ruby*, and the name made her smile.

****

They arrived back at the castle in time for tea, although the duke insisted she rest in her chamber and have tea carried up to her, she refused.

After a warm bath, and a good deal of scolding from Ellen, she allowed her maid to lace her into a pale blue silk tea gown with matching satin slippers. With her clean hair still damp from her bath tied behind her with a silk bow, she descended the stairs on shaky legs.

Papa met her at the bottom with a warm smile and a hug. "What a fright you gave us daughter. I would have your word you will not disappear into the night in such a manner again."

Holding his dear head close to hers, she kissed his cheek. "I am happy to see you, as well." Stepping back, she dropped her gaze. "About the other night…"

Taking her arm in his, he shook his head. "There is nothing to worry about, my dear. The earl is gone, and your dowry has been returned. I do not think he gave my money back out of any conscience for his, er, appearance in your chamber but more out of a concern Lucius would follow through with his threat to shoot him." Papa cleared his throat. "I would like to ask your forgiveness for believing such things of you and for demanding you marry the earl. I knew the situation to be extraordinary but thought marriage would prevent a more unpleasant condition. I made the best of an intolerable situation, thinking in doing so, I protected you. So, I ask again. Do you forgive me, daughter?"

"Of course." Swallowing the lump in her throat, she continued. "'Twas never you, I blamed. All those times you spoke of my situation, I assumed you meant my clumsiness or my lack of gentility. I did not know the real reason until the night of the ball. I stepped outside your chamber to speak with you and Mama and overheard your conversation."

"Then you know I asked your mother for a writ of divorce, and she will be leaving our home in the village once we are returned. Lucius offered her a small cottage with an acre of land for her use on the southernmost part of his property. He will pay her a small stipend once a month to keep her until she dies or remarries. The offer is quite generous of him under the circumstances."

She slowed her footsteps. "And how are you with all of this, Papa?"

A deep sigh escaped him. "I do not regret my choice to marry your mother, for through her, I gained you and Thomas. No greater joy exists than to have you both in my life."

"You shall always have us both. I hope you know this." She meant the words with all her heart. No matter where she traveled or what happened, Papa would always hold a special place in her life.

He nodded as he escorted her to a settee in the gold salon.

They were the first to arrive until Thomas burst into the room a moment later, followed by the duke and Ulysses.

"Ruby!" Her brother hugged her tight around the neck and sat down beside her while the dog sniffed her skirts and sat down at her feet.

"Ulysses whined the second you stepped foot in the castle. I think he wanted to ensure you were recovered from your outing." The duke must have bathed, too. For he wore clean black breeches, a white shirt, and a royal blue vest embroidered with gold. His damp hair glistened in the light of the candles overhead, as did his incredible eyes when he gazed at Rosalind.

Facing the group on the settee, he asked for their attention.

Papa took a seat on the other side of Thomas, and the duke cleared his throat.

"Tonight is Christmas Eve, and the usual program is to burn the remainder of last year's yule log and open gifts. As we have endured a few upsets in the past few days, I thought I would start the festivities a little early. First, I would like to thank the stars and Ulysses for guiding me to Rosalind. I do not know how I could carry on without her as she holds my heart in her hands."

Mama swept into the room in time to hear the last of his statement. Dressed in her best traveling gown and cape, she surveyed the room with her icy gaze. "When did this happen?"

He glanced at Mama. "From the moment we met."

Two footmen walked down the corridor behind her carrying trunks.

Papa rose to his feet with a frown. "Are you leaving, Amelia?"

Her chin rose to a haughty angle as she speared him with her disdain. "Of course. Did you think I would stay and allow you to humiliate me further? I assure you I have no such intention. Just as I am sure you and the duke believe offering me a pitiful monthly stipend and a run-down dowager house quite a gallant gesture, but it is not." She gave him a thin smile. "James left his wife, and I go to meet him in the south of France. Why would I stay here and be subject to your scorn when I can live in luxury in France? Really, Timothy, you underestimate me."

Her gaze flickered to the duke and then to Rosalind. "I shall not worry about you in the slightest, daughter since you managed to trade an old earl in for a wealthy duke. Perhaps there is hope for you after all." She gave a little laugh. "But know I will not lift a finger to help when your enamored duke seeks companionship elsewhere. Men always do. You will get no sympathy from me. I do not enjoy being made a fool of."

Rosalind met her mother's glacial gaze head-on. "You do a fine job of it on your own."

Mama paused. Her gaze narrowed on her daughter's face. "You shall rue the day you crossed swords with me."

Rosalind shrugged and glanced away, uncaring for more conversation, when her gaze dropped to Thomas.

The boy sat on the settee, petting the dog and ignoring the adults around him.

Mama's gaze followed Rosalind's, and she frowned.

"Well, Thomas, what am I to do with you?"

Ulysses growled and rose to his feet, showing Lady Amelia his teeth. This time, the duke did nothing to stop him.

Casting a glance at the duke as if to gauge whether he intended to let the dog attack or not, she gave a tight smile to the boy. "I could send you to a boarding school in Switzerland, I suppose."

Thomas' chin lifted as he patted the dog. "I do not want to come with you. I want to stay with Papa, Cousin Lucius, and Ruby." Sincerity shone from his childish face as he addressed his mother, and the dog growled again.

Mama's hands fluttered at the ribbon tied around her neck as she gave a nervous laugh, her gaze on the animal beside her son. "Then you shall stay. I think the situation for the best, and now I must be off." Turning on her heel, she fled the salon as if concerned the dog would chase after her.

When the heavy front door closed behind her, Papa gave a sigh and regained his seat.

The tension in the air disappeared as chaff before the wind, and Rosalind took a deep breath to clear her mind. No one acted the least upset over Mama's defection, and she tucked the information away.

Her brother straightened and folded his hands in his lap, giving the duke his full attention. "I think Ruby looks pretty." His comment took them all off guard.

The duke recovered first, his gaze flicking over her. A tender smile lit his face. "I do, too, Thomas."

Papa nodded, relaxing into the settee as if nothing important had occurred, and he hadn't just lost his wife to another. Smiling, he nodded at the duke. "What were you saying before Amelia's disturbing interruption?"

The duke's gaze rested on Rosalind's face. "I spoke with your papa earlier, and I have his permission. Allow me to continue."

Heat rose in her cheeks as she guessed his intent. Her body trembled with emotion as he approached and dropped to one knee in front of her.

"I have waited for you my entire life, and now I found you, I shall never let you go."

She gasped when he took a magnificent diamond ring from the pocket of his vest and held it toward her.

"I love you, Rosalind Lillian Chatham, with all my heart and soul. You are the other half of me and the love of my life. No other could be as perfect or as wonderful as you, and I find I cannot do without you in my life. And so, I ask on bended knee if you will marry me and be my duchess? Will you share my life, my wealth, my joy, my heart, and my bed? Everything I have or hope to be, I lay at your feet as I await your answer. Will you make me the happiest of men and join your life with mine?" The sincerity of his tone melted any reservations she may entertain away as if they never existed. The room, the family, and their surroundings disappeared, and there remained the two of them and their love for each other. She gazed into his eyes and knew she would never be the same ordinary girl again, for Lucius loved her, and his love made her special.

With trembling fingers, she placed her hand in his and whispered her answer. "Yes. I love you, too, Lucius, more than I can express."

With a grin, he slid the enormous stone on her third finger and caught her up in his arms. His mouth swooped down to cover hers, and she forgot everything but the feel of his arms around her and the heat of his kiss.

In the background, Papa said something, and Thomas answered.

"I do not want to go out. I want to see Cousin Lucius kiss Ruby. He makes her smile when he kisses her."

Her brother's voice brought her to her senses as the duke lifted his mouth and turned to gaze down at the boy. "Are you certain? I am happy to kiss her again, to be sure."

The boy grinned and nodded his head. "You kissed her in the barn and in the snow. She smiled for the whole day after both times."

Heat rushed to her face, and she shot a quick glance at Papa, who sat back on the settee and nodded at them. "Now we have the matter settled. Shall we have tea?"

Chapter Twenty-One

A knock sounded on her door an hour before dinner, and when Ellen opened it, the footman handed her a gown box for Rosalind.

"His grace sends this gift with his love and asks if Lady Rosalind will wear the gown tonight."

With a bow, the footman disappeared, and Ellen closed the door. She placed the box on the large bed and untied the bow. Lifting the lid and removing the tissue, she lifted out the most beautiful gown Rosalind had ever seen.

Made of red silk with tiny shimmering diamonds sewn to the fabric every few inches, the gown sparkled like fire in the candlelight. With a tight bodice, a full-flowing skirt, and bell sleeves ending at her elbows, the cut of the gown complimented her figure. A tiny row of diamonds were sewn along the neck, the edges of the sleeves, and the hem of the skirt, giving the gown a rich, glittering touch that drew the eye.

He gave her a *red* gown. She blinked back tears as she stared at the gorgeous creation. He must like the color on her as much as she did.

Rosalind sighed with pleasure when the whisper-soft skirt brushed the floor as she turned before her mirror. "I feel like a princess." She held the sparkling diamond on her third finger up to the light. "I cannot believe all this is real, Ellen. First, I dreaded coming here because I knew I would leave with the earl, and I did not want to think of what my life would be then. I could not understand why Papa insisted I marry him or why Mama threatened me with a convent if I did not go through with the wedding. Now, I understand Mama's insistence had nothing to do with me, my clumsiness, or my lack of suitability, and everything to do with her lies about her lover.

"Once I met the duke, I could not help but compare the two men and found the earl more wanting than at first. Lucius was so kind and understanding of Thomas with all his antics, while the earl wanted to beat him into submission. As I sat in the morning room while he read deportment lessons to me from his tiresome book, I knew I could not go through with the wedding. Then Papa asked me to swear I would wed the earl as he asked me to do, and I could not understand his determination when he could see how unsuitable we both were. Biting my tongue had to be one of the hardest things I ever did until the morning I ran away to the convent. You will never know how I felt when I awoke and discovered Lucius. And to hear him speak of love is more than I could ever hope for. I am so happy, Ellen, that I get frightened sometimes."

"Ye deserve to be happy. All the nonsense about Lord Danbury should have never happened. But now ye have the duke, and everything will be fine. Ye shall have the Christmas ye dreamed of." Tucking the last bit of hair into place, she stepped back for one final inspection. "Now, for tonight, I placed all yer gifts downstairs where the activities are. His grace asked me to have ye ready at a specific time. I am to send ye on yer way to dinner now." Ellen fussed around her for another few minutes before shooing her out the door and down the long corridor.

Lifting her skirts with both hands, Rosalind descended the stairs to meet Lucius at the bottom. Dressed in black evening clothes as before, she missed the last step when she glanced at him.

His black hair swept back from his broad forehead, and his blue eyes glittered in the light of the candle. The heated look he gave her sent shimmers of awareness through her trembling body as she sucked in a breath. His cologne assaulted her senses, making her aware of how close he stood. The heat of his body surrounded her, and she resisted the urge to lean closer, afraid he would think her too forward.

His sensual perusal held her spellbound as he took her hand in his and placed a slow kiss on her knuckles. "Good evening, Ruby. You are as beautiful as your name suggests."

Tongue-tied, she stared up at him, unable to think of anything to say for a moment. "You called me Ruby like you did in the cabin."

His smile melted her satin slippers to the polished wood floor. "Thomas gave me permission. The name is to be used by the people who love you the most and no one else."

A smile turned her lips up as emotion created a lump in her throat. "If I am dreaming, please do not wake me."

He chuckled. "I would not think of it. Suppose you asked me to kiss you like you did the day you got locked in the tower. I would miss my chance."

Her eyes widened. "You *did* kiss me? I thought on the situation often and could not discern if the kiss were real or not. You said nothing about the incident, and I assumed I dreamed the whole affair."

"What should I say under the circumstances, darling? You kiss like an angel when you are delirious? You were betrothed to another man, and I could not get the taste of you off my mind?" He shook his head and gave a rueful laugh. "I believed I could resolve the situation by pretending the kiss never happened. My decision worked well until the night in the stable when I had to kiss you again. You tempt me beyond reason, Ruby darling. So, believe me when I say I am ecstatic our wedding day is tomorrow. I do not think I could endure a long engagement. I wish to have the ceremony over before any more earls come searching for a wife. I want the world to know you belong to me and none other."

"We wed tomorrow?" Surprised, she focused on one part of his conversation. In her mind, she supposed they would wed in the spring or summer.

"Why not? We have everything planned, and I see no reason to cancel. You are my Christmas wish, my darling, and I yearn to unwrap my greatest gift. What could be more perfect than to make you mine on Christmas day?"

She had no answer because she felt the same. Their surroundings created a frown of confusion. "Where are we going? I thought the celebration would be in the teal salon."

He smiled and drew her close to his side. "I have a surprise."

Leading her toward the ballroom, the doors opened as they approached, and she stepped through the door to stop dead. Rosalind sucked in a breath of amazement.

The entire room glowed with candles, wreaths, holly

berries, and pine boughs. Mistletoe hung everywhere, and a warm fire blazed on the hearth built on the remains of last year's yule log sprinkled with wine for scent. The room contained dozens of people, all members of the Weston family, and all in evening dress. Long tables stood at the center of the room, and a band of musicians played soft music in the background. Piles of gifts lay beneath the massive twenty-foot Christmas tree lit with flickering candles. The sight took her breath away. And there stood Papa, beaming up at her with his hand on Thomas' shoulder. Ulysses sat beside the boy, who pointed at the admiral's cage sitting on a new shelf mounted to the wall. The boy grinned with pleasure and hopped up and down with excitement.

John appeared at her side and tapped a heavy cane on the floor. "His grace, the Duke of Weston, and Lady Rosalind Lillian Chatham would like the pleasure of your attention."

Everyone rose to their feet, and the ballroom grew quiet as the first snowfall of winter.

Lucius held her hand up, showing off the flash of white fire on her left hand. "It is with great pleasure I announce my engagement to Rosalind Lillian Chatham and invite you all to attend our Christmas wedding on the morrow. For tonight, we will observe the holiday tradition of presenting gifts and burning last year's yule log. Please take your seats while we enjoy the special dinner my cook created for this momentous occasion."

Her breath caught in her throat when he turned to gaze into her eyes. Satisfaction, happiness, and anticipation clung to him like a second skin. If she took in a deep breath, she could taste his desire for her and trembled in reaction.

"Shall we?" Tucking her shaking arm through his, he led her down the stairs to the place of honor to the right of his. Papa sat on his left, and Thomas sat to her right, grinning.

"I told you Christmas wishes come true. I wished for you to marry Cousin Lucius, and you are."

The boy's unwavering faith in the Christmas star delighted her, and she nodded at the admiral. "Is the admiral's shelf a Christmas wish, too?"

The duke turned to join the conversation. "No. I had the shelf made after the ball so the admiral could have a safe place to join family events without creating a fuss."

"I see." Laughter bubbled up as she remembered the chaos at the Christmas ball. "I fear some of the guests will not venture into the castle again."

"On the contrary, everyone knows the admiral holds a special place in my heart for catapulting you into my life. He did jump from your pocket onto my hair, drawing my attention to you, did he not? Without his interference, I shudder to think where my life would be at this precise moment. You would be marrying the earl, and I would have missed my chance at happiness. How could I know how important you would become to me unless providence and the admiral interfered?" Placing his napkin in his lap, he took a sip of the wine served with dinner.

She chuckled and then grew serious as she asked the question she wanted answered most of all. "You believe there is one true love for everyone?" Her gaze swept his handsome face as she held her breath, waiting for him to respond. "You were married before."

He placed his hand over hers where it rested in her lap and laced his fingers with hers, causing her heart to thump loud in her chest. "Lucinda did not love me, nor I her. How can one know what they want unless they know what they do not want? Lucinda is the opposite of you, and what I do not want. I thank whatever force propelled you into my life with all my heart, even if it was the earl. For I have discovered the beginning of every dream I care to have in your eyes and in our future. You are everything I envisioned in the perfect woman and more."

His words filled her heart and soul as they ate their dinner.

When they finished, the duke rose to his feet, took her hand, and led her to a group of seating around the Christmas tree. "Come, my dear. We must greet the family."

So many names and faces passed her way the next hour until they all became a blur. A few of the relatives she knew, but most were names, and now she had a face to associate with the name. Smiling in satisfaction, she settled into the settee as gifts were taken from the tree and delivered to their intended recipient. When the velvet bag containing the precious locket descended on the duke, Rosalind set her own package down to watch him open her gift.

"This gift is from me." Anticipation danced through her as she leaned toward him, hoping he would hurry.

Holding the velvet bag above his open hand, the contents slipped out and sparkled in the light of the chandelier overhead. The gleaming locket sat in the palm of his hand for several long minutes before he flipped the catch and gazed down at his mother's photo. "Where did you find it?" His hoarse voice betrayed his emotions as he turned the locket over.

Her grin widened. "In the tower, after I discovered I

could not get out. I lay down to curl up for warmth and spied the glimmer of gold between the boards. I picked the locket up from the jeweler in the village the day Thomas climbed the tree and could not get down."

"Ahh. And broke young Edward's heart. Thank you, my darling. I believed I possessed everything a man could ask for when you agreed to marry me, but you surprise me yet." He squeezed her fingers and took a box from the pocket of his jacket. "And here is my gift to you."

She lifted the lid with trembling fingers. "You have done so much already. I do not need more." Her breath caught in her throat when she gazed down at a perfect jeweled heart made of ruby dangling from a golden chain.

"I gift you my heart to hang around your neck and keep close to yours." Placing a quick kiss on her cheek, he lifted the heavy stone from the velvet lining and clasped the golden chain around her neck.

The stone hung just above her breasts and soon warmed to her skin. "Thank you. The necklace is beautiful."

"As are you, my darling. An extraordinary woman with remarkable beauty and a fire I yearn to explore."

Heat rushed to her cheeks when an elderly aunt turned and gave them a disapproving glance. "You must behave, Lucius. Public displays of affection are considered in poor taste."

"Then I suggest you wear blinders at the castle from now on, for I plan to display my affection on a regular basis." He grinned when she huffed off in the opposite direction, making some comment about seeking out the more genteel members of the family.

Thomas loved his tunic with the embroidery she stitched for him and threw his arms around her with delight. "I have everything I wished for but one."

No one would guess by his behavior he had lost his mother a few hours earlier, and Rosalind sighed. Though Mama did not show affection, one would suppose she possessed some modicum of feeling if not for her, for Thomas. To learn she did not made her distraught and more than a little angry for the boy's sake.

"And what is this wish?" Lucius ruffled the child's hair with affection. "Tell me, and I will see what I can do about it."

The boy shook his head with a solemn expression. "If I tell, it will not come true. Christmas wishes must be secret."

"Then my wish shall be your last one will come true." Lucius' kindness to the child warmed her heart more and more, for he knew by instinct what to say on every occasion.

A smile of gratitude lit her face as the child galloped away to open another gift

Papa loved his pipe and thanked her with a warm hug.

Mama's muffs lie in the bottom of her wardrobe, and after her mother's departure, she gave the item to Ellen. Who, after much protesting, took the expensive muff, mentioning she would wear the item to the wedding to keep her hands warm.

Everyone had a grand time and after the gift exchange, servants cleared the seating and tables for dancing. Papa let Thomas stay up until ten and then sent him to the nursery. "You must be ready in the morning to go to the chapel with Cousin Lucius and Rosalind.

You will not wake in time if I allow you to stay up."

"Can I take Ulysses to the nursery with me?"

Having been the recipient of those pleading eyes on numerous occasions, she hid her smile and waited for Papa's reaction. No one could deny the child under the same conditions, and she doubted Papa had the fortitude either.

She also knew the boy let the dog out of his kennel every night to sleep on the floor in the nursery but doubted anyone else knew.

Papa submitted to the boy within minutes, and after getting a promise from Rosalind that she would come up to bid him good night, he wandered off to bed.

The ball lasted until well past midnight, and everyone discussed what a wonderful time they had. As the guests filtered out to their assigned wings and chambers, Lucius tucked her arm in his and escorted her to hers.

"One more night, and we shall begin our life together. Have the sweetest rest, my darling, but under no circumstances ask any of the men in your dreams for a kiss, for they all belong to me." Bending, he caught her in his arms and kissed her until they both drew back for breath, flushed and breathing fast. He bent again and this time, kissed the exposed flesh of her chest above the neckline of her gown, clutching her tight against him. "You taste of roses, strawberry wine, and passion. I cannot wait until this time tomorrow night, for I will take you in my arms and show you how much I love you."

He liked the scent of roses. Gazing into his eyes, she sighed with happiness. How could an ordinary girl like her get so lucky?

"Your grace." A footman approached. "Lord

Timothy would like to speak to you in the teal salon. He cannot find Master Thomas, and Nurse has not seen him since he left to go down to dinner."

Rosalind stiffened. Her heart rate sped up in an instant, and fear skittered down her spine. She had been so busy dancing with the duke she had not gone to tuck the boy in as she promised, and now, he was missing. Where could he be? Searching her memory for any recent mention of a tree or a hiding space he might have gotten distracted with, she thought hard and drew a blank.

Lucius glanced at her, and she shook her head, knowing what he would say. "I will not go to bed until I know where my brother is."

Together they made their way to the teal salon and an upset Papa. No one knew the dog's location either.

"If Ulysses is with Thomas, no harm will come to him. He knows the boy is his responsibility and is trained to protect." The duke dispatched footmen to search the castle and grounds for any sign of the child. Papa, Lucius, and she scoured the lower level.

The stable master interrupted their search to report he found Ulysses outside the barn in an unconscious state. "I believe he has been dosed with valerian."

"Why so?" They followed him to the stable where the duke studied the dog's breathing and heart rate.

"I discovered this container beside the water dish, smelling of stinky cheese. The scent is valerian root." The man held out a small porcelain pestle stained with a brown liquid.

The knot in Rosalind's stomach grew larger. "Who would do such a thing?" Without Ulysses, they had no way to track Thomas. He could be in grave danger without the dog's protection.

Lucius stood silent beside her. And then he straightened. "Thomas is not in the castle. The fact the dog is outside tells me the boy is, too. He asked for Ulysses to sleep in the nursery. Something or someone drew the boy outside but who?"

Chapter Twenty-Two

Rosalind nodded, agreeing with his assessment. "Thomas must know the person, or he would not have gone outside. There is no report of the dog barking, and he would attack if my brother were in danger." She could not get the lump in her throat to go down so she could swallow.

"I sent him to bed. Why would he disobey?" Papa scratched his head and walked around the stable, looking for clues.

"We will find him." Lucius turned to the stablemaster. "Send for my woodsmen and have your men search the ground around the stable for clues. I want answers."

"Very good, your grace." The stablemaster bowed and hurried off to give the orders.

"Go inside and change, Rosalind. Thomas will need you once we find him. I will meet you back here as soon as you are ready."

She agreed with her whole heart, racing through the task until she stood beside the duke and Papa twenty minutes later, listening to the stablemaster's report.

There were tracks in the snow where someone waited behind the stable and dosed the dog's water in his kennel. A woman's slipper print walked back and forth over the area.

"This does not make any sense. Ulysses did not get

kenneled tonight because Thomas planned to keep him in the nursery. So how did whoever take Thomas get Ulysses to drink the water?" Rosalind studied the dish and then frowned. "Ulysses never stepped foot in the kennel. The water dish is outside." Wandering around, staring at the ground, she discovered a set of paw prints leading toward the hill where they had their snowball fight. The tracks traveled back and forth several times, and she frowned as she studied them. "Lucius, Papa, look at this."

They did, and with a sharp intake of breath, the duke rose to his feet. "I think I know who took Thomas. The question is, why?" He studied Rosalind's face. "Lucinda threw balls in this area for Ulysses every day before her death. Do you know if Lady Abigail and Thomas were acquainted?"

Lady Abigail! "Thomas spoke to her on his way out of the ballroom. I turned my head to smile at him when he left, and she stopped him. I remember him shaking his head and leaving with Ulysses. Do you think Lady Abigail took him? And if so, why?"

The woman did not like her, she knew, but could not think of any situation where Thomas may have spoken to her unless… "Mama and Lady Abigail spoke quite often. Thomas might be acquainted through her."

"He is. The boy sat in the salon on several occasions while the two of them visited. I did not think anything of the situation until now." Papa's grim tone of voice echoed her own feelings.

"Get my sleigh." Lucius frowned as he went over the scene again. "If Lady Abigail planned this, Ulysses would not bark or consider her a threat since she lived here with us when my wife lived." And then he stopped.

"I believe Abigail remembered how Lucinda played with him and tired the dog out so he would drink the valerian. Once the dog slept, she took the boy."

Rosalind stared at him and the area around them. "Why? He is but a child?"

"I do not know, but we are going to find out." He helped her into the sleigh and sat down beside her. Papa took the other side as Lucius picked up the reins. "Tell the woodsmen to follow as soon as they arrive, and Ulysses if he is able. The potion lasts four hours, and if they dosed him after Thomas left, he has been asleep for two hours. We go to Lady Abigail's."

The stablemaster bowed as they drove across the frozen cobblestones and down the long tree-lined drive.

The cold air nipped at her nose and cheeks until she drew the hood of her cape down over her face and dropped her chin. The furs piled on top of them kept the rest of her warm as she searched for a reason Lady Abigail would take her brother.

They drew to a stop in front of a large two-story stone house two hours later. The light in the lower level lit the windows out front revealing a great deal of activity inside.

Rosalind stared at the cold, dark windows on the upper floor and shivered. If the woman put Thomas up there, she would make her pay with physical pain.

Lucius held a finger to his lips and motioned for Papa to go around back. "I will knock on the front door and see what the lady has to say. You make sure no one escapes through the back door."

Papa nodded and made his way around to the back of the house, sticking to the shadows.

Rosalind threw the furs back and stepped out beside

the duke. "I am coming with you."

He nodded his agreement. "Stand to the side of the door out of sight until I let you know it is safe."

The stone in her belly sunk lower. "Do you think there is danger?"

He stopped and turned to face her. "Lady Abigail did not lift the child into the carriage on her own. She had to have help, especially if Thomas did not want to go."

He made a good point. Nodding, she followed him to the front door and stepped to the side out of sight.

The duke's sharp knock echoed in the silence, followed by a flurry of footsteps and then quiet.

"Open the door, Abigail." Lucius' voice filled the silence until a muffled call answered and Rosalind stepped from her hiding place, ready to kill whoever touched her brother.

The duke's hand rested on her shoulder as he gazed into her eyes. "Trust me. I will retrieve Thomas, but I need you to step out of sight so I know you are safe."

She stared at him for a full ten seconds before nodding and moving back into position beside the door.

The creak of hinges followed, and a butler stood in the entry frowning out at the duke. "Lady Abigail is indisposed. I will give her the message of your visit in the morning when she wakes." He stared down his thin nose and stepped back to close the door.

Lucius struck with lightning speed, setting the old man out of his way and shoving the door open wider.

"How dare you, sir!" The butler spluttered with rage until the duke turned and speared him with icy disdain. "You will stay out of my way and be quiet unless you care to go to jail. The boy you have in there is my brother by marriage, and I will kill anyone who gets in my way."

The truth of his statement sent the old man stumbling backward. He opened his mouth to protest, and Lucius knocked him unconscious.

Striding through the entry hall and down the corridor, the duke strolled into a tiny salon on the left, motioning for Rosalind to follow.

Peeking around the door, she met the furious gaze of her little brother, gagged and tied to a chair with his arms folded tight over his little chest.

Lady Abigail reclined on a white settee in front of the fire, grinning like a cat that just licked up a bowl of cream. She wore nothing but a sheer negligee which left little to the imagination. "Hello, Lucius."

"Abigail. Tell your men to drop their weapons and let the boy go." Lucius rolled his shoulders as he gazed right and then left at two large men on either side of Lady Abigail.

"And if I do not?" Her smile turned sweet as honey as she gazed up at the duke.

"Then I will kill your men and take the boy anyway." His icy tone sent shivers down Rosalind's spine, and she wondered how Lady Abigail could look so relaxed.

The lady's tinkling laugh filled the room. "Oh, Lucius, you have not changed a bit in the last three years, have you? You will not do either of those things, and we both know it. You love me too much. You always have, and this is the reason you sent Lucinda away the day of the storm."

Lucius growled. "I did not send her anywhere. We had this discussion the day you summoned me to the dressmaker a couple weeks ago. I owe you nothing, and

I will not settle your debts again. The stipend I give you every month, as well as the use of this house, are offered because you are my dead wife's sister. Lucinda took a lover and left the castle to be with him. She died in her hurry to get away. You lived with us because my wife asked me to allow you there and for no other reason. I do not love you, and I never have. Now, untie the boy before I get angry."

Rosalind's heart beat high in her throat. She remembered seeing the two of them together at the dressmaker's and assumed they met for other reasons.

Silence filled the salon.

"This is Lady Rosalind's fault. She tricked you into marrying her. Tell me how she accomplished what I failed to do. Did you find her naked in your bed as you did me? Is her Papa making you marry her because he found the two of you together? You would not marry such a milk-faced girl when you could have me unless you were forced. I know she did something, and I want to know what it is." Lady Abigail's eyes had a strange glow to them, indicating the woman did not think as normal people did. Her ability to reason had something wrong with it.

"Lady Rosalind did nothing. I did. I forced my way onto a cabin she occupied in the woods and spent two nights with her there because I love her. I asked her to be my wife, and we will be married tomorrow, Christmas day. Believe me or not, as you choose. Your opinion makes no difference, for either way, I will have the boy." He took a step further into the room and closer to a wide-eyed Thomas.

One of the men slipped a knife from the holster on his belt and glared at the duke, flexing his shoulders.

Rosalind glanced to the right and discovered Papa making his way into the salon behind the men.

"You lie!" Lady Abigail's shrill scream split the air. "You love me! I took the boy because I wanted you to come to me. I knew you would figure out who took him and come to rescue him. Now you have, the village will think you compromised me, and they will force us to wed. I sent my servants for the preacher, who will discover us at any moment and marry us before the shrew in the castle knows what happened. With me in this state—" She waved her hands down at her near-naked body "—they will assume the worst. You see, darling Lucius, you have no choice but to do as I say." She heaved a dramatic sigh. "I would not have to resort to things of this nature if you would marry me like I asked you to do."

Rosalind heard enough. Before the duke could answer, she strolled into the room. "Unless, of course, the preacher discovers me here, too, and you go to prison for abducting my brother." Tilting her head to the side, she studied the other woman and ignored Lucius' attempt to get her to leave the room. "Did you suppose when the villagers burst into the salon to discover Lucius here, they would not see Thomas tied to a chair? Or your two menservants hovering in the corners? I should think a smart lady like you would think the situation over before doing something so stupid."

"You!" Lady Abigail jumped to her feet, hate and jealousy shooting from her green eyes. A scream of outrage filled the room as she rushed at Rosalind with both hands positioned to claw her eyes out.

Lucius stepped forward to intercept Lady Abigail and turned to the side as the first man's knife sailed past his head.

Rosalind used the lady's momentum to tackle her to the floor, ripping the bow from her hair to tie her hands behind her back. When she tied the strips tight, she gazed up to see the men grappling with each other.

Lady Abigail spluttered vile threats as she twisted against the bow binding her arms, and Rosalind glanced around for something to gag her with.

Ulysses' bark bounced through the open front door, growling and snarling as he leaped into the fray.

The second man dove at the duke, but Papa rushed him from behind, knocking him to the floor, where they proceeded to scuffle.

Ulysses leaped at the first man, who stepped over an irate Lady Abigail to confront the duke and clamped his jaws around the man's throat as they fell to the ground.

Rosalind rushed to the boy's side, dropping to her knees beside him before throwing her arms around his thin shoulders. "I am here, Thomas. I am here."

Two seconds later, Lucius cut his binding, and the boy fell against her, hugging her back.

The constable, the preacher, and half the village poured through the front door moment later and stopped short when Ulysses growled, crouched to attack position with his jaws still pinning the first man to the ground.

Lady Abigail screamed and kicked, demanding someone free her. The preacher rushed to her side, muttering soothing words as he helped her to her feet.

Lucius gave a quick explanation of the scene and called the dog off when the constable asked for an explanation. Soon he had both men bound and on their way to jail, while the preacher spoke with Lady Abigail. Relating the sequence of events to the preacher and the other men in the village took a little bit of time, and Rosalind spent precious moments talking to Thomas.

"Lady Abigail asked me to come to the stable before going to the nursery. She said she had a gift for you and wanted to surprise you. I am sorry, Ruby. I did not know she was a bad lady because she talked to Mama all the time."

"I know, Thomas." Brushing his thick hair back, she smiled. "I am sorry I did not come upstairs with you. Then this would not have happened."

He shrugged. "You were kissing Cousin Lucius. A lot."

Rosalind flushed. *Not near enough.* "Did you play ball with Ulysses to make him tired?"

The boy grimaced. "She did. And put something in the water to make Ulysses drink." He swallowed. "I thought he died because he fell over." His gaze dropped to the floor, and his voice grew whisper quiet.

She nodded her head. "You must have been frightened. I am sorry it took me so long to find you."

Thomas gazed up at her with a solemn expression. "Mama gave her money to make Cousin Lucius marry her and not you."

Rosalind's mouth gaped open. "You saw Mama? Tonight?"

He nodded. "She tied me up and laughed with Lady Abigail about you being mad when Cousin Lucius married Lady Abigail. Mama said something about reaping the sew."

Her stomach tightened into another knot. "Reaping what I sow?"

He nodded. "I do not think you ruined anyone's life. You did not mean to tell Papa something wrong. I know you love Mama, and I am glad the old earl went away. I want you to marry Cousin Lucius because he is nice."

"Yes, he is." She did not have to ask. She knew what they said and why. With a sad heart, she turned and met Lucius' raised eyebrow and knew he had heard the entire conversation.

"Come." He helped her to her feet and held a hand toward Thomas. "Let us get you back to the castle and into bed so you can rest. We have had quite a night."

As she turned, a glint of metal caught her attention, and she gaped in horror as Lady Abigail lifted a revolver from under a small pillow on the settee and aimed for Lucius.

"Look out! She has a gun!" Her warning arrived too late, for as the duke turned to shove her out of harm's way, the crack of the shot sliced through the air.

A blur of fur and a vicious growl followed the sound as Ulysses attacked, and Lady Abigail's arm swung up, making her aim high.

Lucius took the bullet in the chest, sending him backward onto the floor at her feet.

Rosalind screamed and rushed forward to drop down beside him, yelling for someone to get the doctor.

Lady Abigail screeched with delight where she lay with the dog's teeth at her throat.

"If you do not marry me, you will not marry anyone."

Glancing down at the demented woman, her gaze swung to the preacher, who gaped at the scene from his position beside her.

"If you did not untie her, she could not have shot the duke. Fetch the doctor, or Lucius will die, and then you will have to commend your soul to heaven as well as

251

his." Her glance dropped to the cackling woman. "If Lucius dies, no one will be able to control his dog. For no one from the castle will call him off. The duke is bleeding all over the floor. Pray Ulysses does not sense how serious his wound is.'

The preacher must have recognized the truth in her eyes. Her words spurred him to action, and he rushed for the door to call for help.

Papa appeared on her other side, handing her a thick piece of linen. "Put this over the wound and press down. We must stop the bleeding."

With trembling hands, she did as he instructed, noting the pallor of Lucius' skin. "Hold on, my love. The doctor has been sent for."

Brushing the hair from his forehead, she gazed down into his pain-filled drooping eyes. "Whatever…happens…know…I…loved…you…more …than…life." Hoarse words rose from his throat as he stared up at her.

"No! You will stay with me. Do you understand? Now I have found my one true love, you cannot leave me! I forbid it!" Her hands trembled, and she swallowed hard to ease the giant lump in her throat. Everything seemed so surreal. This could not be happening. What about Christmas wishes? Her gaze rose to the ceiling. They were *supposed* to come true!

Chapter Twenty-Three

"Let me pass." The doctor's voice rose above the murmur of onlookers, and Rosalind discovered, with a start, people crowded around them on every side.

Thomas huddled beside her, shaking like a newborn foal, and Papa frowned with concern as he searched the base of Lucius' throat for a heartbeat.

Then a gray-haired man took Papa's place and bent over the duke. "Give me space."

Papa took her hand and helped her to her feet. "Let the man see what needs to be done, Rosalind. You cannot help him if you are in the doctor's way." Numb with disbelief, she nodded and leaned against Papa for support.

Thomas' small hand slipped into hers. "I have not received my second wish, Ruby. Cousin Lucius must live. You will see."

She prayed for fortitude as the doctor opened the duke's bloody shirt and inspected the damage. "Hmmmm. We cannot risk moving him, or he will bleed out. Someone fetch my assistant and find me a table covered with clean linen. I need several men to help me lift the duke once the table is in position." He glanced around. "Place the table under the light over there."

Papa took over the situation, sending men running here and there as they gathered what the doctor required, and Rosalind shivered in the heat of the room.

A growl from Ulysses diverted her attention back to Lady Abigail, who surveyed the scene with a smile of satisfaction, unconcerned with the massive dog at her throat.

"Lady Rosalind? If you would call to the dog, we will arrest the lady." Two officers stood on either side of Lady Abigail, too nervous about the snarling animal to get closer than five feet.

Rosalind stared at the woman as she answered. "What charges do you plan to bring against her? They must be serious, or I shall let Ulysses know she killed his master."

The younger of the two removed handcuffs from his belt. "First-degree murder and kidnapping. Lady Abigail shall not see the light of day for years. Everyone in the village loves The Duke of Weston, and many of us owe him our lives. Her trial will not be pretty."

"Fine." Rosalind snapped her fingers at the dog, but his attention focused on the duke.

"Ulysses…tend…Ruby." The whisper soft words, hit her like a runaway sleigh. And she swallowed hard, blinking fast to keep her tears contained.

The dog released his grip on Abigail's throat and trotted over to sit on the floor between Rosalind and Thomas.

"He is out. Lift him now." The doctor's voice snapped out the command like a brigadier general.

Seven men from the village and Papa lifted an unconscious Lucius onto the required table under the light.

The doctor turned to Rosalind. "I must ask you to leave. His grace's condition is quite serious. I must remove the bullet, and you must not be present. The surgery is a delicate procedure and will take some time. I suggest you go back to the castle and get some rest. I will send word one way or the other."

One way or the other. Her heart beat loudly in her head, and she licked her dry lips as she stared at Lucius' prone figure. "Allow me to speak a word to him first."

When the doctor gave a slight nod, she went to the duke's side and whispered in his ear, too cold to the touch for comfort. Then she kissed his cheek and rose to her feet to face the woman who shot her one true love. "Why?"

Lady Abigail stood between both officers with her hands cuffed in front of her and a delighted smile on her face. "Poor Lady Rosalind wants to know why. The matter is quite simple, and I should think an intelligent lady like you would understand. If his grace does not marry me, he will marry no one." Shrugging, she smiled at the two officers. "I shall await news of his grace's death. I hope to be one of the first to hear."

Rosalind's eyes narrowed. "Take her away before I rethink my decision to call Ulysses off."

"He would not hurt me. Even though he pinned me down, I am unscathed. He considers me family."

A low growl from Rosalind's side negated her comment. Glancing down, she discovered the hair on Ulysses' neck stood on end. "I think not." She knew without a doubt if the evil woman blinked in her or Thomas' direction again, the dog would rip her apart.

The ride back to the castle took forever and no time at all. The sound of the horses' hooves on the snow and the slide of the sleigh as they slid over the frozen ground filled the night. Stars twinkled overhead, and their breath hung in the air. The frosty air bit her nose and cheeks, but she paid them no mind. Her thoughts were on the duke.

She waited so long to find her one true love, and now that she did, the universe allowed mere minutes of rapture before whisking him away from her. And on Christmas Eve, too, when wishes and magic permeated the air with anticipation and delight.

"Cousin Lucius will be all right. You will see, Ruby." Thomas tucked his hand in hers and gave her a smile.

Her throat contracted with emotion. His prospects of living were slim. The doctor did not expect him to live the night. She overheard the hurried whispered words between him and Papa when they left Lady Abigail's and did not know how to react. She knew if she let the tears flow, she would not be able to stop them and waited for the privacy of her chamber to express her grief.

How could she tell any of this to the boy when he held onto such hope and belief? With a sad sigh, she stared up at the Christmas star and closed her eyes to wish one final time.

If there is any magic or miracles anywhere in the entire universe, I have need of them at this very moment. I know I have asked much and received more than I deserve in perfect form, but if I could trade everything I have and any future wishes into one, my wish would be to allow the duke to live. I care not what happens to me from this moment on and give all I have or hope to be to this end if you will hear this one last plea, this last time.

Her feelings went up into the twinkling night sky along with her wish, and she opened her eyes to see a falling star flash across the sky in a blaze of color. Her breath caught. Many people said a falling star meant you would be granted your wish, and she allowed hope to flicker in her heart as they turned into the wrought iron gates of Weston Castle.

****

Unable to sleep, Rosalind rose with the sun and rang for Ellen. She listened with half an ear as the woman clucked her tongue and offered her condolences.

"Has there been any word?" Her heart drooped in her chest along with the rest of her body. Having cried every ounce of moisture from her body, she sat dry-eyed in front of the mirror as Ellen brushed her hair.

Puffy eyes, a swollen red nose, and flushed cheeks dominated her heart-shaped face as she stared at her reflection. Her would-be perfect Christmas wedding seemed such a foreign subject she flinched when Ellen asked if she should put the lace gown back in the paper.

Raising her bruised eyes to Ellen's sad ones in the mirror, she answered the only way she could. "Do what you feel is best."

Picking up the skirt of her somber black gown, she descended the stairs to find Papa and see if he had news of the duke. Sadness and grief clung to her like mist in the forest as she focused on putting one slipper in front of the other. Numb to everything around her, she stopped in surprise when a footman touched her elbow to get her attention. "My lady, Lord Timothy waits for you in the morning room with Master Thomas."

She nodded and gazed about in confusion, not remembering which way to go. A frown furrowed her brow as she gaped on one side at the long corridor before her and then the other.

"This way, my lady." The footman took pity on her and escorted her to the appropriate room with a bow.

Rosalind stared at the closed door, not wanting to enter. She dreaded hearing the words confirming her worst fears, for hearing them made the situation real. Nausea rose in her throat, and her hands shook so hard she could not open the door.

"Allow me, my lady." The helpful footman opened the door and stepped back, allowing her to enter.

Hesitating for another minute, she gulped back the pain of loss and discovered she possessed more tears. Her entire life never felt as lonely as she did at this moment. Several Weston relatives entered the corridor and stopped to stare when they spotted her standing so still.

Having no wish to answer questions or hear condolences, she stepped into the morning room and closed the door behind her. Had she known the emotional drama of the past month when she gazed upon Weston Castle for the first time, she would have come anyway. For those fleeting moments of pure joy in the duke's arms were well worth the price she paid.

"Ruby!" Thomas rose from his place on the settee and hurried over to take her hand. "Papa and I have a surprise for you."

She swallowed the lump in her throat, knowing the boy did not understand the seriousness of what had occurred the previous night. Dreading the moment of truth, she smiled down at him and brushed his hair from his eyes. "How nice. Thank you."

The boy's lips scrunched in a frown. "You are welcome, but you do not know what the surprise is yet."

"Then show me." Allowing him to help her across the room, she took a seat in the armchair he indicated. "Where is Papa?" Her gaze wandered the room and fell to the latched window she snuck out of a month and an eternity ago. A sad smile touched her lips as she recalled her surprise when Lucius caught her around the waist. A tear slid down her cheek, and she brushed the offending wetness away before Thomas turned around.

"Papa went to get your surprise. You must close your eyes." The boy grinned and jumped up and down. "And do not peek."

"I promise." Closing her eyes, she dropped her chin and focused on the lump in her throat, preferring the child's glee to the heartbreak he would soon endure. How could she go on when the pain threatened to end her?

Footsteps approached, accompanied by the fast breathing of Ulysses. His wet nose touched her closed fist sitting in her lap, and she gave a start. Rubbing his head, she wrapped both her arms around the animal and buried her face in his fur, fighting for composure.

"Dare I hope you will give me the same ecstatic greeting my dog receives?" The deep voice jerked her back to the present, and her eyes shot open. Rising to her feet in an instant, she gazed up into the dearest, bluest eyes with a cry of disbelief. "Oh, my God! You are alive!"

Throwing both her arms around his neck, she launched her body into his and stopped short of toppling them both over with her enthusiasm.

"Careful, love." His pain-laced words had her stepping back with dismay.

Pale but upright and smiling, he indicated his bent arm held against his chest with a sling. "The bullet went through my shoulder and out the other side. A nicked vein caused all the bleeding, which the doctor cauterized.

He stitched the wound closed and bandaged me up before giving me poppy to make me sleep. I arrived home about an hour ago against the doctor's wishes. He wanted me to stay in bed for a couple of days, but I refused, having more important things to do. Such as marrying the lady I love before she slips through my fingers. If I must stay in bed, I prefer to do so on my honeymoon with my beautiful wife, tending to my every need."

The cloud hanging over her heart lifted with each word, and joy filled her bosom. She could not believe he lived and told him so.

"Ahh, but why would I not when I have the enticement you whispered in my ears, keeping me busy with my thoughts." He gave her a heated once-over causing a blush to rise to her cheeks.

"I believe you promised me two sons and two daughters, and I intend to collect. Your words were, I must live because you planned to have a family, and I am the only man of your acquaintance who passes the requirements to be the father of your children."

Papa chuckled. "We should get you changed and to the wedding if this is the case before the requirements change. I cannot leave my grandchildren lounging too long in heaven, can I?"

Thomas tugged on her sleeve. "I still have a Christmas wish, Ruby. I told you Cousin Lucius would be all right."

She doubted she had any Christmas wishes left but cared not, for the best wish of all stood before her with a smile of tenderness on his face.

"Will you wed this day, darling Ruby, and make all my wishes come true?" His fingers stroked her cheek as if she were the most precious thing in his world and the lump in her throat grew.

Happiness filled her eyes and spilled down her cheeks in a torrent of joy. "Yes." Gulping back a sob, she stood on tiptoes to kiss his cheek. "I will see you at the chapel in an hour's time. If you are not there, I shall make a list of potential replacements."

His gaze darkened. "One hour. If *you* are not there, I shall never stop searching for you. You have my promise." His gaze held hers, and every thought of being plain and ordinary fled from her entire existence, for the gleam in his eye said he found a jewel he intended to possess for the rest of time.

Her heart nearly burst with love. "I shall be there."

And she was.

Somehow, Ellen managed to prepare her for the wedding and get her to the chapel as the first strains of the wedding music floated through the overfull audience to the steps beyond. For years afterward, Rosalind searched her mind for any recollection of being laced into her delicate gown or having her hair dressed and threaded with diamonds but remembered nothing.

Her first realization of the present arrived as she stepped through the chapel doors and gazed down the long petal-laden walkway to the altar where the Duke of Weston stood, resplendent in his full dress uniform laden with medals. Honored for his many battles for king and country, his jacket gleamed in the morning light streaming through the stained-glass windows of the church.

His dark hair swept away from his brow, and piercing blue eyes gazed into hers, sending shivers of anticipation down her spine.

Red roses, mistletoe, and pine boughs draped across every pew and level surface, giving the church an elegant Christmas atmosphere and smell.

As she placed one satin slipper in front of the other, she could not help but thank the gods for this day and this man. She knew everything would be perfect from here on because she married her one true love, and he, her.

Papa squeezed her hand as he led her toward the duke. "I am so happy I give you into Cousin Lucius' hands and not the Earl of Gloucester's. Such a thing should never have been considered, and I offer an apology once again for my part in the situation."

"I have nothing but gratitude in my heart, Papa. Without the earl and a Christmas wedding at the castle, I never would have met the duke. Everything worked out for the best, even Mama. I worried how Thomas would adjust to my absence when he tries Mama's patience so. Now, I do not worry, for he is better off with you."

"And you. Cousin Lucius offered me a large two-story stone house a mile from the castle and a position as head overseer of a large portion of his tenants. With his marriage, he hopes to spend more time at home and needs someone he trusts to help me. I agreed. So, Thomas can go back and forth between us with no worry of danger."

Lucius' thoughtfulness filled her overflowing heart once more, and she smiled up at him as they stopped at the altar steps.

Papa placed her hand in his. "I give her into your care, Cousin, knowing your love for her is greater than mine. Thank you for loving my daughter and making her so happy."

"It is I who thanks you for such a precious gift. I shall care for her as no other." The duke's warm hands took hers in his as he led her up the stairs to the priest.

They gave their vows before the massive congregation, God, and the angels. But Rosalind knew only the love shining from the duke's blue eyes, the heat of his hands holding hers, and the warm musky scent of his skin as he leaned close.

Warmth, happiness, and security surrounded her in a golden bubble as the priest pronounced them man and wife. And then the duke drew her close and placed his warm lips against her own, sealing their union with a kiss.

They turned, and the congregation rose to their feet, expressing their satisfaction with the ceremony and the couple before them.

Rosalind glanced down at a beaming Thomas and smiled.

He grinned in return and pointed to a pillar on her right. Turning, she met the unblinking stare of Admiral Georgeous Frederick Alexander Junior the Third Weston, locked in his cage and eye level. He wore a tiny black bow tied behind his thick neck with a piece of black ribbon.

"Did you know the admiral witnessed our wedding?" She turned to her new husband in concern, glancing around for Ulysses, who on previous occasions accompanied the frog and preceded disaster.

"I placed him there, figuring the admiral would be among the guests either way. If we make a place for him and plan where Ulysses is, we avert catastrophes like the ball." He grinned. "I gave the admiral a place of honor for drawing you to my attention. The added benefit is we made Thomas happy. And before you ask, Ellen made the bow."

The boy beamed with delight, dancing on one foot and then the other beside Papa.

Her ruby heart hung above her own, and she rubbed the smooth stone between her thumb and forefinger as she gazed out at her family with her husband at her side.

Thomas clutched her other hand when they descended the stairs. "Now I have *all* my wishes. I *knew* you would marry Cousin Lucius because Christmas wishes always come true.

And she had all of hers.

Papa smiled and fell into step behind them.

When they arrived at the entrance to the chapel, Rosalind turned to speak to him and discovered him several feet away speaking to a dark-haired woman in a red silk dress.

Papa's eyes glowed with interest as he inclined his head to hear what the lady said. He grinned and waved Rosalind on when he caught her gaze on him.

"Lady Cynthia." The duke explained in her ear, sending a shiver of awareness through her. "She lost her husband a year ago and is one of the sweetest women in the area. Many of the local lords have sought to court her, but she declines their advances before they finish their sentences. Judging from the way she blushes with Timothy, he may not be a bachelor for long following his divorce. Who knows? My cousin may have found the love of his life, as well."

Rosalind hesitated, glancing back at Papa. "How could such a thing be possible? Mama left yesterday."

Lucius patted her hand. "They were never meant to be together, or your mother could not have done what she did. And it is Christmas, darling. Anything is possible. I have it on good authority. Christmas wishes all come true."

She had to agree as later she gazed around the crowded dining hall as their guests enjoyed the wedding feast. Lady Cynthia sat on Papa's right, engrossed in a conversation with him, and Thomas sat on his left, grinning and eating an enormous plate of food as if all were right with his world.

Rosalind's gaze roamed the faces of the relatives, and a glow of happiness filled her heart. The heavy gold band on her finger proclaimed her wed to the love of her life, and the vision of Weston Castle she spied through Papa's carriage window on their arrival no longer embodied the entrance to hell but her private gateway to heaven. Closing her eyes for the briefest moment, she thanked the stars for pointing her in the right direction despite the circumstances and situations required to get her from there to here.

Though the years passed, creating changes and situations in their lives, Rosalind never again doubted the magic of Christmas nor the power of wishing on a star on Christmas Eve.

Epilogue

The Duke and Duchess of Weston lived a long, happy life together, complete with two sets of twins, two girls and two boys. Richard and Ruby were the first set, followed by Timothy and Tabatha. Their joy, laughter, and mischief filled the ancient castle and made the long corridors ring with delight.

Papa married Lady Cynthia the following Christmas and lived out his days in rapture, expressing his gratitude for the winter of 1813 and Rosalind's engagement to the Earl of Gloucester, which propelled him into Lady Cynthia's arms, and she, his.

Thomas grew to be a strong, valiant lord favored by the ruling queen, often spending months in London at her request. Wealthy, handsome, and popular, his sense of humor saved him from dangerous situations on many occasions as he carried out the queen's orders. He later settled in London and married into the royal family.

No one ever mentioned Mama again until years later when Rosalind discovered she perished at sea in a storm on her way to France. Thus, ending the question of how many perfect loves one has in a lifetime. Mama had one, Rosalind's father, and never acquired another, despite Lord Timothy's efforts to make her happy. They were not suited to each other and grew dissatisfied with their union until the universe drew them apart and propelled Papa toward his.

Every Christmas eve after, she would stop and gaze up, offering gratitude for the wishes granted, the happiness she enjoyed, and the family around her. And then she would go find the love of her life.

A word about the author…

I enjoy knitting, crocheting, and quilting. I love roses and the smell of gardenias. I have two large dogs who keep me company while I write. Beethoven is an Aussie/ Great Pyrenees mix and Mozart is a Mastiff/Collie mix.

I occasionally bake when the mood strikes. Not a lot but just enough to get rid of the itch.

My husband of forty-one years is my greatest fan/critic and I don't know what I would do without him. I love my life, and I love my family. Life is a journey and I can't wait to see where it leads me next!

Thank you for purchasing
this publication of The Wild Rose Press, Inc.

For questions or more information
contact us at
info@thewildrosepress.com.

The Wild Rose Press, Inc.
www.thewildrosepress.com